ANTON HANSEN TAMMSAARE (1878-1940) is widely regarded as Estonia's greatest writer. The son of a farmer, Tammsaare's education at the University of Tartu was cut short when he was diagnosed with tuberculosis, which led to a stay in the Caucasus. Following Estonian independence in 1918 he moved to Tallinn, where he lived for the rest of his life. His early literary works reflected a poetic rural realism, although he also wrote several urban novels and collections of short stories: the contrast between urban bourgeoisie and hard-working peasantry would prove to be one of the enduring themes of his writing.

His epic five-volume sequence of novels, *Tõde ja õigus* (Trust and Justice; 1926-1933), tracing the development of Estonia from tsarist province to independent state is considered the great masterpiece of twentieth-century Estonian literature. According to Tammsaare himself, the first volume depicts man's struggle with the earth, the second with God, the third with society, the fourth with himself - while the fifth ends with resignation. The early volumes are partly autobiographical, and the work is deeply rooted in Estonian history, but it deals with many of the same literary and philosophical issues that concern his contemporaries Thomas Mann and John Galsworthy.

Although a realist at heart, Tammsaare used allegorical fantasy in his stories, most notably in his final novel *Põrgupõhja uus vanapagan* (1939; *The Misadventures of the New Satan*). Here he combines a satire on the inequalities of rural life and absurdities of rigid social attitudes with biblical themes, mythology, and bawdy folklore. The resulting novel has proved to be an enduring classic of European literature.

Some other books from Norvik Press

Juhani Aho: *The Railroad* (translated by Owen Witesman)

Johan Borgen: *Little Lord* (translated by Janet Garton)

Jens Bjørneboe: *Moment of Freedom* (translated by Esther Greenleaf Mürer)

Jens Bjørneboe: *Powderhouse* (translated by Esther Greenleaf Mürer)

Jens Bjørneboe: *The Silence* (translated by Esther Greenleaf Mürer)

Vigdis Hjorth: *A House in Norway* (translated by Charlotte Barslund)

Jógvan Isaksen: *Walpurgis Tide* (translated by John Keithsson)

Svava Jakobsdóttir: *Gunnlöth's Tale* (translated by Oliver Watts)

Selma Lagerlöf: *Mårbacka* (translated by Sarah Death)

Viivi Luik: *The Beauty of History* (translated by Hildi Hawkins)

Christopher Moseley (ed.): *From Baltic Shores*

Amalie Skram: *Lucie* (translated by Katherine Hanson and Judith Messick)

Ilmar Taska: *Pobeda 1946: A Car Called Victory* (translated by Christopher Moseley)

Kirsten Thorup: *The God of Chance* (translated by Janet Garton)

Dorrit Willumsen: *Bang: A Novel about the Danish Writer* (translated by Marina Allemano)

The Misadventures
of the New Satan

by

Anton Tammsaare

Translated from the Estonian by
Olga Shartze and Christopher Moseley

Norvik Press
2018

Originally published in Estonian in 1939 as *Põrgupõhja uus vanapagan* (literal translation: The New Devil of Hellsbottom).

Original translation © Olga Shartze 1978; revisions © Christopher Moseley 2008.

A catalogue record for this book is available from the British Library.
ISBN: 978-1-909408-43-2

First published in 2009 by Norvik Press, Department of Scandinavian Studies, University College London, Gower Street, London, WC1E 6BT. This edition first published in 2018.

Norvik Press gratefully acknowledges the invaluable contributions made towards this publication by Eesti Kultuurkapital (The Estonian Cultural Endownment Fund), the Estonian Literature Information Centre and the Anton Hansen Tammsaare Museum.

Norvik Press
Department of Scandinavian Studies
University College London
Gower Street
London WC1E 6BT
United Kingdom

Website: www.norvikpress.com
E-mail address: norvik.press@ucl.ac.uk

Managing editors: Elettra Carbone, Sarah Death, Janet Garton, C. Claire Thomson.

Cover image: Olenka Kotyk 2016, unsplash.com
Cover design: Essi Viitanen
Printed in the UK by Lightning Source UK Ltd.

CONTENTS

Prologue 7

Chapter 1 14

Chapter 2 31

Chapter 3 43

Chapter 4 54

Chapter 5 66

Chapter 6 76

Chapter 7 88

Chapter 8 100

Chapter 9 111

Chapter 10 122

Chapter 11 129

Chapter 12 140

Chapter 13 150

Chapter 14 160

Chapter 15 171

Chapter 16 181

Chapter 17 189

Chapter 18 197

Chapter 19 206

Chapter 20 216

Chapter 21 226

Chapter 22 236

Epilogue 253

＊ ＊ ＊

PROLOGUE

This was the annual day of reckoning in heaven, a routine business of sorting out the souls – so many to go to paradise, and so many to hell. Satan had been at the gate since early morning, expecting to go in as soon as the messenger-angel appeared. But this time he had a long wait – the angel was certainly taking his time. It was well past midday, and finally Satan worked up the courage to knock, very softly at first, then a bit louder. As no one came to open the gate for him, he started banging on it with all his might, and the entire firmament reverberated as though thunder were crashing in the clear blue sky. The noise brought the Apostle Peter to the gate, he opened the peephole, saw Satan and asked as formally as if he were addressing a total stranger:

'What can I do for you?'

The tone and the question made Satan see red, coming on top of the humiliation of being kept waiting.

'Gatekeepers are getting more conceited than their masters themselves, I see,' he said angrily. 'Since when have you stopped recognising me?'

'Since today,' Peter replied coolly, and attempted to close the peephole. But Satan was quicker and, sticking his fingers into the hole, he prevented it from shutting all the way.

'Hold on a moment, Peter, this is soul-sorting day, isn't it?' he spoke into the peephole where all he could see above his fingers was Peter's right eye.

'There's no such thing as soul-sorting days any more,' Peter said, and added in explanation: 'It's all different now.'

'How d'you mean, different!' Satan cried in consternation. 'I've a contract, you know!'

'It's not valid any longer,' Peter told him.

'Not valid, you say?!' Satan screamed, more alarmed than surprised now. 'Both sides signed the contract, so one side can't break it.'

'It has been broken nevertheless,' Peter said. 'There's no distributing today, no accounting, no souls.'

'Don't talk rubbish, Peter,' Satan said in friendly admonition.

'I'd ask you to keep a civil tongue in your head,' Peter replied in a frigid tone. 'We don't know each other.'

'Hell's bells!' Satan roared, almost out of his mind. 'Why, I've known you and you've known me from that very moment when you denied your Lord. If we two don't know each other, who does!'

'Such are my orders, and that's all I know,' Peter said. 'Kindly remove your fingers so I can close the peephole.'

The manner in which Peter spoke to him convinced Satan at last that some new winds were blowing in heaven. 'What's going to happen to hell and my chaps if the inflow of souls is stopped?' he said anxiously to himself. 'Why should I bother with that sooty, smoky hole then?'

'Hey you, clodhopper, let go of the peephole while I'm asking you nicely, otherwise I'm going to have to resort to new measures!' Peter rudely broke in upon his meditations.

'Peter, my dear old friend,' Satan said in a tone of entreaty.

'I'm not your friend any more,' Peter cut him short.

'But you were, once,' Satan persisted. 'And in the name of our former friendship, I beg you: open the gate a slit and let me in, so that I can get this business really clear in my head.'

'My orders are not to let you in any more,' Peter said in a friendlier tone.

'Maybe you could come out yourself for a couple of minutes and we'd have a nice chat like in the good old days?' Satan wheedled. 'You've got to see that I daren't go home like this. What shall I tell the old woman and the boys if I come back empty-handed?'

Peter thought it over, and said:

'All right, I'll come out, only let go of the peephole first.'

'Promise you'll come out?' Satan asked suspiciously.

'I promise,' Peter said curtly and firmly.

Satan drew back his hand, and the peephole snapped shut.

A lot of time passed, and still Peter did not come out. The hours dragged terribly, so terribly that Satan began to doubt his former friend's word and thought he'd have to start banging on the gate again.

When Peter appeared at last Satan sighed and said: 'How time drags on in heaven these days!'

'I wanted to bring some papers along, but I could't wait for them any longer, so I came without,' Peter said by way of explanation. He sat down on the top rung of the celestial stairway, and with a gesture invited Satan to sit beside him.

'What papers are you talking about, if no souls are forthcoming anyway,' Satan grumbled.

'But they are the papers where the new rules and procedure in obtaining souls are set out in black on white!'

'Does it mean I'll still be able to get my souls?' Satan asked, cheering up.

'The contract, of course, remains in effect, only...'

'Only what, if the contract remains in effect?' Satan cried impatiently. 'The contract stands, but evidently they don't want to hold to it. Is that it?'

'It will be upheld on one condition: you have to take the shape of a human on earth, and...'

'Be born of woman, right?'

'Not necessarily,' Peter replied matter-of-factly. 'You can be born of woman or anyone else you like, it's your choice. Or you can simply appear on earth, as it used to be done.'

'I don't understand a thing,' Satan said. 'What's new about my going down to earth? I've been there before lots of times.'

'You went as the Devil before, and now you'll be going as a human being. Get this straight: as a human being, an ordinary mortal. See the difference?'

'And die?'

'And die.'

'No, I won't do it.'

'Very well,' Peter replied calmly. 'No one's forcing you.'

'But what about my souls?' Satan asked.

'There won't be any for you unless you go down to earth in the shape of a man.'

'And if I do go?'

'Then you'll get them, I suppose.'

'Why "suppose"?'

'Well, you see, there's the rub. If, living on earth as a mortal, you quality for heaven, you'll have the right to obtain all the souls you want for ever after. But if, living and dying as a mortal, you yourself quality for hell, you'll forfeit this right for ever. What's more, you'll be required to hand over the souls you have already received, so there'll be no one left in hell at all.'

'The wisest and most reasonable thing to do then is for heaven to take hell over entirely.'

'No, we don't want to do that yet,' said Peter.

Satan smirked inwardly: 'I like that! Not yet!' But, thinking the matter over for a minute, he once again addressed Peter as an old friend:

'What you've been telling me is all very interesting, but in every business there has to be a purpose, if you know what I mean. Even on earth they don't skin good friends alive for no good reason, let alone in heaven. So why are you planning to destroy my domain? Why delete hell from the world economy? I gave you no cause for that, I'm sure.'

'The reasons lie much deeper,' Peter said.

'You mean higher.'

'You could put it that way, if you like.'

'Won't you tell me about it in more detail?'

'No, it's a secret,' said Peter

'Good heavens above!' Satan cried. 'I've never yet given away a heavenly secret, and I don't intend to start now. True, no one keeps his promises nowadays, but Satan will keep his, he's that sort! And so, tell me, O Peter, why does the Lord want to change me into a man and send me down to earth?'

'The Lord has begun to doubt men, that's why,' Peter replied.

'But it's the Lord Himself who created them!'

'To be sure, but...'

'In other words, the Lord has begun to doubt his own creation, his own self.'

'Maybe so. Doubt has been voiced in heaven as to whether, given the way man is made, he's capable of living righteously. If he is not, is it fair to send him to hell when he dies?'

'You mean that robbers, murderers, and such like should be sent to paradise, or what?'

'No, but...'

'There's no third choice, you know,' interjected Satan. 'Either a man goes to paradise or he goes to hell.'

'A third choice has been found.'

'What is it?' Satan asked with mounting curiosity.

'If it is proved that the way man is made means that he's altogether incapable of living righteously, that is, if the creation is found wanting, then it'll have to be withdrawn,' Peter explained.

'What will?' Satan asked, puzzled.

'Mankind.'

'Whatever can you mean?'

'Just this: the entire human race will be exterminated, and then the souls of what were once men will be gathered together – from paradise, from hell, from wherever – and despatched to where they came from originally.'

'You're joking, aren't you?' Satan asked.

But Peter replied as solemnly as before: 'In heaven, we don't make jokes.'

'That would mean an end to all our undertakings, efforts and achievements,' Satan said thoughtfully.

'Apparently so,' Peter nodded, and then said softly: 'That's why it's so important for you to go down to earth as a human and see if there isn't some way of earning salvation. In other words, what you have to do as a mortal is confirm that it isn't the Lord who made a failure of his creation, but men themselves who err in their lives and, this being so, it is our right, nay, our duty, to send their souls to hell.'

'Are you sure there'll be no other conditions for me getting my souls?' Satan asked, to test his old friend.

11

'There's no fear of that, no.'

'All right then, I'll go down to earth in the shape of a man,' he said, his mind made up.

'I'm pleased, and the heavenly host will be pleased,' Peter drew a sigh of relief. He wanted to get up and go, but Satan put his hand on his knee and held him back.

'I'll only keep you another minute. I've a small question to ask: may I take my old woman along with me?'

'If you are certain she won't be a burden,' Peter replied.

'I don't think she'll be a burden, but if she is I'll send her back to hell, pronto.'

'Very well. I believe you will receive permission.'

'One more thing: what do you think I'd be better be off being on earth – a peasant, a merchant, an industrialist, a worker, a diplomat, a scientist, a writer, an artist, or a preacher? Who will achieve salvation easiest these days?'

'That's hard, very hard to say,' Peter said thoughtfully. 'In my day I was a fisherman, and you know as well as I do what happened. Farming is a good occupation, because if war breaks out, laying waste the land, burning down all the buildings, destroying your livestock, and killing your wife and children, you'll certainly go to heaven, seeing that you couldn't expect any mercy or charity from anyone but God. Now, if war doesn't break out and you start growing rich quickly, thanks to all manner of government subsidies and wanting to live in the style of an industrialist or a merchant, thriving on the high prices set in the name of the fatherland, you'd do better to forget about saving your immortal soul, though you might attend church as regularly as respectability demands, and pay your church dues without the intervention of the police.

'I would't advise you to become a worker. That breed is too cocksure these days because of its vast numbers, and paradise doesn't seem to be much of an attraction. Now, if idle talk is all you're interested in, diplomacy would be the right field, because actually the stockbrokers and arms manufacturers do nothing. Spiritual work is no good either. Once upon a time the spirit exerted its influence on those in power, but now it's the other way round. Supposing you were a scientist, a writer, or an artist, how could you possibly come close to God if Mammon rules the powers that be, and the powers that be rule you? There's the clergy, of course. But I don't have to tell you that all they care about is church rites, prayers, and gilded crosses, and not good deeds, not by a long chalk. You'd have to swim against the current to earn salvation by righteous living, and I'm afraid they'd stone you to death if you did that. I have spoken my mind.'

'Will I be able to change my occupation if I want to?' Satan asked.

'You will,' Peter replied. 'If you feel like it, you might even devise something entirely new and more suited to your nature.'

'Good. I'll begin as a farmer, and then we'll see,' Satan said resolutely.

'But remember this well: if you return without accomplishing your mission on earth, hell will never obtain another soul again.'

'I understand. I'm staking everything on this.'

'Not you alone, but also all of us here, in heaven,' Peter stressed this point, and rose to go. 'What I've told you today will be set down in writing in clear, precise terms within the next few days.' Saying this, he vanished behind the heavenly gates.

'Clear and precise,' Satan repeated, standing alone on the stairs. 'The crazy ideas they get! Imagine, changing me into a human being and sending me down to earth! We're in for hard times, very hard indeed!'

CHAPTER ONE

In the forest wilds, far from the roads and human habitation stood a solitary farm, called the Pit. It was generally known that no one had lived there for years. The old owner had died, and no one seemed to want to take the place over.

But one fine day, a villager who happened to be passing that way noticed a wisp of smoke trailing from the chimney. Obviously some people had settled there, but who those people were didn't interest anyone much: after all, who cared if the Pit had a new tenant? Some time passed, and finally the news reached the authorities, and the new tenant was interviewed. His papers were found to be in order. His name was Jürka, he had a wife named Lisete, they had been married in church, and they were childless.

'Who gave you permission to move into the Pit?' he was asked.

'It was God's will,' Jürka replied.

'But it's not God who owns the place!'

'Who else?' asked Jürka.

From Jürka's replies it was concluded that he and his wife belonged to some kind of sect, and that they both had a screw loose. Actually, they were the right sort for the Pit, because people who are in their right mind usually seek the company of their own kind.

'How did you know that the Pit was untenanted?' Jürka was asked.

'Because there were no people there,' Jürka replied.

'And there were people in all the other places,' Lisete explained.

'Well, do you like it there?'

'I guess so.'

'And the name of the place, too?' the official asked, smiling ironically.

'The name more than anything else,' Jürka replied gravely.

'Well, if that's how you feel, you may stay on at the Pit and feel at home there with your missus, like Old Nick himself would. No one's going to bother you.'

'Like Old Nick and his missus,' Jürka repeated, and gave a roar of laughter that sounded like a horse's neigh coming from an empty barrel.

The official stared at Jürka in astonishment. He had never heard anything like this before: surely a human throat couldn't have made that noise?

And as he stared at Jürka it occurred to him that he had never seen anyone like him before either. Jürka was as broad across the shoulders as he was tall. His arms stuck out as though avoiding contact with his body. His face was broad and pockmarked; the forehead was low and sort of concave; the head was large and round, and the hair was red and curly. In front of the ears it merged with a beard, the same red colour, and the growth covered not just his neck but, apparently, his chest as well. In fact, it was difficult to tell where the growth ended. Even his legs seemed to be covered with matted fur.

The slight, somewhat stooped woman with coal-black hair looked strangely ill-matched with her bulky, hairy man. How did they happen to marry, and how did they get along? But they weren't newlyweds, so obviously they must get along.

'I see you've no children,' the official said. 'You should have children, otherwise there's no sense in taking over land and toiling on it.'

'There will be children,' Jürka said.

'They'll come if there's bread enough,' said Lisete, to affirm her husband's words.

'And there hasn't been until now?' the official asked.

'Obviously. Seeing as we're childless,' Lisete replied.

'Too true,' Jürka mumbled into his beard.

'If the Lord sends you children, He'll send you bread too,' the official continued.

'I guess so,' Jürka said.

The formalities took some time, but this did not worry the new tenants of the Pit in the slightest. They seemed to have all the time in the world, they did not fuss or fret, just calmly sat and waited. Lisete started saying something to her husband every now and again, but he always cut short her attempts at conversation, saying: 'Shut up, you're bothering the gentleman.'

Sitting so nicely and quietly made Jürka terribly sleepy. But the moment he dropped off and gave his first tentative snore, his wife jabbed him in the ribs with an elbow and scolded:

'Have you no shame? A fine time to snore! Can't you behave like a good Christian?'

'What's that?' Jürka started up, his eyes popping.

'Don't snore, you hear me?'

The formalities were finally over, and the new tenants of the Pit were free to go home, but Jürka sprawled comfortably in his chair again, reluctant to leave this place, evidently liking it here. Lisete stood beside him for a minute, and then said:

'Come on, let's go, shall we? Time to go home.'

'I guess so,' Jürka replied, without budging.

'Come on, get up, what are you waiting for?' Lisete said, but as her husband did not so much as stir, she grabbed hold of his sleeve and started tugging him, saying with every tug: 'Get up, time to go, get up, time to go!'

'I guess it is,' Jürka said, and heaved himself up from his chair.

He went out of the door first, with his wife coming after him. And that's how they strode down the road – the husband in front, and the wife behind. They were both silent at first, and then the old woman began to nag:

'We've a roof over our heads now, but we've neither a pig, nor a lamb, nor a calf, nor a cock and hen. It would be nice to get a baby pig to start with, we could put it in the pen, and it would go grunt-grunt, grunt-grunt.'

Jürka strode on without saying anything, but suddenly he stopped the first woman they met and said:

'My old woman would like to get a young pig.'

'Dear man, I've nothing, neither a young pig nor anything else, alas,' the woman replied. 'The last pig I had was about ten years ago, but he went down with the fever and died, and never rose again.'

'Do they sometimes rise?' Jürka asked.

'The master's hog did. He quite died in the night, and in the morning he was as good as new and, eating out of the trough. It gave everyone a turn, it did, it seemed the end of the world was near. People couldn't have long till Doomsday, if animals had started rising from the dead.'

'Your pig didn't rise from the dead, eh?'

'No, my good man, it hasn't risen to this day,' the woman replied.

'Oh well, good day to you, then,' Jürka said, and strode on his way with Lisete trotting behind, and the woman watching them go.

Before long they met an old man, and Jürka approached him with the same words:

'My old woman wants to get a young pig...'

The old peasant gave Jürka a startled look, as if he didn't quite understand him, and then asked:

'You mean you'd like to buy a young pig?'

'I guess so,' Jürka replied.

'You don't hail from these parts, do you?' the peasant inquired.

'No, we're from afar... my old woman and me...'

'Farmers, are you?'

'I guess so.'

'And you've no pigs of your own?'

'I guess not.'

'Is yours a large farm?'

'I guess so.'

'And what is it called?'

'The Pit.'

17

'Oh, so you're the new tenant!'

'I guess so.'

'And you're looking for a young pig?'

'I guess so.'

'Have you got yourself a cow already?'

'No.'

'A horse?'

'No, no horse.'

'A sheep?'

'No, no sheep.'

'What will you do with a young pig if you've nothing else? What are you going to feed it with? You must get a cow first, and only after that buy a pig. The hen clucks first, and only then will the rooster sing.'

Having told Jürka what he ought to know, the peasant went on his way. Jürka gazed after him, as though expecting the man to turn round, and when he didn't, called out:

'What about the pig, eh?'

The old peasant stopped, turned round and said:

'I have no young pigs. All I have is a horse, and if the price was good I'd sell it.'

He said this, and continued on his way. But no sooner did Jürka and Lisete start down the road than he shouted after them:

'What about the horse? Sure you won't buy it?'

This time it was Jürka who stopped. He turned round, thought for a moment, and said:

'I guess not.'

He said this, and continued on his way with his old woman following.

'If you don't take it, you'll be making a foolish mistake,' the peasant shouted, but Jürka ignored it.

'A good man, his manner and talk couldn't be better, but he doesn't have a young pig ,' Jürka said, after a while.

'Sure, he acts good and well-mannered so as to palm his nag off on us,' said Lisete.

'I guess you're right,' Jürka agreed.

For a long time after this no sound was heard from them but

the heavy thud of Jürka's feet – stomp, stomp, and, breaking
into it, the patter of Lisete's mincing steps: tip-top, tip-top.
They remained silent until they encountered a sprightly young
village wife. And Jürka said to her:

'My old woman would like to get a young pig.'

'Are you looking for young pigs? Why, our neighbours have
a very good sow. She's just had a farrow of a dozen or maybe a
baker's dozen, and the piglets are each one better than the other,
lovely things!'

'That's where we could get one then,' Lisete said
confidently.

'What a hope!' the young woman cried. 'I wanted to buy a
couple for myself, but I tried in vain, and so I had to go to the
fair for them. What can you do if your neighbours won't sell?'

'D'you mean they've kept them all?' Jürka asked.

'The whole farrow, if you please! It'll be a good thing if they
can rear two or three. A piglet won't grow at all, and...'

'Seems there's little hope of getting one there?' Lisete
interrupted the flow.

'None, not this year, not the next one, not ever! Unless they
get another sow. But the old miser won't, no use counting on it.
He's that kind of person: if he says no, he means no. He told me
personally, in front of people too, that he didn't care if his sow
overlay or trampled all her farrow, he'd just take her back to the
boar again, that's all! People grow wiser with age, he says, so
maybe the sow would get more sense in her head, too, and learn
not to trample or overlie her young.'

'The mother herself, fancy that!' Lisete and Jürka gasped
together.

'The mother herself,' the young woman confirmed and,
coming a step closer, dropped her voice as though she were
imparting a secret to them: 'She killed the lot, squashing them in
her sleep or stepping on them. All but one, and that one must
have died a natural death. The mistress says it's either because
he was lonely without the others, or because he had overeaten.
She's a big sow, you know, her teats are bursting with milk, and
that one got it all, there were no others, you see. Only better keep

19

mum about it, because there's talk of an evil eye, and the mistress says that if anyone did put a blight on her sow it must have been us. But, heavens above, what have we got to do with it? No one had even seen the piggies alive except me! But the mistress goes on telling everybody that my mother-in-law saw the sow just before she was farrowed and said: "A fine sow you have there, she'll soon give you a nice litter of young." And where's that nice litter now, I ask you? And so the mistress says that it's my mother-in-law who put the blight on the pigs, and seeing as I stuck up for her I was no better myself. And so I said to her: "What's wrong with my mother-in-law? She's a kind old soul, we get on ever so well." And the mistress went on again: "How can she be kind when she has brown eyes?" And I said: "Oh well, what if she does have brown eyes? If it's a blemish, then, of course..."'

'Well, good day to you,' Jürka said, anxious to be on his way.

'And to you, too,' the young woman said, breaking off her tale, and quickly added: 'D'you want a kitten, while you're looking for a pig? We have some, they're sweet little grey kittens. Our cat had five, we drowned three in the pail and kept two, one of them we can give away for free, if we're giving it into good hands. Children can never let a kitten be, and it's only elderly people who can rear a real cat. How many children do you have, I wonder?'

'We haven't any yet,' Lisete told her.

'Our kitten couldn't find a better home then! Would you like to come with me now and take it, it's not heavy to carry.'

'What d'you say, old woman?' Jürka asked his wife.

'If we can't get a pig, we might make do with a kitten,' Lisete replied.

The three of them went to fetch the kitten. Lisete was glad there'd be another living creature in the house besides the two of them. But things turned out not quite as Jürka and his wife expected, and not as the young woman told them it would be. Although her husband was considered the master of the house, it was actually his mother who ruled the household. The chatterbox of a young wife had only this one right – to chatter, but when it came to acting, she couldn't do a thing without her mother-in-law's approval. When the older woman heard what the strangers had come for, she started pelting them with questions right away:

'Have you a cow?'

'I guess not,' replied Jürka.

'You guess not? Yes or no?'

'Not yet,' Lisete said.

'What will you feed the kitten, I'd like to know? Fresh milk is what it needs, it'll die without it.'

'I'll fetch milk from the village. A kitten can't want much,' Lisete said reasonably.

'But it's all of two or three kilometres from the Pit to the village!' the mother-in-law said.

'Never mind,' Jürka said. 'My old woman has the legs for it, none better.'

'No, it's no use,' the old mistress decided. 'Get a cow first, and then come for the kitten.'

'I guess you're right,' Jürka muttered, and turned to go.

Lisete, however, wasn't going to give in so easily. She felt so lonely, she told the mother-in-law, she'd love the kitten so and take such good care of it!

'I'll take it along when I go for the milk, and let the darling drink it fresh and warm: lap it up, pussy, lap it to your heart's content! Believe me, mistress, you couldn't find a better home for your kitten in the whole wide world,' she concluded her lengthy wheedling.

The mistress thought it over, and asked her daughter-in-law:

'What do you say, Leeni, shall we let them have it?'

'I would, if it were up to me.'

'Do that then,' the mother-in-law said, feeling well pleased that the newcomers addressed her as 'mistress' and not her daughter-in-law, and that her daughter-in-law had herself implied to the newcomers who the mistress was. 'Put the kitten in a basket with something nice and soft for bedding.'

This was done at once. The only hitch was finding something to tie the basket with. There was not a rag the old mistress would spare to go with the kitten and the ancient basket. These people were strangers, after all, so how could one be sure they'd ever return anything? And here Lisete had a brainwave.

'Take off your neckerchief,' she told Jürka. 'It's so dark and grimy, it'll do very well.'

While he was wondering whether he ought to take his neckerchief off or not, Lisete went to work with her hands and, before he knew what was happening, she had the neckerchief wrapped round the basket.

'There, my darling pussy, there, my precious dear,' she crooned as she tied the knot. 'You'll like living with us, you'll do anything you please... If birds sing in front of the door, go after them; if mice scurry across the floor just grab them with a paw; and if rats start running between the barn and the house, go ahead and...'

The mother-in-law sprang forward and snatched the basket from Lisete's hands.

'What's this I hear? You have rats and you think I'll let you take my kitten there? Not on your life! If there's no old cat to defend the kitten, the nasty things will gobble it up straight away. Leeni, take the kitten and carry it home.'

The daughter-in-law did as she was told.

'Heaven forbid! Would I let the rats get at pussy?' Lisete cried in protest. 'Won't I be there to protect it?'

But the old mistress remained deaf to her protestations. And so Lisete and Jürka had to continue on their way empty-handed, with neither a young pig nor a kitten.

'Crazy people,' Lisete grumbled as they walked out of the yard. 'We've mice and rats, and so they won't let us have their cat. If we had a cow, they would have. Sit under the cow all day, pussy dear, and lap up the milk!'

'Don't run on so!' Jürka said. 'It's you who told them that we have rats and mice running about the house. People didn't know.'

'Should I have told them we've bears running about the house?'

'I guess you should. A bear won't savage a kitten, it's too

22

small, but it would clout you on the head sure enough.'

On hearing this, Lisete stared fixedly at her husband.

'Where's your neckerchief, I'd like to know, you dumb cluck?'

'You took it off yourself and tied it round the basket!'

'Some people!' Lisete fumed. 'They won't give us the kitten, but they pinch our neckerchief! What are you waiting for, why don't you go back for it?' she turned on Jürka.

'I won't go back.'

'D'you want to lose your neckerchief for good?'

'I guess so,' Jürka replied calmly.

'Then I'll go and get it back!' Lisete declared.

'If you get it back,' Jürka sounded doubtful.

'If they don't return it, I'll simply take it.'

She started back to the farm. But everything turned out to be much simpler and nicer than they anticipated: no sooner had Lisete pushed open the gate than Leeni came rushing past her mother-in-law who stood in the middle of the yard, shouting in a ringing voice:

'Here, good people, you've forgotten your neckerchief!' Thrusting the neckerchief at Lisete, she said under her breath: 'Here, take it quickly together with the kitten, my mother-in-law won't see. Never mind if it wets the neckerchief a bit.'

Without uttering a word, Lisete hurried away with her precious bundle.

'When you've poisoned all the rats, come back for the cat,' Leeni called out, laughing, as she closed the gate behind Lisete.

'And get a cow if you want to rear a cat,' the mother-in-law added, pleased with what Leeni said.

'They're nice people,' Leeni was smiling happily.

'What's so nice about them?' her mother-in-law said. 'They're fools, that's what they are.'

'Of course, they're fools,' Leeni burst out laughing, and the sound reached Lisete and Jürka. The mother-in-law was laughing together with Leeni.

'Listen to them roaring,' Jürka remarked resentfully.

'They've good reason,' Lisete said.

'I guess so.'

'But you don't know why. Look!' Lisete told him, and, knowing that they couldn't be seen now from the place they had left, she showed him the kitten, bundled up in his neckerchief, which she had been hiding under her apron. 'This is why.'

Jürka merely grunted, but when Lisete told him the whole story, he burst out laughing in his turn, and his roars certainly reverberated a good deal farther than the laughing of the mother and daughter-in-law.

'I wish we had a daughter-in-law like her,' Jürka said after a while.

'Like *her*? Why, she'd give away everything you owned right in front of your nose, and strip you bare!'

'But look how she laughs,' Jürka persisted.

'She's laughing at the person she robbed, stupid.'

'I guess you're right.'

Of course, she had laughed not at him but at her mother-in-law, and the mother-in-law had laughed at herself. The realisation gave him courage and confidence. 'My old woman has her kitten now, so maybe we'll find a young pig too,' he said to himself. To make their dream come true quicker, he stopped every person they met, and got into quite a long conversation with a girl who was tending cows near the road. Jürka and Lisete believed they were on the right track, but again their hopes were dashed: the people for whom this girl tended cows did have two young pigs, but they wanted to keep them, and the rest of the farrow they had sold ages ago. The footsore couple didn't break their hearts over this. While talking with the girl they sat on a hummock and rested, which was something, at least.

They continued on their way, addressing everyone they met on the subject of the young pig, and at last they reached the farmsteads nearest to their home. And it was only here that a lame hunchback – a shoemaker or a tailor, it was hard to say – told them that if they needed anything it was best to go straight to Cunning Ants, for he had everything, and he could fix anything too.

'You think we can get a young pig from him?' Jürka asked.

'That too,' replied the lame hunchback who was either a tailor or a shoemaker.

'Does he own any cows?'

'Cows too.'

'And a horse?'

'And a horse.'

'And what's he like himself?'

'And what sort of bird are you if you don't know Cunning Ants?' the hunchback asked instead of answering.

They took a good look at one another – the hefty Jürka, and the hunchback, who was no bigger than a fly in comparison.

'You go straight from here, then you turn right, then left, until you come to a birch with two trunks,' the hunchback said. 'Walk on a little way, and then you'll see Cunning Ants' house. Anyone you ask will show you the way, everybody knows Ants, and you'll know him too once you've been there.'

Jürka, followed by his old woman hugging the kitten, went to look for the birch with two trunks. They did what the hunchback told them to do: first they turned right, then left, and there was the birch, further on there was Cunning Ants' house, just off the road, and Ants himself standing at the gate. Jürka, however, could not have known that this was Ants, and so he asked:

'Is this where Cunning Ants lives? My old woman wants to get a young pig.'

'I see, I see,' Ants chuckled. 'What else can an old woman want but a young pig and a lamb!'

'A heifer wouldn't go amiss either,' Jürka said.

'Obviously,' Ants chuckled again. 'Nor would a horse, eh?'

'I guess not,' Jürka said.

'Where are you from?'

'From the Pit.'

'Oh, so it's your chimney the smoke's trailing from, so people say?'

'I guess so. It's the old woman's doing,' Jürka added as an afterthought.

'I see, I see,' Ants said again, and scratched the meagre beard sprouting from his chin. 'Your papers in order?'

'That's what we went for today.'

'Well, well, well, so the Pit has got a new tenant. The last one came to be called Old Nick; let's see how you make out. Are you going to follow in his footsteps?'

'What's in a nickname? What we need is a young pig,' Jürka said.

'The Old Nick ended up by owning no pig, and the new one starts with getting one,' Ants chuckled. 'You look pretty tough, strong enough to take on the real Old Nick. That's the kind of master the Pit wants, a punier man wouldn't do. The last tenant was on the weak side.'

A silence fell between them.

'How about that young pig?' Jürka asked after a while.

'Don't you need a lamb and a heifer as well?' Ants replied with a question.

'Just a pig will do for a start,' Jürka said.

'He'd grunt so nicely in his pen,' Lisete added.

'Oh well, you have the right idea,' Ants said, chuckling again. 'Pity the master is not at home just now...'

'Ants, you mean?'

'Who else? It's Ants you're looking for, isn't it?'

'And what might you be, his farm hand?'

'Not quite. I live in his house.'

'It's the right place then,' Jürka said with relief.

'The very place,' Ants said. 'Now, about that young pig this is what we'll do: I'll try sounding out the master, and if it's all right I'll send you message or come over myself to spare you the trudge. On your way from here, when you reach the big birch tree don't go straight on, as you did before, because that's the longer, roundabout way, but turn left, cutting across the meadow, and you'll come out on to the road running to the Pit. That's a short cut. The other Old Nick always came that way to see Cunning Ants. He was the one who trod the path.'

Jürka did as the man told him, and on reaching the birch he turned left. Lisete followed close behind.

'He's a good man, friendly too. I'd like to know what his

master is like,' Jürka said when they had crossed the meadow.

'You'll see when you go to fetch the pig,' Lisete told him.

'Who knows,' Jürka muttered.

'What's there to know?'

'Whether we get the pig or not.'

'If we don't, what use is Ants to you?'

'Because that farm hand, or whoever he was, spoke about a lamb, a heifer and a horse.'

'And you believed him? Your mouth watered, did it? Let's see if we get the young pig or not. And thank the Lord for the kitten, though we did get it by trickery, and hope to God that the mother-in-law doesn't come after us. Your precious neckerchief, by the way, is wet through...'

Talking so nicely, they came out on to the road and shuffled along it to their house. Once there, Lisete remembered that there wasn't a drop of milk for the kitten in the house. Picking up the old fish can with the string handle which served as a pail, she rushed back to the village as fast as her legs would go. She gave the kitten to Jürka, telling him to handle the little darling gently and not to let go of it for a minute, because the naughty thing might escape and there'd be no catching it afterwards.

'Don't worry,' Jürka told her. 'It won't get away from me!'

Saying this, he sat down on the step with the late afternoon sun upon him, and, holding the kitten in his left hand, began to stroke it with his right hand, crooning:

'Ah, you tiny little pussy cat! You don't like being bundled up in that neckerchief, do you? Scratch-scratch, here we go pushing out one paw, and now the second one, here comes the third one, and scratch-scratch the...'

Before he could say the 'fourth', the kitten jumped down, and while Jürka was heaving himself up from the threshold the naughty thing had already scrambled up the wall to the attic. Jürka stood there, staring hard at the place where the kitten had disappeared. What would the old woman say when she came back with the milk? The worst thing was the shame of it: he was a big, tough man, and he couldn't hold a kitten! As if he didn't have the strength or the sense.

He decided to climb up into the attic* and catch the kitten before his wife came back. He took off his jacket, just in case he had any clambering to do. He did not doubt that he'd catch the kitten, because how could a little animal escape a man, inside a building too!

But once he was in the attic, he realised that it wouldn't be as simple as he imagined. After the sunlit yard it seemed very dark in here with the light barely trickling in through the chimney and the chink along the eaves. In order to get to the kitten, to that part of the attic which was above their living quarters, he had to walk across a floor of planks. Maybe there never was any decent flooring here, or perhaps someone had pulled out a lot of the planks, but, either way, walking wasn't any too safe as you were liable to crash through the planks down to the hard mud floor below.

There was nothing for it but to go down on all fours and crawl. The tall, angular and sooty platform made by the barn section barred his way like some sprawling monster. It meant either clambering over it or squeezing around it. Jürka chose the latter course. He clung to the roof where tufts of straw, on which soot and dust had accumulated over the years, hung down between the laths. The dirty straw brushed against his face and the sleeves of his white shirt, but Jürka didn't care. He crawled on, and at last reached the attic over their dwelling rooms. It was so dark here, that at first he could not make out a thing, though he heard the soft patter of running paws. Jürka crouched. Two eyes burning like hot coals seemed to stare at him from the gloom. Ah, there it was!

'You just wait, you rascal,' Jürka whispered. 'I'll throw my hat over you, then you won't get away.'

He crept towards the burning eyes, holding his hat at the ready, when suddenly the twin lights went out and, in the light seeping

---

* In an Estonian farmhouse, the dwelling, the barn and the threshing floor were under one roof. In this case, the barn where the sheaves were put to dry was between the dwelling and the threshing floor and had the highest ceiling of the three, forming a raised platform in the middle of the attic floor.

in close to the eaves, Jürka saw the kitten leap across to the other side of the attic and race back along the planks. So Jürka had to squeeze through between the roof and the platform again, collecting more soot and grime. When he got to the section above the threshing floor he saw that there were no planks at all here, and none but a cat could leap across. He crawled back the way he had come, wasting so much time that there was no telling where the kitten might have got to by now. However, on reaching the part of the attic where it was lighter he saw the kitten sitting on a plank close to the ladder, watching something down below. Jürka took off his hat and threw it at the kitten, hoping that it would escape to the ground where it was easier to catch. But the hat missed it and the kitten ran to the opposite end of the attic above the threshing floor. Jürka crawled over with the greatest difficulty because what planks there were started rolling away when he put his hand or knees on them. In the meantime the kitten had run to the darkest corner near the eaves, and Jürka went after it.

'Well, dearie, you won't get away from me now,' he gloated, creeping closer to the fugitive, but just as he reached for it the kitten slipped under the edge of the roof, apparently meaning to jump down to the ground. But to his surprise Jürka discovered that there was another small attic there, belonging to an annex built on to the rear wall of the dwelling section. The kitten was safe there, there was no reaching it in that small attic. Jürka went down the ladder and tried poking a long, thin stick into the chinks, but it only made the kitten escape to the main attic again. When Jürka tried to catch it there, it slipped away into the small attic. Jürka clambered up the ladder, then hurried down and poked with the stick, and up the ladder again. This went on until his patience snapped, and he decided to pull the annex apart, because he had to catch the kitten, didn't he? Just as he started tearing the first planks away, he heard Lisete's voice from around the corner of the building.

'Old man! Where are you? Give me the kitten, I've brought the milk.'

He had to leave the annex alone, worse luck. What was he to do, and what to tell his wife? And then she started calling him again, and he had to come out and face her.

'My, what a scarecrow!' Lisete screamed when she saw what a sight he was. 'You're sweating as though you'd been threshing all day! What have you been up to? And look at your shirt! It was snow-white when I gave it to you this morning.'

Jürka was unable to utter a word.

'And where's the kitten? Where's it gone? You've let it get away, I suppose?'

'I guess so,' Jürka spoke at last.

'And here I am, hurrying home with the milk, all out of breath,' Lisete wailed. 'But what happened, where's the cat?'

'Up in the attic.'

'Did you go after it?'

'I guess so.'

'You didn't catch it?'

'I guess not.'

'Some husband I have! He can't even be trusted to watch a kitten!' Lisete wailed even louder. 'And what were you doing at the back of the house, I'd like to know?'

'Pulling it down, so as to...'

'To catch the kitten?'

'I guess so.'

'Oh merciful God!' Lisete screamed. 'I leave him alone for a minute and he starts pulling the house down right away!'

'But there was no other way of catching it...'

'Where is the kitten anyway?'

At last Jürka was able to tell his wife where the kitten was now and where it had been before, how it had got where it was, and what Jürka himself had been doing and what he meant to do next. The two of them went after the kitten together – the old woman climbed up into the attic with the milk, while Jürka stationed himself at the back of the house with the long stick. And what do you think! When the kitten saw the bowl of milk, it ran to it and started lapping it up, and Lisete grabbed hold of it without any difficulty at all! This was the first great joy to befall the new tenants of the Pit.

.

CHAPTER TWO

On a clear, sunny day the mistress of the Pit was sitting on a log beside the front door and watching the kitten lapping up its milk. Before giving it to the darling she had tasted the white stuff herself for fear it had gone sour in the night and might upset the kitty's stomach. The milk had seemed fresh enough, and so she had poured it into a bowl of sorts, which was actually the remains of a broken earthenware bowl left behind by the former owners, and pushed the kitty's nose into it.

Jürka, the new master of the Pit, returned just then from the forest with another load of stakes: the fence around the yard had collapsed and wanted fixing. This wasn't Jürka's first trip to the forest: he had brought home several bundles of firewood, and then as many bundles of stakes and timber for repairs. When he saw his wife with the kitten he tried to put down his burden quietly, but still the clatter was so awful that the kitten would have certainly bolted from fright had not Lisete's quick hand caught hold of it.

'Must you raise such a racket?' Lisete began to scold. 'You'd like to drive the kitten up into the attic again, I shouldn't wonder.'

'He's got mettle, for all that he's such a mite,' Jürka marvelled, and came a step closer to look at the kitten which had gone back to lapping up the milk. Man and wife sat in silence for a while. Jürka collected his thoughts at last and spoke:

'Well, mother, what do you think of our life here? We came looking for a roof, and now we're master and mistress of this place. And we already own a cat, too.'

'Seems we'll just have to bear the cross, now that we've come here,' Lisete said. 'We do have a cat but we've no milk for it. You'll be going to the forest for firewood, and I'll be going to the

31

village for milk.'

'If we could come to an arrangement with Cunning Ants, then maybe...'

No sooner were these words out than Ants himself walked into the yard and, with a chuckle, said to Jürka:

'Hello, Old Nick! Yesterday, you called at our place, and today I'm returning the call, because I'm curious to see how you're getting on the Pit. I had some business in the forest, and so I thought I'd drop in, hoping you wouldn't mind.'

'How about the piglet?' Jürka asked.

'What's the rush?' Ants asked in his turn.

'Have you spoken to Ants, your master?'

'Naturally,' replied Ants whom Jürka still believed to be a farm hand.

'And what did he say?'

'Well, Ants reasoned like this: who knows what sort of person this Old Nick is? We knew the one before you, but he went and died. He kept his livestock and poultry to feed on, it seems, and as for feeding them he didn't take the trouble. So, it's best to wait and see how the new Old Nick makes out. Supposing you're given a piglet, you might have to be given a sack of feed as well, so it doesn't starve to death... You spoke about a horse yesterday, and though there's no trace of a wheel or a runner here I see you've a fresh stack of firewood. How did it get here?'

'I brought it on my back,' Jürka explained.

'Must have taken you days, eh?'

'No, only this morning.'

Ants gave him a look, and grinned.

'Pulling my leg, are you? Old Nick had no use for jokes.'

'I haven't either,' Jürka said.

'Are you seriously trying to tell me that you brought more firewood on your back in one morning than two horses harnessed into a cart could haul in a day?'

'I guess so.'

'Well, well,' Ants scratched his chin. 'The Pit, it seems, is going to be in better hands now. Are you thinking of fixing up the fence?'

'I guess so.'

'And how will you till the fields if you've no horse?'

'If only I had a plough...'

'You're in a bad way if you don't even own a plough. What are you about? You've nothing at all, and yet you took the land to work!'

'Why, we have a cat,' Lisete put in.

'So I see. And the milk, too. Got it in the village, did you?'

'I've no cow of my own to milk,' Lisete replied.

'Nor can you produce any kittens yourself, and you have to beg the village folk for one,' Ants said.

'A kitten might stray to the door and cry, but milk has neither legs nor voice.'

'That's very true,' Ants agreed and, turning to Jürka, added: 'Your missus is pretty sharp, and the one before you had a ninny for a wife.'

Jürka burst out laughing raucously, and now Ants stared at him earnestly. Anyone with a roar like that might well have the strength to lug a ton of damp wood on his back.

'To come back to the pig. D'you still want one?' Ants asked.

'I guess so,' Jürka replied.

'For cash, or how?'

'How else?'

'There are different ways of making a bargain,' Ants said, scratching at his chin. 'The former master of the Pit never paid cash for anything. He'd bring a measure of grain, or a sack of potatoes, a pound of wool, half a pood of flax, a bit of firewood from the forest, or maybe he'd cart manure, dig up the potatoes, reap and thresh the wheat, bring in the hay, scutch the flax, or suchlike, and pay that way. It's all money anyway. He didn't like to part with the real kind that rustles and jingles. Ah well, he was made that way – a meek, quiet character. But then, of course, it takes all kinds...'

'The pig I'd buy for cash anyway, but as for the rest...'

'Why buy it from Ants then? You can buy it from anyone for cash, you might even bring it from town and choose any pig you like, the biggest.'

'At first I'll buy things for cash, and then for jobs. I don't have enough cash for everything,' Jürka explained.

'You mean you want to get a ewe, and a heifer, and a horse, and a plough, and a cart?'

'I guess so.'

'They'd all come in useful,' Lisete added.

'Ants will arrange it for you, he'll find a way out. He'll find a pinch of flour he can spare, and a handful of beans or peas, and maybe a slice of bacon fat, and a tuft or two of flax – you'll need a bit of everything in the household.'

About three days after this long talk, Jürka and Lisete decided to call on Cunning Ants himself to have a chat with him and see for themselves how the land lay. And weren't they surprised to discover that the man they'd been speaking to was Ants himself! Jürka was so stunned that he wanted to turn and go at once, because if a thing began with deceit no good would come of it ever. But Ants hastened to set his mind at rest, and said:

'It was just a little game, no harm meant. I wanted to see what sort of people you were, and if it was worth my while to get mixed up with you at all. I see now that it is.'

'Is it?' Jürka asked.

'Of course, and it's the honest truth,' Ants assured him.

'I guess it is,' Jürka confirmed.

'So we'll get our piglet now?' Lisete asked.

'The piglet and everything else, whatever you want,' Ants replied.

And he did keep his word. When Jürka and Lisete were ready to go home to the Pit they were the proud owners of a dilapidated cart and a nag. They hoisted a plough on to the cart, and placed a ewe with her lamb on a bed of straw between the handles, then a box with a grunting young pig, and a sack filled with all sorts of good things. A cow was tethered to the rear end of the cart – a scraggy, dry cow it was, to be sure, but maybe there'd be enough milk for the kitten and the piglet. One would think that Jürka and Lisete had every reason to feel overjoyed, yet strangely they felt no joy at all.

'I was happier about the kitten,' said Lisete at length.

'I guess so,' her husband replied thoughtfully.

'He was our first when we started building up our household, that's why he was such a joy,' Lisete continued. 'He'll have his fresh milk now, and that's when he'll start growing big and strong.'

Lisete spoke of the kitten as if it was on him that the future of their entire household depended. Jürka listened and urged on the horse. His silence seemed to be one of complete agreement with what his wife was saying.

However, the kitten wasn't to enjoy the fresh milk for very long. A few days later, Lisete took the cow out to pasture on the forest edge, where it could nibble last year's grass, when suddenly a bear appeared from the thickets. He hadn't had anything to eat yet after hibernating, and there and then he savaged the poor cow in full view of her stricken mistress. It was a good thing that Lisete herself got safely away together with the ewe and the lamb. She had such a fright that she couldn't utter a word when she came rushing home, and just flapped her arms and pointed at the forest.

'Huh?' Jürka said.

'A bear,' Lisete blurted out at last. 'A bear's savaged the cow.'

'Nonsense,' Jürka said.

'It's true, it's true! Pity we've no rifle.'

Jürka took his axe with the long handle, and growled: 'Where? Come along, show me where.'

'Oh, don't go, my precious, my darling!' Lisete implored him. 'Not with just an axe! Better let the bear devour the cow, because if you go he'll eat you up too, and I'll be left alone with the kitten!'

Turning a deaf ear to the woman's pleas, Jürka hoisted the axe on his shoulder and strode off to the forest.

'He's a huge black bear, so shaggy and ferocious. I'm still weak at the knees from fright,' Lisete wailed, keeping close behind her husband.

'Show me where,' Jürka told her.

Neither the bear nor the cow were where Lisete had left them. The bear must have dragged his prey into the thickets. Jürka plunged into the forest, and the bear growled on hearing him. The thickets were so dense that he couldn't swing his axe there, and so

35

Jürka went in a circle round the bear, looking for a spot where the trees were thinner.

'Step back,' he told Lisete. 'Women have no business here.'

'I won't step back,' Lisete replied. 'If he savages you, let him kill me and the kitten too.'

Jürka hadn't noticed before that she had the kitten in her arms.

'All right, we'll all three go for it – you, me, and the cat,' Jürka conceded.

'And there are two of *them* – the bear and the dead cow,' Lisete said, and the kitten miaowed.

'Better stand back so I don't hit you before I axe the bear.'

Lisete fell back a little as her husband went straight for the bear, holding the axe at the ready. The bear stopped tearing at the dead cow, and came out into the open.

'Come on, come closer, I'll get a better swing,' Jürka muttered.

The man and the beast were coming closer. Lisete covered the kitten's eyes with a hand and shut her own eyes tight so as not to see the horror of it. But actually nothing frightening happened – Jürka brought the axe down on the bear's head, and when the beast collapsed in a heap he proceeded to pull the axe out of the skull.

'I split it like a turnip, and now I can't get the axe out,' Jürka grumbled as he tugged.

Lisete's fear of the bear evaporated.

'Felling a bear is as easy for you as kneading dough,' she said to her husband, walking right up to the bear. Letting the kitten walk over the dead beast, she crooned over him: 'See, you silly darling, we got the better of a bear, the three of us, see?'

Jürka was taking a good look at the dead cow.

'A neat kill, this,' he said. 'He bled her to the last drop, everything's just right. The beef can be salted, and the hide's only slightly damaged close to the neck.'

'What are we going to do with the bear?' his wife wanted to know.

'We'll skin him like the cow, and what else is there?'

'Is the flesh no good?'

'We'll see. After all, he had nothing but his paw to suck all

36

winter.'

Jürka took out the knife he carried tucked behind his belt, and got down to work. His wife helped him, and the kitten looked on. When the animals had been skinned and the flesh chopped up, Jürka went home, harnessed the nag into the cart and drove back to collect the hides and the meat.

'Our possessions are increasing,' Lisete said when Jürka returned with the horse and cart. 'We have now got our meat and hides, too.'

'I guess so,' Jürka muttered.

On the following morning he went to Ants's place to tell him that a bear had savaged his cow.

'Did you actually see the bear doing it?' Ants asked.

'I did. And my old woman saw it too.'

'It's all right then. If it had been a wolf it would have been quite a different matter. The government pays if it's a bear, because bears are state property, you know, there for the bigwigs to hunt. Now, anyone who owns livestock is bound to feed it, and so the bears have a free choice of food, it might be a cow, or a bull or a horse.'

Ants spoke of the hunting laws and hunting practice very knowledgeably, and Jürka listened open-mouthed and didn't have to say a word. And so Ants never learnt that Jürka had felled the bear with an axe, skinned it and stretched the skin to dry on the wall of his house. All this came out only after the authorities demanded proof from Jürka that it was indeed a bear who had savaged his cow. The whole story sounded rather doubtful, because according to the forest guard there was not a single bear in these parts, for if there were the hunters would have gone for its lair in the winter. So what was all this about a bear who, what is more, was alleged to have killed a cow! Where? Under what circumstances? Nobody had seen the cow: it had been skinned and chopped up before the investigation.

'Did you truly see the bear with your own eyes?' Jürka was asked.

'I did,' Jürka assured them.

'And did you see it savage the cow?'

'My missus saw it.'

'And when did *you* see the bear?'

'When I was killing it.'

Everyone gaped and glanced suspiciously at Jürka.

'He was eating the cow, and I hit him with my axe,' Jürka explained.

'Tell us another!' someone said, and everyone laughed.

'I have the hide at home, stretched on the wall,' Jürka told them.

'And yet you want to be reimbursed for the cow?'

'You killed that bear during the fence months.'

'But how else was I to get the cow away from him?' Jürka asked. 'My missus saw it: the bear went for me, and what was I supposed to do? I only hit him that once with the axe. I never meant to kill him, I thought I'd give him a scare, but he...'

'All right, we'll leave it at that,' Jürka was told. Still, the bearskin was requisitioned. True, he was reimbursed for the cow, but it was Ants who took the money and also the hide, so all that was left to Jürka were the chunks of bear flesh which he tried to salt, and some lean beef, and that only because Ants said that he and his family wouldn't eat the beef of a cow savaged by a bear: he ceded the honour to Old Nick from the Pit. Lisete was saddened and disappointed, but Jürka's reasoning comforted her.

'Thank God that I got out of it so easily. It was clever of me to tell them that I never meant to kill the beast and only wanted to frighten him a bit. Killing a bear isn't a small thing, seeing that...'

'But giving the toffs' bears a fright is allowed, you mean?' Lisete asked.

'I guess so.'

'And if they don't take fright, you're allowed to kill them, are you?'

'I guess you are.'

'And where are we to get another cow from? There'll be no milk for the kitten and the pig, you know.'

'Ants has promised to fix it.'

'He certainly has a heart of gold, Cunning Ants has, making our troubles his own,' Lisete murmured sentimentally.

'I guess he has...'

And they were right. A few days later a message was brought to the Pit that if the master and mistress wanted to have another cow they could come for it. Jürka and Lisete went. This cow was a bag of bones, even scraggier than the other one.

'What d'you want a good cow for if you're going to graze in the forest? Another bear might savage her, there are more bears in the forest, that one wasn't alone. Above all else see that no wolves attack her, because their food is not provided by the worldly authorities but just by the merciful God in heaven,' Ants told them.

'Oh wolves, I'll scare them away with my screams,' Lisete said.

'In that case you've nothing to fear,' Ants said. 'A bear now, that's a useful beast.'

Feeling much the wiser for Ants's lecture, Jürka and Lisete went home with the cow. Jürka led her on a tether, and Lisete urged her on from behind, scolding all the while because the silly animal refused to come after her master.

'What do you think about all this?' she asked Jürka when she got tired of scolding the cow.

'About all what?'

'The new cow and everything else. What if a bear savages this one too? Ants warned us, you know.'

'I guess he did.'

'And you'd kill the bear again?'

'I can't tell now... Well, if he doesn't take fright...'

'And if he does?'

'Shut up, will you.'

'You'd like me to do all my talking with the cow, I s'pose,' she snapped, and relapsed into a hurt silence, but not for long. 'We'll soon start working for Ants in payment,' she said, as though talking to herself.

'He told me to come tomorrow,' Jürka said.

'Merciful God! Tomorrow?' Lisete cried. 'Why, you were supposed to start only next week!'

'It's the second cow, that's why.'

'Too true,' Lisete sighed. 'I won't know where to begin all by myself! There's the kitten to watch, the pig to feed, the cow and the ewe to graze in the forest. And who's going to go for the bear if he attacks the cow?'

'Come to Ants's place for me, what else could you do?'

'You think the bear will wait for you to come?'

'That he will if he starts on the cow.'

And that's how they lived from then on: Jürka worked at Ants's place all the time, and Lisete managed the household. The only time Jürka could get anything done round the house was at night or on Sunday. Even so, Ants wanted Lisete to come and help occasionally because the debt would never be paid with just Jürka's labour. Lisete, however, refused to comply: there'd be no one to look after the house, so it couldn't done.

'Who's going to watch the kitten with me gone?' she demanded.

But events took an unexpected turn at the Pit, nearly providing a solution to this problem. One fine day, the young woman who gave Lisete the kitten came to ask for it back.

'My mother-in-law keeps calling me a cat-thief morning, noon and night,' the young woman told Lisete. 'If it were a horse I'd stolen, but stealing cats! I can't live down the shame.'

'How does your mother-in-law know that it was you who pinched her kitten?' Lisete asked.

'She doesn't know, she suspects it.'

'There you are! If you bring the kitten back she'll *know* it was you.'

'I'll sneak it in.'

'Well. I'm not giving the kitten back to you, even if you put the law on me. I wouldn't tell the truth in court either, I wouldn't tell them I got it from you. So do whatever you wish. Let your mother-in-law scold all she likes, it won't kill you. Let her come here, and I'll tell her where I got the kitten.'

'And you won't give me away?'

'D'you take me for a fool or what?'

'Well, goodbye then,' the young woman said happily and, climbing over the fence, started for the forest. 'I'm going through the forest because of my mother-in-law,' she shouted from the other side of the fence.

Two days after this the mother-in-law herself descended upon Lisete.

'And what's new in the village?' Lisete asked, inviting her guest indoors.

'Our kitten has been stolen, and people say there's one exactly like it at the Pit. A grey kitten with stripes.'

'Like the one I'm holding now?'

'Exactly like it. Why, it is our kitten.'

'And there aren't any like it in the whole wide world!'

'Why not? There are, naturally. Where did you get it?'

'I didn't. He came here himself.'

'A tiny kitten like that came to the Pit all by himself?'

'Not by himself, with his mother,' Lisete replied.

'Rubbish!' the mother-in-law snorted. 'And where is his mother, I'd like to know?'

'She was here one minute and gone the next. She found a nice home for her baby son, and vanished. Maybe the rats got her, or maybe a bear. A bear did savage our cow, you know, so why couldn't one savage a cat? He'd strike her once, and that would be the end of it.'

'You'd better own up that it was my daughter-in-law who brought you the kitten.'

'What daughter-in-law?' Lisete asked innocently.

'You don't know that either, eh? You don't remember the woman who offered you the kitten, do you? Lord, what a bitch that woman is! She'll cheat you before your very eyes, and rob you of what you own! And why is it this kind of women that men fall for? If I didn't keep my eyes and ears open I don't know what would become of my son. Believe it or not, I've lost sleep, I keep awake day and night, making my rounds to see that nothing's gone. And still things get stolen, whatever I do. Now, if only I could get to the bottom of this – how did she bring the kitten to you and when?'

'You mustn't blame your daughter-in-law. She may be bad through and through, but she never brought the kitten here.'

'Good heavens above, how did he get here then?' the mother-in-law wailed.

'Maybe there are rats in your house like there are in ours, and maybe it's they who got your kitten?'

'Who can tell about those pests,' the mother-in-law said, starting to waver. 'Only I haven't noticed any rats about. Can you swear by your immortal soul that the kitten came here by himself?'

'I can,' Lisete replied. 'He came with his mother, where from I don't know, and where the mother's gone I don't know either.'

Still, the older woman would not believe Lisete, though swear she did by her immortal soul. The grudge she had against her daughter-in-law wouldn't let her. That wench was at the bottom of everything that went wrong in the household or went against the mistress's wishes!

No sooner was the old woman out of the gate than in she walked again to have another go at Lisete and catch her off her guard. She'd let her keep the kitten if Lisete owned up.

But Lisete stood her ground.

'I swore that it wasn't your daughter-in-law who brought me the kitten. I did see a kitten in her hands that time we came to your place, but that's all I know, if the Lord God Himself were to ask me.'

'Well, that's whom we shall have to ask,' the older woman said. 'There's a fortune teller I know, a devout soul, she goes to church first and prays and only after that she lays out the cards and reads them. I'll go and see her, I won't give up until I get to the bottom of this business. People must reap what they sow, I always say.'

She said this and left.

'Did you hear me perjuring my immortal soul for you, you silly darling?' Lisete murmured, fondling and kissing the kitten. 'When you're worth no more than a darning needle. But then, my swearing an oath is worth as little. See, how I love you?'

CHAPTER THREE

Jürka and Lisete were driven harder and harder as spring came and sowing time loomed near. Ants threatened to take away the livestock and tools he sold them if they didn't hurry up and settle their debt to him. And since working off the debt took Jürka's entire time, his own home and plot were left untended. And once again it was Ants who pointed the way out for them.

'You'll have to hire a farm hand, there's nothing for it,' he told Jürka. 'It'll pay if you hire a lad to help the missus round the house, and then you'll be able to work fulltime for me and square your debt. You'll see how things go, maybe you'll hire a girl later on and then you'll have a proper farmstead with a master and mistress, a farm hand and a girl servant.'

'We'll be short of a shepherd,' Jürka said.

'Get a herd first,' Ants admonished him. 'Keeping a shepherd to tend just one cow, one ewe and one kitten is too much of a good thing. You'll go hungry yourself.'

'I guess so.'

And so a farm hand was hired. While he pottered on Jürka's strip of land, Jürka slaved for Ants – a farm hand himself. He thought it might be a good idea if he sent the lad over to Ants to work in his place and pay off his debt for the horse and everything else, but Ants refused quite flatly.

'No, it's you who bought the horse and cow from me, so it's you and none other who must work off the debt. That's the way it's done.'

So Jürka remained with Ants, and the farm hand moved into the Pit with Lisete, and lived there as if she were his and not Jürka's missus.

Day followed day and week followed week, and Jürka did not even rightly know what was happening at home, at the Pit. The little he heard was mainly from Ants, who sometimes stopped at the Pit when business took him to those forest parts. Jürka grew worried, and one night he decided to go home. He found the door bolted. He knocked, but no one opened the door, and he broke it in. As he stepped into the room, the farm hand jumped out of the window. Jürka dashed after him, but the window was too small and he got stuck. In his rage he started wrenching at the boards to widen it, but pulled himself up in time: a no-good farm hand was not worth smashing a house for. He rushed out through the door he had broken in, and started after the lad who made for the forest. Jürka gave up the chase and went back to the house. He came and stood over his wife's bed. Lisete was fast asleep, sleeping the sleep of the righteous.

'Wake up, woman!' Jürka's yell made the walls tremble.

'Oh, it's you, my darling husband!' Lisete opened her eyes and cried in the sweetest voice Jürka had ever heard from her. 'I've just had a dream about you, as if you came here on a great, black stallion, and the stallion had smoke and fire pouring from his nostrils...'

'What was that no-good farm hand doing in your room?'

'What farm hand, dearest, what are you talking about? It's you I saw in my dream.'

'Why didn't you open the door when I knocked?'

'So help me, I never heard it!'

'I broke down the door, and the farm hand jumped out of the window.'

'The stupid lout!' Lisete said angrily. 'I left the window open when I went to bed to sleep better with the fresh air. He'll get it from me in the morning!'

'Tell him that next time I catch him in your room I'll knock him dead.'

'That's right, dear, serves him right, it's all he deserves. Maybe he's not even worth this effort, because you can't skin him like a bear, can you?'

'There's no point in skinning a bear either, somebody else will get the skin.'

'Next time you kill a bear we'll hang the skin up in the attic to dry. No one will think of looking for it there,' Lisete said to placate Jürka. 'It would be nice if you could get a bit of shut-eye here with me, but who's going to fix the door? That farm hand is no good at such things. And even though it's summer, we can't do without a door, you know.'

'I guess not,' Jürka said, and got down to the job in the semi-dark of a summer night. The door fixed, he hurried back to Ants where people rose early. So much for his visit home – he smashed and fixed the front door, that's all.

'I might at least have beaten up that farm hand,' he thought with regret as he hurried back. The endless jobs he was expected to do left him no time for meditating, and before long he forgot his regret.

The nights had already become longer by the time he was able to get away to the Pit again. He tiptoed into the house – the door stood open – groped for the bed, and found it empty. Where was his wife? Could she have run off with the farm hand?

Jürka left the house and climbed up into the attic where the lad slept, but there was no one there either. He went into the barn – the horse, the cow and the ewe were all there. In the yard he came across the kitten who shot behind the house in a panic. Jürka stopped to wonder about it and then lost patience and started shouting for his wife, and his voice rang louder and louder with every shout. At long last Lisete appeared from round the house where the kitten went.

'What are you doing out at night?' Jürka roared.

'You're quite a joker, husband dear. You steal into the house like a thief in the night, and pounce on me at once – Where did I go? I went where you go if you have to in the middle of the night.'

'Where is the farm hand?'

'In the attic, where else? What d'you want him for?'

'I'm asking you where he is? He's not in the attic.'

'Must have gone for a walk.'

'I guess he has too. You're out walking, so why shouldn't the farm hand go out walking too, leaving the house wide open and deserted.'

'Why deserted, when I'm here?' Lisete asked innocently.

Here Jürka remembered the barn on the edge of the field, a few dozen yards from the house, and it occurred to him that his wife might have come from there. Deliberately, he strode towards that barn.

'Where are you going?' Lisete asked.

'I want to see how much hay we've left.'

'You can see it later, come into the house for a bit first.'

'No, I want to see it now,' Jürka replied, and strode on.

Lisete came behind him, scolding at the top of her voice:

'What's got into you, checking on the hay in the middle of the night! There's not much of it in the barn, not all the ricks have been brought in yet.'

Jürka broke into a run. Lisete rushed after him, screaming: 'Have you gone mad? Have you gone mad?'

He had, indeed, gone mad. Wheezing and puffing he reached the door of the barn and all but collided with the farm hand. Grabbing the lad by the scruff of his neck, Jürka hurled him back into the barn, and began stacking firewood in the doorway, working at great speed.

'What's on your mind, you madman?' Lisete screamed.

'You'll see in a minute,' Jürka replied.

'Then let me in there too!' Lisete shrieked, making a dash for the opening.

'I'll finish you off too, never worry,' Jürka wheezed, pushing her away.

When the doorway was completely blocked, he got his steel and flint out of his pocket. Lisete begged and pleaded but he took no notice of her pleas and set fire to an eave of the barn. The wind was quite strong, and soon the barn, stocked with hay, turned into a roaring sea of fire. Tongues of fire leaped high, and the nearby junipers began to crackle merrily. Jürka roared with laughter as he watched the leaping flames, and gradually quieted down. Lisete was sitting on the ground and crying. When everything was finished and all that remained of the barn were red-hot coals and smouldering fire-brands, Jürka walked to where his wife sat and muttered:

'Come on, wife, let's go home now.'

Lisete leapt to her feet, turned a tear-stained face to him and suddenly threw her arms around his neck.

'You know now that you still love me!' she said.

'I guess so,' Jürka grunted, and after a thoughtful pause added: 'When I've knocked the stuffing out of you, I'll love you even more. Pity about the barn, though.'

'Never mind. Maybe it's all for the best, who knows,' Lisete consoled him.

When Jürka came to work in the morning, he told Ants that someone had set fire to his barn on the edge of the field, and a lot of hay stored there had perished. The house might have caught on if the wind had been blowing that way. He and his wife had put their heads together, wondering who might have done it, and somehow things pointed to their farm hand with his everlasting smoking. That evening he had said something about wanting to sleep on fresh hay, and when the fire broke out they couldn't find him anywhere. Would he turn up for work in the morning, they wondered?

But the farm hand did not turn up. Lisete came over at midday to tell her husband and Ants. The police was notified, but it was decided to wait a little for the fire to die completely before starting the search for the body, because how could anyone rake it now? A downpour would be a good thing, of course, it would stop all the smouldering at once.

Still, policemen did come to the Pit that evening and started digging in the ashes of the burnt down barn. Down below they discovered some hay which the fire had not reached, and under the hay – the farm hand, who was dead, of course. Why and when did he bury himself in the hay, when he might have jumped out of the burning barn? This was truly difficult to explain. If the fire had broken out when he was fast asleep and moreover if there had been no way of escaping with his life, then he wouldn't have been lying *under* the hay. There was one thing, however, that was beyond any doubt: the lad was to blame for the fire, as there was no one else there. When did the master and mistress awake? The master hadn't gone to bed at all; he was on his way home to see his wife and noticed the fire from afar. He started running then, thinking that it was the house that was burning, but when he approached he saw that it was only the barn. He banged on the door to rouse his wife who was fast asleep and didn't know anything was wrong.

'My legs gave way when I heard there was a fire,' Lisete said brokenly.

There was an inquest, there was questioning and cross-questioning, and that's as far as it went. Jürka was obliged to find a new farm hand. Talking it over with Ants, he said:

'I'd rather not take on another lad, he might set the house on fire with his smoking.'

'What do you think about our Juula?' Ants asked.

'Juula, you say?' Jürka said reflectively.

Of course she suited him. Juula had a powerful body, big hands and thick legs. She could harness a horse and do any of the men's jobs. Apart from everything else, she was very clever at stacking hay. True, she was generally considered a bit gawky. Jürka once helped her down from a huge, new stack, as only he had the strength to lift a wench her size in his arms. Afterwards they both laughed like mad. And Jürka caught himself wishing that he had a woman like Juula for a wife. She could take a lot, he'd bet, not like Lisete.

'Juula works like a man, but you may be sure she won't go lighting a cigarette or a pipe to set your house on fire,' Ants told him.

'I guess not,' Jürka said.

The matter was settled: Juula was to go to the Pit and work in place of the lad who'd perished in the fire, and Jürka was to go on slaving for Ants to square his debt.

'Let's see if I get burnt alive at the Pit,' Juula giggled foolishly, as she made ready for the road.

'Mind you don't start the burning yourself, no one else will,' Jürka told her.

'Master, why don't you take me to the Pit yourself, eh?' Juula said, laughing.

'You think he'd waste a whole day on you? You can find your own way,' Ants told her. 'It so happens that we're going to cart the boulders from the fallow land today, and who can I put on the job if Jürka drives you to the Pit?'

Ants was quite right, of course. No one could take Jürka's place. There were no men as strong as him in the whole world – Juula had felt it in that brief moment when Jürka's arms lifted her down from that stack. And that's why she was laughing like mad. How wonderful that there was a man like Jürka in the world! When he grabbed you, you felt as though you were in a vice.

No sooner did Juula leave for the Pit than a remarkable change came over Jürka: he grew homesick. He didn't seem to miss his wife before, and now he couldn't do without her. It was actually others who noticed the change in him.

'You're always running home these days, is anything wrong?' Ants asked him.

'The womenfolk are by themselves there, that's why,' Jürka replied.

'You're always having worries – first with the farm hand, and now with the wench.'

'Yeah, I guess I have.'

Lisete, however, misunderstood the situation.

'What a helper you've given me!' she said to her husband one day. 'Maybe she's not too brainy, but she does the work of two men, that she certainly does! She's already begun to push me on too, as if she and not I were the mistress in this house.'

Jürka did not say a word, but his heart leapt for joy. Thereafter, he appeared less often at the Pit. Very soon, Lisete was struck by Juula's strangely sleepy look, and took to watching the wench. Every night, instead of going to bed, Juula slipped out of the house. Where did she go? Lisete wondered. Next time Jürka came home, she told him that the wench stayed out all night, and could hardly keep awake in the daytime.

'I'll speak to her,' Jürka said.

'No, for heavens' sake, don't breathe a word to her, or she'll pounce on me when we're left alone. She'll guess at once that it's

I who told on her. I didn't mean anything, it's just that I don't know who she spends her nights with and where...'

'What business is it of yours anyway?' Jürka asked.

'None, but since she lives in the house she sort of belongs to the family,' Lisete replied primly.

For the moment they left it at that. Jürka promised not to say a word to the wench. And Juula, for all that she looked sleepy some days, worked so hard as though it were her own household she was doing her best for, and not just an employer's. Weeks passed. And then Lisete noticed that Juula was off her food, and was sick all the time. Driven into a corner by her mistress's prying questions, Juula admitted that she had been with someone. But who? That, Juula would not tell. She simply could not.

Lisete told Jürka everything when next she saw him, and asked him what they were to do about it. Jürka didn't turn a hair at the news, and after pondering the matter pronounced:

'Oh well, it's the times we're living in. If the wives can't have children, the unmarried girls might as well have them. You keep an eye on her, see she doesn't strain a gut, because you never know...'

'I like that!' Lisete gasped. 'Just because I've no children of my own you expect me to mind someone else's kids even before they are born?'

'I guess I do,' Jürka replied. 'Since you've no children either by your husband or by anybody else, you'll...'

'I haven't, and I don't want to have any,' Lisete interrupted his slow speech. 'I don't want to live in this world at all, so why should I bring children into it?'

'D'you want to go straight to heaven?'

'Why not? I might go there too.'

'Go anywhere you like, to hell if you want, but while you're living in this world you'd better be good to children. Since you've none of your own, mind other people's.'

'Listen, my old man, why this sudden love for children?'

'I'm a man and I'm mortal, I want to save my soul – that's why.'

'Did you get this wise stuff from Ants, or where?'

'I go to church. I was taught this wisdom there.'

'Look at that! Old Nick from the Pit has become a church-goer!'

'And I'm also learning to sing in the choir.'

Lisete gave a peal of laughter, thinking that her man was joking, but then she saw that he was in dead earnest. This frightened her. How was she to finish her span of life on earth when Jürka, living among people, had grown so strange? As Juula's time approached, Lisete's anxiety mounted because Jürka was showing more and more concern for the wench. At first Lisete believed that it was to see her that Jürka came home whenever he could get off, but then the truth stared her in the face: he came because of that wench, because of the baby, soon to be born. And suspicion crept into her soul: could her husband be the father of the baby, was it with him that Juula had spent the summer nights in the forest? How stupid of her not to guess at the time, when she might have caught them in the act.

'I know now who's the father of your child,' she said to Juula.

'And I've not an inkling,' Juula replied.

'It's Jürka!' Lisete cried.

'Did he tell you himself?' Juula asked.

'Why else would he fuss over you so? But do you know what Jürka is? He's Old Nick. You're carrying the child of Satan.'

Juula burst out laughing, and then said:

'All the masters of the Pit were called Old Nick, and yet their children are like other people's.'

'But Jürka *is* Old Nick,' Lisete persisted.

'They call him the new Old Nick,' Juula said. 'But for all I care he might be the Lord God Himself. What matters is that he's a strong man, stronger than me even, and I hate saps. He does with me whatever he wants, and I can't lift so much as a finger to resist him.'

'You shameless bitch!' Lisete screamed in a terrible rage.

'No, mistress, I'm not a bitch, because I'm going to have a child and not a pup. And maybe twins, at that.'

There's no imagining what Lisete might have done in anger remembering what Jürka had done to the farm hand, but Jürka himself came home just then, and she vented her fury on him.

'This shameless hussy says that you're the father of her child!' Lisete went on the attack.

'It's not I who told her,' Juula said. 'The mistress keeps saying that the master told her that he was the father of my child, and all I said was that maybe I'd have twins.'

Jürka stood there waiting to see how the brawl would end.

'Why don't you say something, has the cat got your tongue?' Lisete screamed at him.

'I guess so.'

'That's why you fussed over Juula,' Lisete screamed the louder.

'Maybe,' Jürka grunted.

'You ought to be burnt alive, both of you!' Lisete yelled.

'I'd better go while the going is good,' Juula said.

'No. You're staying,' Jürka told her.

'If anyone must go, it's me! And as for you, husband dear, you wait and see what I'll do!'

'You won't,' Jürka said. 'I'll kill you first.'

'Let her live,' Juula said, and touched Jürka's arm.

'See, I'm letting you live because this woman has asked me,' Jürka uttered gravely.

'Thanks for nothing!' Lisete fumed. 'Go on, kill me, kill me now! I'd rather go to hell than stay here.'

'Go ahead then, if you don't want to live on this earth,' Jürka told her.

'And I will, too! And, Juula, I want you to know this: it's Jürka who set fire to his barn and burnt that farm hand alive, he stood there and watched so the lad shouldn't get out.'

No one spoke for some minutes. And then Juula waddled up to Jürka and asked:

'Is it true?'

'It is.'

'What for?'

'For sleeping with my old woman.'

'And Juula slept with you, so she should be burnt alive too!' Lisete was off again.

'Juula is carrying a child, and you've borne no fruit till this day,' Jürka said.

'And where did you get this from? The church, I suppose?'

'Yes, from the Holy Bible. God said: 'Be fruitful and multiply'.'

'Juula, are you going to stick with this murderer?' Lisete turned to the girl.

'He is the father of my child.'

'Very well. I'll hand you both over to the police,' Lisete said grimly.

'What for?' Juula asked.

'For burning the farmhand alive.'

'I didn't do it,' Jürka said.

'Why, you just told Juula you did!'

'First time I head of it,' Juula stated flatly. 'Was it you, perhaps, who set that barn on fire? Maybe it's you who should be handed over to the police.'

Lisete was stunned: those two had joined forces against her.

'You'll drive me to my grave,' she moaned.

'Your own spite will,' Juula told her.

Lisete did not fight back any longer. She took to her bed and said that she would wait for death to come. Let others live if they wanted to, she'd had enough, she'd known nothing but deceit in her life. The days rolled on, and Lisete lay on her bed, taking neither food nor water from Juula's hands. She did not speak a word, nor did she respond when she was spoken to. Even when Jürka came to visit her, she remained deaf and mute. She lay thus on her bed until one fine day Juula found her dead. Oh well. Juula heated up some water and washed the body, which was the decent thing to do before laying it in the coffin. Juula managed all by herself, she didn't need help – the mistress was skinny when she was alive, and now that she was dead she was skinnier still. When she had finished washing the body, she went to tell Jürka that the dead mistress had stayed behind alone to watch over the house. That's exactly how she put it herself.

CHAPTER FOUR

When Jürka heard that his wife had died, he told Ants about it. Ants, who liked things done properly, gave Jürka some boards and nails, also a handsaw and a plane, so he might make a coffin for his wife with his own hands. Jürka and Juula started back home – the man striding ahead with his load, and the woman behind him. And everything would have gone off beautifully, if trouble hadn't struck out of the blue.

Jürka came to the church to tell the pastor that his wife had died and to ask him to toll the bells and do whatever else was done for a person's soul. The pastor laid out several bulky volumes, and started leafing through them, one after the other, looking for something and muttering under his breath: 'Not here, not here, not here.'

'What d'you mean not here? I myself made the coffin for her!' Jürka burst out.

'Yes, my beloved son, the coffin is here, but the soul is not,' said the pastor.

Jürka flopped down on a chair and stared stonily at the floor. His stricken look puzzled the pastor who hastened to clarify his point:

'Neither you nor your missus are here.'

'But I *am* here!' Jürka exclaimed, and stood up.

'Your body is, but your soul isn't,' the pastor smiled.

'Where is it then, my soul, I mean?' Jürka stammered.

'In some other place, in some other parish register. And, incidentally, who are you, my beloved son? I don't remember seeing you before.'

'I've been to church several times.'

'When did you last take the eucharist, my beloved son?'

Jürka had never taken the eucharist.

'And where's your home, my beloved son?'

'The Pit is my home.'

'Oh, I see,' the pastor said thoughtfully. 'Well, well. I'm at last beginning to understand.'

Jürka didn't understand a thing, and stared at the pastor dumbly.

'The former master of the Pit was called Old Nick, and what about you?' the pastor asked with a small smile.

'The former master was called that, and I am actually Old Nick,' Jürka replied.

'D'you mean to say that you, my beloved son, are really Satan?'

'As real as they come,' Jürka confirmed readily.

The pastor thought it so funny that he laughed wholeheartedly. Jürka didn't see the joke, but for the sake of politeness gave a small guffaw. The ear-shattering roar that might have come from an empty barrel shocked the pastor into silence, and he peered closely at Jürka as though he were really seeing Satan in the flesh before him.

'If you really are Satan, why did you come down to earth?' he asked after a little, watching Jürka closely all the time.

'It was Heaven's will.'

'I see. But what was the idea anyway?'

'To earn salvation.'

'If you want to earn salvation, my beloved son, you must not believe that you are Satan.'

'But I am.'

'Satan can't be saved, my beloved son.'

'And if he is a human?'

'If he is a human, he has to believe that he is a human.'

'But if I *am* Satan, just the same?'

'Then you have to believe in the impossible, and if you do you will earn salvation.'

'I shall earn it, I believe in that, because otherwise people will stop coming to hell.'

This made no sense whatever to the pastor.

'How can that be, my beloved son?' he was curious to hear more.

'Apostle Peter said so.'

'Precisely what did this Peter say?'

'Peter said: man is sinful; he cannot save his soul, he is that sinful. He'd like to but he can't. But what if he doesn't want to save it? And so it was decided, up there in heaven, to find out if he wants to or not, if he can or can't. That's why when I came to collect my souls Peter told me I was not entitled to any more. 'If you want to get some,' he said to me, 'go down to earth in the shape of a man and see if you can earn salvation. If you can, people can too, and it means they simply don't want to. But if you can't, it'll mean that people can't either, much as they'd like to. And so, if man can but doesn't want to he will be sent down to you, to hell, and if he'd like to but can't he'll go to heaven, and you'll never see another soul again.' That's what Peter said. And here I am.'

The pastor was literally dumbfounded by Jürka's story, and when at last he found his voice again, he uttered:

'But, my beloved son, there's the matter of redemption, you know!'

The pastor sank down on a chair. He believed that feeble-mindedness was a guarantee of ultimate bliss in the hereafter, and when he was younger he enjoyed visiting lunatic asylums. There he met men who thought they were the son of God, or a Chinese emperor, or a haystack, a garbage bin, a clucking hen, a gust of wind or simply a nothing, but until now he had never met Satan either in the madhouse, or at large. Martin Luther and the other teachers were much luckier than himself, for they had met the Devil tête-à-tête. And now his great moment had come: there, sitting before him, was Satan in the flesh. The only thing he regretted at the moment was that no one in the world – not himself nor others – any longer possessed that profound and unassailable faith which enabled the believer to take things as perceived by his senses. Why were people prey to this perpetual, nagging doubt about everything, why did they always feel compelled to get to the bottom of everything with their reason? Why couldn't he see this burly creature as Satan, but must regard him as simply a candidate for the madhouse? Heavens, how small, how shabby the world and man himself had become! Why, take himself: here was Satan in the flesh before him, and all his emotions boiled down to was a panicky fear of what might happen if the peasant sitting before him should go berserk! Thank God there was the writing table piled with books between them, and behind his back, at arm's reach, the door. He was therefore able to address Jürka quite calmly, although his heart did flutter a little.

'How are you to save your soul if you don't believe in redemption? We, humans, trust only in redemption.'

'And you shall perish, as Peter said.'

'Yes, it does sound like Peter,' the pastor said vaguely. He was afraid he might anger Jürka if he replied more firmly and clearly, but inflammatorily. However, he need not have been so cautious. Jürka was calm and confident, and the pastor's remark simply missed him.

'In heaven that time I didn't get a chance to speak to anyone else,' he said quite candidly.

'And where is heaven?' the pastor also attempted a tone as candid.

'Why, don't you know where?' Jürka said, instead of answering.

From this the pastor concluded that it was a waste of breath discussing religious questions with Jürka, and so he said:

'I'm afraid this conversation will lead us nowhere. And so, let us dwell on the matter in hand. You told me that you want a burial service for your deceased wife. But in our parish register neither you nor your late wife are listed. Where were you born?'

Jürka told him where, and even produced his identification paper from which the pastor took down some particulars. Everything seemed to be in order, and Jürka could go ahead with the funeral. At last, the pastor came up to him, placed a hand on his shoulder, and said:

'My beloved son, you did well to confess to me who you

really are, but don't tell it to everyone you meet, because people never believe what they are told, and they might laugh at you. This matter concerns the soul, and I understand you because I am a pastor of souls. Still, you should believe in redemption if you want salvation. And now, go in peace, your woman is waiting for you in her coffin.'

Jürka left. He felt sorry for the pastor and embarrassed for him, too, because by his parting words he revealed his utter ignorance and obtuseness. Talking about the soul to Satan, there in the flesh before him! And how little he knew about his old woman! His wife would be waiting for him, ha-ha! Jürka wanted to roar with laughter at the pastor's ignorance. But the old chap was right about one thing – there was no sense in telling people about himself, they wouldn't believe him anyway. The pastor himself didn't. Jürka had sensed it.

However, everything went off without a hitch. The mistress of the Pit was buried properly with the bells tolling, and all the other trimmings. There was just one flaw in the ceremony: the coffin lid had been nailed down, and none of the curious gathered in church could see how the dead woman looked. Juula told them that she had changed so terribly that Jürka did not want to show her to people. This only whetted the imagination of the curious, and everyone clamoured to see how badly death had disfigured the mistress of the Pit. Jürka was adamant, however, and the lid nailed down with long nails stayed put.

Soon after the funeral, however, everyone started saying that Lisete had not died a natural death. The talk rose to an outcry when Juula gave birth to twins. It was she who must have killed her mistress in order to usurp her place. As for Jürka, he either did not know or had helped Juula to keep the funeral quiet. People now remembered the burnt-down barn and the strange death of the farm hand, and everyone wanted to know what had been going on at the Pit since the new Old Nick had appeared from nowhere to take up abode there. Suspicion ran so high, that finally the police had to step in, and the body was exhumed. But there *was* no body! The coffin was filled with earth and stones. Jürka and Juula were called to answer: how could they explain this? They didn't even try, and only sat staring at each other.

'Who filled the coffin with earth and stones?' they were asked.

'I did,' Jürka replied.

'Why?'

'Because there was no body in it.'

'What happened to it?'

'I don't know.'

'Did your wife die or didn't she?'

'I guess she did.'

'Did you see her dead?'

'I guess not.'

'Who saw her?'

'Juula.'

Juula was interrogated thoroughly. She swore that her mistress had indeed died a natural death and she had washed the body.

'What was she ill with?'

'St. Anthony's Fire, or something.'

'And what had caused the illness?'

'Spite.'

'What had roused her spite so?'

'My being with child by Jürka, and also my saying to her that maybe there'd be twins. And twins they are, fancy that!'

'Did she die from that?'

'No, not from that.'

'What then?'

'She lay ill in bed, and she wouldn't eat and she wouldn't drink. Not a mouthful, not a gulp of anything, nothing at all.'

'Maybe you didn't give her anything to eat and drink?'

'Why shouldn't I? I brought her food every day.'

Jürka confirmed her statement. He, too, had asked his wife to eat and drink something, but she flatly rejected everything he offered.

'Could she have starved to death?'

'I guess she could,' Jürka opined.

'But where could her body have gone?'

'I washed the body, laid it out on the bench, and went off to tell the master,' Juula told her story. 'And when we came back –

the master carried the boards for the coffin on his back and the nails in his pocket – she was no longer there.'

'Where did you say you left her?'

'In the front room.'

'Did you find the door shut when you came back?'

'It was ajar,' Jürka and Juula spoke up together.

'I take it you didn't lock it when you left?'

'There is no lock on our door, it can only be bolted from inside.'

'Did you shut the door tight when you left?'

'I think so,' Juula said, but on second thought added: 'But it's just as likely I didn't, because on my way to Jürka I said to myself that the late mistress had stayed behind to watch over the house.'

'What do you mean by that?'

'Why, who'd go into a house where someone was dead? I guess I left the door so she'd feel better there, the dead, you know, like it cool.'

'Well then...'

'That's all I know.'

'And what did you think when you arrived home to find the body gone? Didn't strike you as strange or suspicious?'

'No,' Jürka replied.

'It didn't at all?'

'No, because master told me right away that she'd gone straight to hell,' Juula volunteered.

'That's right, that's what did happen,' Jürka confirmed. 'My old woman didn't like the idea of being buried in the ground for fear she might be taken to heaven from there. She always said that she'd go straight to hell. And she did, so what's the fuss?'

'Why didn't you report it to the police at once?'

'We were afraid,' Jürka replied.

'Afraid of what?'

'There's no telling what they'd think, maybe they wouldn't believe me and try pinning something on me.'

'Do you yourself believe that your wife has gone straight to hell?'

'I guess so.'

'You mean she got up from the bench and went?'

'Why not? I heard the pastor saying in church that the dead would arise, so why shouldn't my old woman arise, seeing that she was dead. And she had to be dead, because how else could have Juula washed her body?'

'I washed her with my own hands,' Juula said in confirmation.

'So, you see, she must have been dead, because if she were alive she'd never had let Juula wash her,' Jürka added.

'But it's not Doomsday yet, when the dead will arise,' one of the officials attempted to argue, but Jürka simply said:

'I guess it was for my old woman.'

The officials realised that it was quite senseless trying to argue with Jürka, while Jürka, for his part, saw that the officials did not know a thing about matters such as this. What good would it do to tell them what his old woman was, what he himself was and what was the purpose of his coming to the Pit? Maybe he would tell them some other time, but not just yet, because they didn't believe him, he saw it.

'Can you be sure you didn't see any animal traces in front of the house when you came back?'

'What animal traces?'

'It doesn't matter what animal. Were there any footprints at all?'

'It was already dark when we got back,' Juula said. 'There was snow and wind that night, and by morning even our footprints were gone.'

'I take it, you didn't look for footprints when you got home?'

'No,' Jürka said.

'But I told you it was dark,' Juula added.

Now the officials said to Jürka: 'If you believed your old woman had gone to hell you could have gone after her by following her footprints.'

'No footprints are left on the way to hell,' Jürka said.

'What makes you think so?'

'If there were, hell would have been located long ago.'

This was reasonable enough. To be sure, no footprints were left when one went to hell, whether by a short cut or via the grave. Even if one went to heaven first, there'd be no footprints left. The investigation had to be suspended. True, there remained the question of whether Jürka and Juula ought to be detained or not, but finally it was decided to let them go because the information obtained from Ants and other people suggested that although the case did smack of crime it was hardly plausible that one of them had committed it. Jürka had to go back to Ants's farm, and there he could be kept under surveillance until some light was thrown on this shady business. In these cold winter months Juula would be house-bound at the Pit with her two babies. It would be a different matter when spring came with its warm rains, green grass and gentle breezes. Oh well, by that time the truth would be out, the snow would divulge its secret.

What worried the officials was the matter of the gaping grave. What had better be done about it? Should the empty coffin be lowered into it and the grave filled in with earth? Or should it be filled in without the coffin? Or, perhaps, left gaping till spring when the truth may be out? The pious held that the coffin should be re-buried and the grave filled in, seeing that everything was done right and proper at the funeral, with church-bells tolling, prayers read, and everything else.

A consecrated coffin had to rest in consecrated soil and nowhere else. Others insisted that since church-bells were tolled and a funeral service sung over the coffin with the earth and stones in it, instead of the body, they were consecrated and as such should remain in the consecrated coffin. There were objections to this too: the earth and the stones could not be left in the coffin because they were the instruments of deceit. Hereat a new question arose: can deceit be qualified as deceit if it has been consecrated? After all, the bells had been tolled not for the coffin as such but for what was inside it – the earth and the stones. The pious were unable to come to a unanimous decision on this question. In the hope of unravelling these tricky knots, great and bulky volumes had to be burrowed in, but since these holy books also differed in opinion from one another, the solution did not seem to be forthcoming very soon. This being so, the police resolved as follows: the grave was not to be filled in but it was to be covered with something lest someone fall into it accidentally and break his neck or a limb; the coffin together with the earth and stones was to be placed at the disposal of the authorities as material evidence.

The case was accordingly suspended. However, investigation was resumed in the spring because some bones were found in the forest. They did not lie in a pile, but were scattered all over the place. These bones were collected and sent to the experts for examination in order to establish whether they were human or animal, and if the former whether they belonged to an old person or a young one, male or female. The experts began by studying the age of these bones to ascertain if they belonged to the same period, and if not then which of them had an earlier and which a later origin. If they belonged to different epochs, how far apart were these epochs? Tied up with the age factor was another rather essential problem: if all or part of the bones belonged to an animal, what animal was it? Moreover, if more than one animal was involved, which bone belonged to which animal? And for another thing: did a particular bone belong to a male or a female, a young or an old animal? And what was the approximate age of that young and that old animal? It was also important to establish if the bones had been lying *on* the ground all the time or if they had lain *in* the ground to begin with and had then, for reasons unknown, appeared on the surface. These cardinal questions and also a great many side-issues, arising in the course of the laboratory research, had to be satisfactorily resolved before the experts could submit their opinion to the appropriate authorities.

Jürka was quite bewildered by this whole business, though he and Juula, carrying the twins, had gone looking for these scattered bones together with the others. To Jürka's mind, Lisete could not have possibly strewn her bones about the forest before going to hell. Because, how could she have walked without her bones?

The experts made a very thorough analysis and, as usual in these cases, each one arrived at an entirely different conclusion. Actually, there was not a single point on which they agreed. Such a divergence of views was largely due to the fact that each expert had his own pet line, which he pursued in preference to everything else. To give an instance: one of them found that the bones were so badly gnawed it was difficult to say anything definite about them at all. The important thing was to ascertain who had been at the bones – a bear, a wolf, or a dog? If more than one animal had taken a nibble, then how did the nibbling go – that is, who was last? Another expert held that a rational solution of the food problem was a matter of global importance, and so in his analysis of the bones he was mainly concerned with ascertaining what their owner ate.

As a result of the lengthy debates and speculations, a general resolution was drawn up which, however, went contrary to the conclusions arrived at by each of the experts separately. One of these experts, reserved his opinion on every single point. Consequently, the conclusion was submitted to the authorities concerned who, on the basis of it, established that the bones were human bones and belonged to someone who was past his or her prime. An addendum was made to this: although it was impossible to establish who the bones belonged to – a man or a woman, it should be accepted, considering the circumstances, that they could belong only to a woman.

And so, one problem was solved: the bones, found in the forest, belonged to the mistress of the Pit; they could be placed in the coffin instead of the earth and stones; the coffin could be lowered into the grave, and the grave filled in. The pious were again beset by doubt: ought the bones to have the bells tolled for them, and the 'dust to dust' said again, and all the rest of it? Would it be sufficient just placing them in a coffin that had been consecrated once before? Taking Juula's advice, Jürka quickly resolved their doubts: he wanted the bells tolled again, the psalms read, and everything done all over again, though he was quite certain that the bones belonged to anyone but Lisete. However, he wanted the business to be over and done with, and that's why he asked for a repetition of the funeral service.

The situation in which the authorities found themselves was much more complicated. To be sure, the origin of the bones was established, but the question remained – what was the cause of the woman's death, and how did her bones come to be scattered in the forest? There was much room for suspicion here, but there were also considerations which allowed it to be assumed that there was no crime at all. Surely it was improbable that Juula, pregnant with twins and her time coming in a fortnight, could do violence to a woman whose help she was going to need so badly and so soon? Surely she could not have gone to fetch Jürka after this, walking quite calmly, according to witnesses, and then making him carry those boards for the coffin on his back, a trudge of several kilometres, with no body there to put in the coffin? Incredible! It was quite another matter if from the start Juula had acted hand in glove with Jürka, that was certainly quite another matter, but there was no evidence to support an assumption such as this. Therefore, the only way out of the deadlock was to close the case.

CHAPTER FIVE

While Jürka and Juula were busy with the complications following Lisete's unannounced departure for hell, a new trouble was looming.

Jürka wanted his twins to be entered in the parish register, and went to see the pastor about it. He hated the thought that one day they might be subjected to the embarrassment he himself had suffered: standing there before the pastor on his own two feet, as alive as anyone could be, and suddenly being told that he wasn't there! Oh no, he'd have his children put in that register, and he'd know for certain that they each had a soul. This was most important because he trusted that if his children had souls the salvation he was so anxious to achieve would include them as well.

'Aha! Here comes Old Nick from the Pit!' the pastor cried before Jürka had even said good-morning. 'I know you now! You came just when I wanted to see you.'

'But it's I who wanted to see you,' Jürka mumbled, but the pastor ignored the interruption and continued:

'I was going to send for you, and now you've saved me the trouble. Look here, what's all this about? I mean, the parish registers where you and your late wife are listed. That time you came to see me I asked you where you were born and I sent an inquiry there, and now they've replied that neither of you is listed in that parish!'

'Yes, but my old woman has died, you know,' Jürka muttered for lack of anything to say.

'So what if she has died, the soul does not die, it is immortal, and so it should be listed in the parish register. Oh well, never

66

mind about your wife, let's leave the dead in peace, if you'd rather, because their reckoning is, after all, kept in heaven...'

'The reckoning of their souls, you mean,' Jürka put in.

'Yes, quite right, the reckoning of their souls,' the pastor nodded. 'But what's to be done about registering your soul, you're alive, aren't you? You should be registered on this earth, seeing that you're still here.'

'I am still here, and I've children now, so...' Jürka said in an effort to get down to brass tacks at last.

But the pastor refused to be diverted.

'Would you show me your identification certificate once more? Have you got it with you?'

'Must have,' Jürka said, delving in his pockets. He handed the bit of paper to the priest who scrutinised it carefully.

'It looks in order,' he said. 'The stamps and signatures are there, and yet the parish I sent my inquiry to answered that you do not exist.'

'But I do, don't I?' Jürka said confidently.

'I don't know, I don't know,' the pastor said, wondering who was making a mistake, and in an effort to see his way a little more clearly asked Jürka: 'Who gave you this certificate?'

'Peter,' Jürka replied without a moment's hesitation.

'Peter who?' the pastor faltered.

'Why, Peter who guards the gates to heaven,' Jürka said, as sure of his grounds as ever.

Well, well, well, the pastor thought. So we're back to heaven and hell, as last time. He still thinks he's Satan.

'Did Peter give it to you himself, with his own hands?' he asked matter-of-factly, as though they were speaking of the most ordinary things.

'No,' Jürka replied.

'Who did then?'

'An angel brought it.'

'Why didn't he hand it to you himself when you went to see him?'

'They didn't know for sure yet if I'd be going down to earth or not.'

'Why didn't they know for sure?'

'You see, I wanted to talk it over with my old woman first. I didn't know if salvation was worth turning into a human for.'

'And your wife, I take it, decided it was worth it.'

'I guess so.'

'Was it after this that Peter sent you the certificate?'

'Yes, that's right.'

'What's all this silly talk I hear about your wife's funeral?'

'Why silly?'

'She hasn't even been in her coffin.'

'How could she be there if she went straight to hell? But no one believes it, you see.'

'Too true, faith in men is weakening,' the pastor sighed. 'You'll have no end of trouble with your certificate, my beloved son, I am afraid, because nobody will believe it either. They'll say it's a fake.'

'A fake!' Jürka was indignant. 'Peter himself sent it to me!'

'Peter's signature is not on it, that's the trouble. Didn't you take a look at it?'

'No.'

'Peter's signature is not there, take a look now.'

'I can't read.'

'Pity, because if you could read you'd see for yourself how dubious this certificate would appear to anyone. You tell me you received it from Peter, but his signature is not on it, instead there is the stamp of some district office and the scrawl of the clerk there, but it's so illegible that you can't be sure what it is.'

'A fake, you say,' Jürka muttered, pondering the accusation. 'In other words Peter is a cheat.'

'Judging from this certificate, he seems to be.'

'And angels are cheats too...' Jürka said reflectively.

'It still remains to be proved who cheated you – Peter or the angel who brought you the certificate,' explained the pastor, trying to help Jürka out of the deadlock, but his efforts were futile.

'Peter himself said to me,' Jürka launched into his word-for-word account. 'He said: 'If you want to be born on earth, it's all right with us. You won't need any papers then, because none are asked of the newly born, they don't have to explain where they'd come from. But if you appear on earth without being born there, you'll need a paper certifying that you were born at such and such a place, and so on and so forth.' And I said to him: 'Give me the paper, I think I'll go down to earth without being born there.' And he said: 'It's safer that way actually. The world's come to such a pass that though the women do conceive they can't be delivered, and what children are born are sure to be premature. You, too, might be aborted, and then you'd have to start all over again. And there's another hazard – you might not get born at all, because the entire human race might vanish from the face of the earth with you still in somebody's womb."

'Ah yes, my beloved son, a grim time is upon us,' the pastor said gravely.

'I'd have a proper birth certificate now if I had agreed to be born of a woman,' Jürka said with a regretful sigh. 'Ah Peter, Peter!'

Jürka was indeed in a quandary.

'Let's forget it for the moment. I'll go into the matter thoroughly, perhaps it's simply a mistake,' the pastor promised.

'Mistake nothing! Peter's signature is not on it, so it's a fake, a swindle!'

'You have to tread very carefully in such matters,' the pastor said persuasively. 'Don't let it upset you so, I'll try to settle everything with Peter.'

His kind words had such a soothing effect on Jürka that he mumbled his thanks and started for the door. The pastor, however, called him back when he was halfway there.

'I say, you came to see me about something, didn't you? It wasn't about this paper, obviously.'

Jürka stopped, reflected for a moment, and walked back into the room.

'What's worrying you, my beloved son?' the latter asked very gently. He felt sorry for Jürka. He was such a big, strong fellow, he believed he was Satan, and yet he was so honest and sincere that he was shocked speechless by his first encounter with a faked document, a mere scrap of paper! Evidently, he very much wanted to be human.

'Reverend, I came to you to have my children entered in the parish book,' Jürka told him.

'But, son, your wife is dead, so who bore you the children?' the pastor asked in dismay.

'Juula did.'

'And who might Juula be?'

'My wife.'

'But your wife is dead, we've just been talking about it with you!'

'It's not Juula who died, it's Lisete who went straight to hell.'

'When did you marry Juula?'

'Lisete was still living, that's when we...'

'Who married you?'

'We did ourselves.'

'Where?'

'In the forest.'

It came home to the pastor at last that by 'marriage' they did not mean the same thing.

'D'you mean to say it happened while your wife was living?'

'Yes, Reverend.'

'And did your wife know?'

'I guess so.'

'Did you talk about it?'

'And how!'

'And the three of you lived together?'

'No, my old woman got mad, she took to her bed and died. She said she'd rather go straight to hell. And she did.'

'There is a sin upon your soul, dear Jürka. Why did you do it?'

'Lisete was barren.'

'Are you certain it was her fault?'

'Who else's?'

'Yours, perhaps.'

'She didn't click with other men either.'

'My beloved son, how do you know?'

'She slept with the farm hand, didn't she?'

'Are you quite sure?'

'I wouldn't have burnt him alive if I wasn't.'

The pastor felt his flesh creep. He remembered how nicely he had just treated Jürka, and squirmed from the shameful memory. However, he mastered his reaction, and asked:

'Where?'

'In the barn. I burnt him together with the barn and the hay in it.'

'And nobody saw you, I presume?'

'My missus saw me, she watched.'

'What did she say?'

'Nothing much. She cried. She was sorry for the farm hand. And then she hugged me and said that I must love her, after all.'

Very curious! It sounded like the truth. Once, as a young and more hot-blooded man, he beat up his wife's lover, she, too, cried and then clung to him – she did not throw her arms around him, no – and asked... What exactly did she say? Ah, yes! She asked: 'Do you believe *now* that you love me?' Those were her very words. He had not believed that then or later. With his fists he had defended only his own honour and the honour of his profession. It was an interesting thought: what if he had... not burnt alive, of course, but killed or shot his rival that time? He might have done it, the law would not condemn him for it, he could hardly carry on as a pastor, though, because say what you like he would have been a murderer... He wondered if his wife would have thrown her arms around him, like this poor Satan's woman?

He came to with a start. Jürka still stood before him.

'And did you really love her?' the pastor asked.

'I love her more now that she's dead.'

'Why?'

'She told me: who do I take her for, wanting her to produce human young.'

'What other kind are there?'

'Imps, that's what.'

'And Juula's children, were they fathered by a human?'

'Who else?' the question baffled Jürka. 'Juula's human, isn't she, and I too am a human now, and I want to save my soul.'

'Tell me, my beloved son, how can you dream of saving your

71

soul here, in the shape of a man, if as you yourself have admitted you burn other men alive, your brothers in Christ, and if you violate the sanctity of holy wedlock?'

'I wanted children, and now I have them.'

'But legally they are not yours, my beloved son.'

'Who else's? I fathered them, didn't I?'

'They are not yours, they're Juula's. Juula herself has to register their birth. They are the children of a spinster, and not of man and wife.'

'Are you telling me I've no children?' Jürka asked in alarm.

'You have none because Juula is not your wife.'

'She is my wife, we have two children, she and I.'

'You don't. She has children by you.'

'You know what, Reverend? I sort of itch to set this house on fire.'

'For shame, for shame, my beloved son, talking like that to your pastor!'

'But, look, if the children are Juula's only, then...'

'Then you should enter lawfully into holy matrimony with Juula, so that her children would become your children as well, and that's all there is to it, my son. It's much simpler than setting houses on fire, because no matter how many you burnt down, the children of a spinster would still remain hers alone. And so, go home to the Pit, and...'

'Maybe you'll register the children first anyway? They're twins, two boys...'

'Oh no, no, my beloved son, there's nothing we can do about it now because, as I have already told you, at present, your children are Juula's alone.'

'Juula alone could never produce children, never in her life,' Jürka protested.

'According to the law, she can,' the pastor said sternly. And here Jürka suddenly remembered hearing something like this from this very same pastor in church, and asked quietly:

'Like the Virgin Mary?'

'Yes, I suppose so, if I can't make you understand any other way,' the pastor felt too frustrated to explain further. 'And now,

remember what I tell you: go home, and come back in two days'
time, in your best clothes...'

'I have no better clothes,' Jürka said sullenly.

'It doesn't matter, wear what you're wearing now, take Juula
and...'

'The twins?'

'No, not this time, because...'

'But if Juula comes here who's going to suckle the twins at
home?'

'All right, bring them along. The four of you will come, and I'll
register you and your Juula as an engaged couple, and put up the
banns. For three weeks I'll announce your engagement from the
pulpit, and then I'll be able to marry you.'

'And I'll have children?' Jürka cried joyfully.

'You will have children, and twins too, that is if Juula's boys
are twins.'

'They are, that's right.'

'That's settled then, and I want you to come here with Juula the
day after tomorrow.'

When Jürka left, the pastor mopped his perspiring brow. What
would happen, if his entire flock were like Jürka? What if all the
parishioners imagined they were Satan come down to earth to
save his soul? What if they believed that their wives went straight
to hell, angry with the husbands for getting their farm maids in the
family way? What if these husbands – the Satans in human guise
– took to burning alive their farm hands and other philanderers
together with their farm buildings? What if all this happened in
reality and was not simply an invention of this poor soul, suffering
from a religious mania? To think of the number of barns that
would have to be built anew every year! O divine faith! He
believed that he was Satan, but being a man he strove for salvation
and at the same time committed murder, arson, and adultery. His
crimes failed to shock him, but the trifling matter of a faked
certificate caused him heartache! Ah, ye blind guides, which strain
at a gnat and swallow a camel! Man was truly an amazing
creature.

While the pastor sat musing thus, Jürka strode home in the

happiest of moods, for he also had something to chew on. 'He's a good man, that pastor,' he was thinking. 'Understanding, and nice spoken, and kind. He means well, and when he asks you something you always know what to answer. And he doesn't mind anything you say. I wish there were more people like him.'

His spirits were dampened a bit when, before he hardly entered the house, Juula demanded if he had registered the boys.

Jürka told her he had not.

'Why ever not?'

'I have no children, that's why.'

'And the twins, whose are they?'

'Yours.'

'Is that what the pastor said?'

'The pastor said you were something like the Virgin Mary.'

'Don't be stupid!'

'Well, I said it first, and then the pastor...'

'You'd say any silly thing, but I can't believe the pastor...'

'It's the honest truth! He said: "All right, it will be clearer that way."'

'What will be clearer?'

'That you're a sort of Virgin Mary.'

'No, dear man, what the pastor wanted to say was that I was a wench with a couple of bastards, but he didn't dare.'

'What was he afraid of?'

'Of you. You might have killed him.'

'I only threatened to set his house on fire!'

'You shouldn't have done that.'

'What could I do if he wouldn't come across?'

'You could walk out, that's all. I'd have gone myself.'

'He said we must both come.'

'Why both? The twins are mine only.'

'The pastor will fix it so that they're mine too.'

'Does he want to marry us in church, or what?'

'He wants to put up the banns or some such thing.'

Juula was silent for a minute, and when she spoke it was very softly, but Jürka could feel that she was pleased.

'That's the best way, of course. The pastor is right.'

'The pastor is right,' Jürka repeated.

And as arranged the time came, Jürka harnessed his horse into the cart and climbed up in front to drive and whip the nag on, while Juula sat behind him with the twins in her lap. This time, she left her knitting at home because she had her hands full with the babies who were far more trouble and wanting to be suckled or changed all the time. What with this and that, Juula hardly noticed the journey.

As soon as the banns were put up, Jürka asked the pastor to register his sons, but he wouldn't do it. Their proposed marriage had to be announced three times, then there had to be the wedding ceremony, and only after that could the children be registered. There was nothing for it but to wait. At last all the formalities were completed, and there was every reason to hope that peace and quiet would come to stay at the Pit, and that the unpleasantness and worry of all those investigations and interrogations was over and done with.

CHAPTER SIX

A load was taken off Jürka's mind when he heard that the case of his vanished wife was closed by order of the authorities. It wasn't on his own account so much as on others' that he welcomed the news. What worried him was that Juula couldn't quite believe that Lisete had really gone straight to hell, and kept asking: supposing she couldn't find the way in the snowstorm and was still wandering like a ghost in the forest? And what if she came back home, as the dead were known to do even when buried properly?

'My milk would go bad from fright, and the twins' tummies would ache,' Juula said to him.

'Oh, you scaredy-cat,' Jürka tried to laugh off her fears. 'You weren't afraid of her when she was living, and now that she's dead why fear her at all?'

'I guess my blood's thin, that's why.'

He was taken aback: to think that a woman as strong and healthy as Juula should have thin blood! The thought that she was a timid sort really, touched Jürka profoundly.

'Don't worry, I know my missus, she did go to hell, she had nowhere else to go. And if she does come back it will be straight from hell. Well, she'll have me to deal with then!'

Still, Juula felt uneasy, it kept on troubling her.

'You wouldn't like to go to the cemetery, would you?' she asked him.

'What for?' Jürka asked, and seeing Juula's embarrassment added gruffly: 'I might, I guess.'

After a while, to change the subject Juula said:

'People are funny, really.'

'What people?'

'Oh, the police and such, thinking that it was I who sent your wife to the nether world!'

'Oh, them!' Jürka dismissed them contemptuously. 'I call it the limit, their deciding that the bones were Lisete's!'

'They might be, don't be so sure.'

'You mean, you also believe that...'

'I don't believe anything. It's simply that, seeing how it is... it would be a good idea for you to go to the cemetery – people do, you know. The thing to do is dig three holes with your heel in the earth where her feet are, spit three times in each hole, repeating as you spit: 'So you can't get up, so you can't get up, so you can't get up.' I'd go myself, but I wouldn't be much use. It's you who ought to go: she's your wife, so it's for you to speak the words.'

Jürka listened to her open-mouthed, startled by the wisdom he hadn't know she possessed. With every day he was discovering anew what a treasure he had got himself for a wife. A jewel, that's what she was.

'You mean if I go, make the holes, spit in them and speak the charm she'll never get out any more?' he asked thoughtfully.

'Others didn't, and she won't,' Juula declared. 'The spell's been tried and tested.'

'But she isn't there, you know...' Jürka faltered.

'Of course she isn't. But just supposing she is and wants to get out, we've got to stop her. People are sure she's there in the grave, and with everyone believing in it so strongly she might be really there, who knows... After all, you'd be doing it for our children.'

Saying this, Juula began to suckle the babies – one at her left breast, and the other at her right. This had such a powerful effect on Jürka, that he instantly succumbed and said: 'All right.'

'You mean, you'll go?'

'I guess so.'

'The boys' tummies won't be upset then,' Juula said, smiling down on the busily suckling twins.

And after that life flowed on serenely at the Pit, they were cloudless years, really. Jürka and Juula didn't just sit twirling their thumbs, of course, and toiled from dawn till dusk. It was especially hard on Juula who was always either nursing a baby or carrying one – some years doing both things at the same time. But that's how it had to be, she reasoned. As far as she could see, everything in the world was continually multiplying all the time. Otherwise there'd be no life on earth, she supposed.

Jürka worked mainly for Ants in settlement of his old debt. But in the meantime, he was compelled to make new debts, and it seemed he'd never get free of the yoke. If this went on, Jürka's children, too, would be slaving for Ants. Ants must have had it in mind when he said the first time he saw Jürka's twins:

'You're rearing a couple of shepherds for me, I see.'

And for the first time in his life, Jürka felt stung to the heart.

'I guess I'll need them myself,' he said gruffly.

'One for you, and one for me,' Ants grinned.

The thought rankled that Ants was already sizing up his boys, his twins, who were especially dear to Jürka. One day, sitting with Juula on the threshold and watching them play in the grass, he said:

'Ants has an eye on the lads.'

'Our boys, you mean?'

'Who else's?'

'What does he want them for?'

'For shepherds.'

'Huh, we've our own cow and sheep to tend!'

'That's what I say, too.'

Both fell silent. The children were wrestling in play on the grass. Their world ended at the kitchen garden. Now and again their father appeared from the world beyond, and then vanished there again.

'You'll have to talk to Ants, maybe he'll let you off,' Juula said.

'I tried. He won't.'

'Send the farm hand in your place.'

'He says there's no better farm hand than me.'

'And no better master either. So you have to work for him, eh?'

'I guess so.'

'We mustn't borrow any more from Ants.'

'If only we needn't!' Jürka sighed.

'We'll manage. We've got to manage,' Juula said. 'He's making a slave of you with that debt. And your children are the children of a slave.'

'I am my own master,' Jürka protested.

'You are Ants's slave. And I am the wife of a slave.'

Jürka found nothing to say to this.

'Where did you get this stuff from?' he asked after a lengthy silence.

'I used to work for Ants myself, so that's where I got it.'

Until now the master and mistress of the Pit had never engaged in a discussion of such major issues. They might not have known before that such issues existed at all. After this Jürka gave Ants no peace, demanding to be let off. Ants was forced to meet him halfway, and it was agreed that Jürka and his farm hand would take turns – a week each. This was a big step forward, and it gave Jürka a chance to tackle the work waiting at the Pit with new strength and vigour. Even the expression on Juula's face changed. However, they didn't succeed in passing the entire lod of Ants's work on to their farm hand. Ants threatened to call in witnesses if he didn't see reason.

'Who's been putting these notions in your head to make you so damned stubborn? Can it be Juula?' Ants asked.

'The kids are growing,' Jürka replied.

'What's wrong with that? Let the kids grow, we need workers! You're a fiend for work, Juula's a toiler in a hundred, and your children will be hard-working too.'

'Hard-working or not they'll have to sweat for some bastard or other.'

'Look at that! Hear Old Nick talking,' Ants chuckled. 'Did you pick it up from me, or where?'

'From you, I guess.'

'If you go on like this you'll develop into a rebel!'

'I'd rather be a farmer.'

'But you are a farmer now.'

'And yet I work for another master.'

'Well, that's how it goes in the world,' Ants said instructively. 'A small man slaves for a big man, a weak one for a strong one, a fool for a clever man. It's God Himself who arranged it like that. And whoever goes against this order, goes against God, and anyone who goes against God shall perish. Remember this well, Jürka, and teach this truth to your children. And then you shall build your house on rock, and your herds shall graze in rich pastures.'

Jürka heard him out and said to himself: 'You keep runnning up against God everywhere, and He's always on the side of whoever's stronger and smarter.' He remembered his encounter with the bear, and thought: 'God was on my side that time because I had more sense than the bear. I came at him with my axe, the axe has a long handle, and that's what proved that I was the smarter, because what does the bear have? Just his teeth and his claws, with never a handle to them. That shows he's stupid. And so I got the better of him.'

Very soon, however, Jürka discovered that one couldn't always tell whose side God was on. It struck him particularly when a snake in the rye bit his three-year-old son and the poor kid died. True, their dog came running and tore the snake to pieces, but it didn't do much good because the child died anyway. Poor Old Nick, this was the first time that his heart bled like a human's. The worst thing was that for the life of him he could not understand why the child's death should cause him such terrible anguish. He had plenty of other children, with a new one appearing every year or a year and a half. Tears welled from his eyes when he lowered the little coffin into the grave, and when the clods of earth fell with a hollow thud on the lid. Jürka's tears were the talk of the village, for it was a sight no one ever expected to see – imagine that huge bear of a man weeping!

'Even Old Nick can't help crying when his child dies,' some said without malice, while others jeered: 'He didn't like burying him, more likely. How much nicer to despatch people straight to hell, like he did with his wife!'

Jürka, quite unaware of what people were saying behind his

back, was making his slow way home. The cart wasn't wide enough to seat him and Juula side by side, and so they sat back to back – Jürka facing forward, and Juula facing back. Juula usually knitted on their way to church, but now her hands seemed to freeze in her lap. Her knitting lay there, it is true, but she didn't touch it. Somehow, they couldn't even talk, although talking things over would have done both of them good. Even when they got home they did not say a word to each other. Jürka sat down on the bench, Juula perched beside him, and they just sat like that in silence for a little while, and then they rose and went their ways. There was no helping it with life continuing on its course and chores waiting to be done.

There was one thing that Jürka knew very clearly now – one's own children meant something entirely different from the calves and lambs one had, from baby birds in the nest, from new, tender shoots on a tree, from grass sprouting in the woods and rye in the fields. None of this had ever brought tears to his eyes.

He was to know a father's feeling at its strongest the following summer when the whole family went berrying into the woods. They came to a clearing where it was nice and sunny, and Juula sat down on a tree stump to nurse her youngest. In that moment a mother bear with her two cubs emerged from the thickets. The children ran to Juula in fright. Jürka rose to his feet from the grass on which he had sprawled.

'Let's go away,' Juula said to her husband quietly.

'On account of the bear?' Jürka asked.

'Well, who else?

'I'm not leaving,' Jürka said resolutely. 'If that bear wants to, let her sun herself a bit, and I'll stay too.'

'Supposing she attacks us?'

'I have my knife,' Jürka told her. 'Pity I don't have my axe with the long handle.'

'The axe would come in very handy just now,' Juula agreed.

The bear was slowly approaching them as though oblivious of their presence. Jürka gave a thunderous bellow to frighten her off. Juula and the children also shouted at the top of their voices. The bear gave a snarl, but did not turn back and walked on towards them as slowly as before.

'Let's go away,' Juula said again.

'Not me,' Jürka replied angrily and, taking off his trouser belt, started winding it round his left arm from the wrist up.

The bear was inexorably drawing nearer. With the belt wound round his arm, Jürka stepped forward and pulled out his long knife. The blade flashed in the sun.

'Old man, don't go,' Juula begged him, and the children all started yelling. But Jürka took no heed, and continued across the clearing.

Juula then laid down her baby on the moss at the foot of the tree stump, and went after Jürka, crying: 'If you go at the beast, I will, too!'

She was some distance behind him when he picked up a hefty branch and threw it straight at the bear's head. Enraged, the beast attacked, with its mouth wide open. Jürka thrust his left fist deep into the bear's throat, and stabbed it again and again with his knife. Man and beast rolled on the ground. The beast was suffocating with its throat blocked by man's fist. Suddenly the knife slipped from Jürka's fingers. Juula dived for it and stuck it with all her might into the bear's side where she believed the heart was. The pain made the bear release Jürka and clutch at the wound, inadvertently thrusting the blade all the way in. The bear gave a jerk, its front legs drooped limply, and then with a mighty twist it pushed Jürka's hand out of its throat.

Leaving Jürka alone, the bear went back to her cubs. She sniffed them, licked them with her bleeding tongue, and then turned to her enemy once more. After only a few steps, however, she collapsed and could not rise again. The cubs waddled up to their mother and pushed their noses into her warm blood. It was an entirely novel experience in their young lives.

Jürka was bleeding too. The bear had mauled his left arm somewhat, despite the protective belt, and with her claws had ripped his clothes and the skin on his legs and ribs. The ugliest was on the left side of his chest where the flesh, in places, was torn away down to the bone.

The bigger children ran to their parents to see what had

happened.

'God was on our side,' Jürka said, rising from the ground.

'The bear was alone, and there were two of us,' Juula said. 'We had a knife.'

'And the bear had claws and teeth.'

'Father got the better of a bear,' the twins said, digesting the impressive fact, and would have discussed something else of no smaller significance if their mother had not ordered them to pee in turns on their father's wounds. This, she believed, was a better remedy than cobweb or milfoil, and was almost as good as homebrew. The boys administered the treatment very earnestly, and afterwards they were certain that it was they who had saved their father's life. The only fly in the ointment was that for all their trying the spurts they made were not as long as their mother wanted them to be.

After bandaging Jürka's wounds as best she could, Juula asked him:

'What shall we do with the bear and her cubs?'

'Leave them as they are,' Jürka replied. 'No use skinning the bear, we won't be allowed to keep the skin anyway, let alone the cubs.'

'What about our knife?'

'We'll leave the knife too, then people will see that it was us who killed the bear.'

'Wouldn't they believe us without it?'

'There's no knowing what people will believe.'

'But you're bleeding all over!'

'It just shows you that every time you go to the forest you must take the big axe along.'

With a start Juula remembered the baby. Where was it? What had the big boys done with it? The twins had left it lying where it was because their mother wanted them to come and do something that urgently needed doing. Of course, Juula agreed, if they hadn't done it there's no knowing what would have happened to their father.

The baby had not come to any harm – it lay in the sun beside the tree stump, happily kicking its tiny legs and poking its fingers into its mouth or its eyes. The sky was clear and blue above with whisps of white clouds trailing across it, but the baby could not know yet that the sky was blue and the clouds were white. The mite didn't even know that these things really existed, and was therefore quite content with its fingers that kept getting into its mouth and eyes.

'That nasty bear didn't let baby have a proper meal,' Juula cooed, picking up the baby.

'But the bear got what was coming to it,' Jürka said.

'You did, too,' Juula pointed out.

'That I did.'

'Can you walk home, d'you think?'

'I guess so.'

His usual reply set her mind at rest. He wasn't in such a bad way if he could talk in that casual tone. And, true enough, there seemed nothing wrong with him on the walk back, and when they got home he went to bed at once and was soon snoring lustily. Juula hurried off to the forester to tell him about the bear. The forester passed on the news at once, and within a few hours the authorities descended on the Pit. They wanted to be shown the site of the happening, and since Jürka couldn't go Juula went, grudging the authorities the hours she had to waste.

The cubs were playing close to their dead mother. One of them would climb on to her body, and the other one would chase him away. They took turns at this. The game was in full swing because their mother, always enduring their pranks with patience, had really outdone herself that day, letting them do anything they liked. It was fun, but the cubs were beginning to feel hungry, and there was nothing to eat: their mother's teats were empty and strangely cold. It struck them now that their mother was cold all over, a thing that had never happened to her before.

Now and then the cubs bumped noses and sniffed one another, as if to make sure that they hadn't turned cold as well. No, they were quite warm, and only their mother remained cold in spite of the hot sun.

When people appeared on the clearing, the cubs wanted to run away, but people came from everywhere and surrounded them.

The cubs were caught. And there and then, before their very eyes, these people skinned their black, shaggy mother and made her smooth and shiny. The most astonishing thing of all was that she let them, she did not even stir. The people went on doing something to her and calling out to one another as if she didn't count at all. The cubs did not know that there was a god who had turned away from their mother and from themselves, for he sided with the stronger.

Juula watched the fussing men until she got her knife back. She wiped it on the moss, scraped the bear's blood off the blade, and went home. Why stay in the forest longer? She and Jürka had done their bit: they killed the bear.

However, matters did not rest there. A few days later, an official came to the Pit for a more detailed account of precisely how the bear was killed. The fact that Jürka had wound his belt round his left arm before going at the bear roused the official's suspicions. He said he'd like to see the belt in question.

'But it's a saddle girth!' he exclaimed when he saw it.

'That it is,' Jürka replied.

'Why did you take it along with you?'

'To hold up my pants.'

'With a saddle girth?!'

'I have no other belt.'

'Did you have one before? Perhaps it's only now that you don't have a belt, yet you had one before? Perhaps you mislaid it?'

'What belt are you talking about?' Jürka asked, baffled.

'That's what I am asking you: did you or did you not have a belt, was it mislaid or was it not?'

'I don't get it.'

'What, then, have we been talking about all this time?' the official demanded.

'How should I know?'

'I am asking you: did you ever own a belt for you pants and if so has it become lost or has it not?'

'Where?'

'Here, at the Pit.'

'How could it get lost when it never was?'

'Am I to understand that you never had one?'

'No, not here.'

'But where else could it be if not here?'

'At Ants's place.'

'And what happened to it?'

'That's for Ants to know.'

'The belt, you mean, remained with Ants?'

'Sure, it's his belt.'

'And you have been wearing it?'

'I have.'

'But you were not wearing it that day?'

'You don't wear two belts at the same time.'

'Why did you wear a saddle girth and not a belt on that particular day, the day you went bear hunting?'

'I went a-berrying and not bear hunting!' Jürka protested.

'Nevertheless you did kill a bear, and wound the saddle girth round arm for the purpose.'

'But what was I to do?' Jürka asked.

'Not kill the bear.'

'But then the bear would have killed me.'

'You could have gone away.'

'There were young children with me, I couldn't.'

'And the bear had her cubs with her, so she couldn't either.'

'I guess not.'

'You haven't answered my question: why did you wear a saddle girth on that particular day?'

'So what should I have put on?'

'A proper belt.'

'But it's Ants's belt.'

'How come? Your belt has suddenly become Ants's belt!'

'It never was mine.'

'Who does it belong to, seeing that it's yours to wear?'

'I told you – to Ants.'

'And so, you wear Ants's belt?'

'I wear Ants's belt.'

'Then why didn't you wear it when you went bear hunting?'

'I didn't go to the forest to kill that bear, it's the bear that wanted to kill me.'

'Now this is the question that has to be investigated: did the bear want to kill you, or did you want kill the bear? This is how the case appears to me: you intentionally belted your trousers with the saddle girth so as to have a length of leather to wind round your arm, because you probably knew where to find the bear and her cubs. You had it all worked out beforehand: if you walked at the bear and teased it, it would certainly pounce on you and then you'd be able to kill it. And your plan worked.'

'Why didn't I take my axe along then?' Jürka asked.

'That first time you killed with an axe, and it was too easy a kill – you hit the bear once, and that was that. Small pleasure for you. The second time you went armed with a knife and a saddle girth, for you must have been very sure of your strength. The third time, I think, you'll go bear hunting with your bare hands, without even a knife or a saddle girth.'

'No fear. And it wasn't me either who killed this bear, it was Juula.'

'Juula?' the official cried in amazement.

'She took the knife and stuck it into the bear, and then the beast itself helped to push it in.'

'According to you, the bear killed itself.'

'If you don't believe me, ask Juula.'

'Oh yes, we shall.'

Juula was interrogated, and it was from her statements that the whole story was pieced together at last: how the bear crushed Jürka under, how deep were Jürka's wounds, and what was done to stop the bleeding. The twins made their very timely appearance just then, and shouted: 'We squirted our pee all over him.'

This last statement apparently made the whole case clear. The official was compelled to admit that the matter of the saddle girth and trousers belt played a role of little or no importance in the case. And Jürka's one and only fervent wish was to be left alone.

CHAPTER SEVEN

But this was when the trouble really started. The police suddenly realised – either prompted by the pastor or using what brains they had – that Jürka's identification certificate was a fake. Jürka, naturally, remained Jürka whether his certificate was genuine or fake, whether he had one or none at all. The point, as everyone agreed, was that unless the matter of the certificate was cleared up there would be no getting to the bottom of Jürka himself. And a faked document was a real headache.

And so the police came to the Pit or else summoned Jürka to their office and pressed him for an explanation of his certificate and, in fact, of himself. They also wanted to know if the woman, named Lisete, who died so strangely and was buried under even stranger circumstances, was indeed his wife, and if not what was she to him?

'My wife she was,' Jürka replied to the last question.

'What proof have you?'

'But you know that she went straight to hell.'

'Did your wife have to go straight to hell?'

'Where else?'

'Why not to heaven?'

'Because Peter wouldn't let her in.'

'What makes you think so?'

'Peter's no fool, he wouldn't let my missus into heaven.'

'Was she so wicked?'

'Why wicked?'

'Why are you so sure then that she couldn't go to heaven?'

'What's heaven got to do with it when she went straight to hell?'

'But it's you who said that Peter wouldn't let her in.'

'Nor would he!'

'Why ever not? That's what I'd like to know. Why wouldn't he let her in?'

'I explained to the pastor, but he didn't believe me. I don't want to talk about it any more, no one will believe me anyway.'

The police officer coaxed him and threatened him, but all in vain: Jürka had closed up, he wasn't going to explain anything again, because people wouldn't understand and, therefore, wouldn't believe him. It seemed that believing depended on understanding, just that and nothing more.

It was decided to interrogate the pastor, for there seemed no other way. The officer, however, wanted to clear up some points with Jürka first.

'Did you go to the pastor to confess your sins?' he asked.

'I went to register our twins.'

'It wasn't your sins then?'

'What sins?'

'The sins you wanted to confess.'

'I told you, I went on account of the twins.'

'That's all right then,' the officer said soothingly, as Jürka was obviously vexed by these questions to which everybody knew the answers.

As a matter of fact, the interrogation might have been ended there because in the course of it the officer had ascertained that Jürka had never made an auricular confession and therefore the pastor need have no compunction about passing the information on to the authorities. However, he was curious about the twins, and asked.

'Who is the mother of your twins if your wife is dead?'

'Juula, not my late wife.'

'And who might this Juula be?'

'Juula? Why, it's because of her that my late wife went to hell.'

The officer, recently transferred to the local police force had but a superficial knowledge of the circumstances attending the death and burial of Jürka's wife, and he wished to hear the whole story from Jürka himself, but the man refused to comply, saying that he had confessed everything to the pastor. Since no one believed him, why waste breath? There was nothing for it, but to go to the pastor who proved quite willing to relate everything he knew about Jürka, as Satan, and about Peter who supplied him with a faked certificate.

These details, in the officer's opinion, were most important and characteristic of Jürka, unless they were trumped up, which it was up to him to find out.

The pastor believed that Jürka had told the truth. Whether this truth sufficed the officer was another matter, or, to put it more correctly, would it not lead him astray because Jürka's truth had to be accepted on trust, and for some this wasn't good enough, while for others it was too much. Jürka believed that he was Satan, come down to earth in the shape of man to save his soul. Was it not a true sign of the times that even a man who believed he was Satan should crave salvation? Even a man who hardly realised that he had an immortal soul instinctively longed for immortality. Even a dumb creature wanted to be without sin, and yet our secular mind could not be bothered with such things as sinfulness and the forgiveness of sins. If there was no sin who would guide the flock? Who if not the officials in their thousands? That is why the pastor regarded Jürka as a star shining in the utter darkness, although the light it shed was slightly out of true. What had caused this divine light to stray from the straight and narrow path was a question deserving of study, and in this particular case the pastor believed not so much in punishment as in instruction, admonition and remonstration.

The officer, who had had his fill of the pastor's discourse, took advantage of a pause to say:

'It seems to me this Jürka person is slightly feebleminded.'

'You're right,' the pastor agreed. 'He is feeble in mind but strong in his faith. Thas is what I meant by the wonderful sign of the times.'

The officer, however, had his own considerations from which he meant to proceed in this case. What interested him was not what someone imagined himself to be, but what he actually was. And so, he resumed his interrogation of Jürka.

'You told the pastor that you were Satan. Were you joking or do you really believe it?'

'What's believing got to do with it?'

'And that your wife came from the same clan?'

'Where else?'

'Listen, Jürka, take my advice: stop clowning and tell me who you are, where you got your identification, and who faked it.'

'But I told the pastor already.'

'It was Peter or his angel, right?'

'Who else?'

'And you do believe it?'

'I guess so.'

'Can't you understand that it's impossible?' the officer cried. 'There is no firmament, just blue air. And if there's no such thing as a firmament how did you get up there to see Peter?'

'There's no firmament for those who don't believe in it,' Jürka responded calmly. 'How could there be if you don't believe in it?'

'Oh, go to hell, you and your belief!' the officer shouted in exasperation.

'I mean to, only first I'll get my soul's salvation,' Jürka said.

'Salvation? You want salvation to go to hell?' the officer shouted. 'Do you think before you speak or don't you?'

'What's there to think?'

'But the saved go to heaven, if they go anywhere at all!'

'If not to heaven, then to hell,' Jürka said.

'If there's no heaven there's no hell either.'

'Hell there is.'

'Have you been there?'

'That's where I came from in the shape of man in order to achieve salvation.'

'The same old story again!' the officer cursed inwardly, and was silent for a while, thinking what to say next. He had tried various subtle approaches, but they invariably led to the same thing: heaven, hell, Peter, his angel. The only 'earthly' piece of information was that Jürka had been working for Ants for some time. This gave the officer a glimmer of hope, it was something to get his teeth into anyway. All he wanted was to be done with this mess in some decent manner, because actually he didn't care who this bird really was or where he had obtained his faked document.

The officer's problem merely amused Ants.

'You have to know how to handle him with understanding, you know,' Ants said, and promised to probe Jürka. Chances were, he hoped, that he'd be able to clear up the matter.

'Try handling with understanding someone who doesn't understand anything at all,' grumbled the officer.

'What I say is that those who are empowered to educate people and guide them should first learn how to rear domestic animals and how to drive them. And we begin by twisting the bull's tail,' Ants concluded.

When the officer left, Ants asked Jürka what the police wanted of him.

'They don't believe anything anyone says, and that's why they don't understand a damn thing,' Jürka replied confidently.

'That's because you're telling the truth,' Ants explained.

'But what can I do?' asked Jürka, rather taken aback.

'Tell lies.'

'And then they'll believe me and understand?'

'Right away.'

'But I don't know how to lie.'

'You must learn. What kind of man are you if you can't lie?'

'I seek salvation, so how can lies help me?'

'They might, if told properly...'

'Then teach me, Ants, how to tell lies properly.'

And Ants did. He did because he had become attached to Jürka as to a domestic animal. The poor dumb animal had dug a hole for himself, and if left to use his own brains he'd never get out. Realising this Ants had to hurry to the rescue.

'You told the pastor you were Satan,' Ants began as a preamble, but Jürka rudely interrupted him saying:

'That I am.'

'It doesn't matter. The main thing is not to talk about it and not to be what you are, because a man must never really be himself. He must re-fashion himself every day, he must be born anew in order to adapt himself to his surroundings and the current

92

circumstances.'

'But I wasn't born here, you know, I simply came down.'

'In that case, get born in order to become a real man. If you really are Satan and want to go to hell, then just lie back and gaze at the sky. If you are as strong as a bear, which you really are, tell people that your strength comes from your unshakable faith and your trust in God. Supposing you burnt your farm hand alive – tell people that the farm hand did it himself; supposing you killed your old woman – tell people that she wished death on herself because of Juula's twins.'

'I didn't kill my old wife.'

'That's beside the point. I said 'supposing' you killed your old wife.'

'But if I didn't kill her, must I tell people I did?'

'Of course, if you want to save Juula for the sake of her twins.'

'But Juula didn't do it either, so what am I supposed to tell?'

'Nothing. Keep quiet and weep over your old wife, even though you're glad you got rid of her. And now listen to what I'm going to tell you and try to remember it: you came here straight from hell...'

'That's right,' Jürka nodded.

'Not another word to anybody about it, understand? If anyone asks you why you gabbled about it before, just answer that it must be because of that bear. You killed it with a knife but it mauled you badly. Your ribs showed through the flesh, that's why you thought you were in hell, and all the rest of it. And right away add that you have sneaked in from Russia where someone had hit you over the head with a bottle of moonshine or, say, a weight, a stake, or some other hard and heavy object. And it's also in Russia that you got your certificate, and not from Peter or an angel, understand? Deny Peter just as he himself denied Jesus Christ: you never saw him, heard about him, or know anything about him at all. The same goes for the angel who handed you the document. If you're asked why you mentioned some Peter or other, tell them that you knew a man called Peter in Russia – a priest or perhaps a blacksmith he was. Why did you flee from Russia? Because the churches have been closed down (it's a lie, but never mind), and you were afraid

93

for your soul. You came here for the salvation of your soul because there are churches here and new ones opening every day, so there's sure to be salvation. If you're asked why you kept the truth back before, tell them that you were afraid you'd be sent back to Russia where there were no churches and no salvation. If you answer like that all the clever people – and everyone thinks he's clever – will say: aha, so Russia is the hell he meant, and Peter was a policeman or a frontier guard or someone.'

'And the angel, who'll he be?'

'Since there's no Peter, the angel is also out.'

'And what about my certificate?'

'You bought it, that's all. You bought it from a Jew, blaming Jews is the fashion nowadays. You can pile anything you like on Jews. If you're asked something you can't answer, just say you've forgotten, your missus knew but she has died. It's her memory that wouldn't let her live. And remember this: the less you talk the better, because people take most of the words you say wrongly. True, they might even misinterpret your silence, but still it happens less often. So, the fewer words the better. As for your soul's salvation, you can talk all you want about it, no one will take you seriously anyway.'

'But I myself do.'

'Never mind, others will think you don't mean it. These days, believing in salvation is as indecent as blowing your nose with your fingers.'

'I do that,' Jürka said.

'I do, too. But not everyone belongs to the chosen people like you and I,' Ants said. 'I want salvation as much as you do, but not everyone does. Nowadays the whole world believes in one thing only: the hotter the hell on earth, the nearer is heaven... That's why it's made so hot for people, big nations and small...'

Listening to Ants's talk made Jürka's head spin. How on earth could he remember everything? But very soon he stopped trying, remembering Ants's main commandment: if you're asked something you can't answer, just say you've forgotten, your missus knew but she has died. He could bravely go and see the police officer now, and besides Ants had promised to put in a word for him and explain things.

The officer was all smiles when Jürka entered his office, and said most pleasantly:

'We didn't get anywhere last time, did we? With luck, we'll understand each other better today. Well then to begin with, are you going to tell me where you got your identification certificate?'

'I bought it.'

'From whom?'

'From a Jew.'

'Peter, was it?'

'I don't remember.'

'Last time you said it was Peter.'

'That was another Peter.'

'Another Peter?'

'Either a priest or a blacksmith he was.'

'It was from him you bought your certificate?'

'I bought it from a Jew.'

'But Peter is a Jew, you know.'

'I know no such Peter, I don't remember.'

'And what Peter do you remember?'

'The one who was a priest or a blacksmith.'

'I don't get it,' said the officer. 'You are insisting that you bought your certificate from a Jew, and yesterday you said his name was Peter. Now then: did you or did you not buy it from Peter?'

'No, from a Jew.'

'But isn't Peter a Jew?'

'He is, but not that one.'

'Which then?'

'I don't remember.'

'What don't you remember?'

'His name.'

'You're telling me you don't remember the name of the Jew from whom you bought the certificate?'

'My missus remembered, but she went and died.'

'I see, I see it a lot better now. Tell me, where did that Jew live?'

'I forgot.'

'Have you also forgotten in what country?'

'In Russia.'

'Did you and your wife leave Russia together?'

'I guess so.'

'Why didn't you say so at once?'

'I was hit over the head, that's why.'

'Who hit you?'

'I don't remember.'

'Where did it happen?'

'I forgot. My missus remembered, but she died from too much remembering.'

'But surely you must remember where it happened – here or in Russia?'

'In Russia.'

'Why did you leave it?'

'I wanted salvation for my soul.'

'And there isn't any in Russia?'

'They closed the churches down.'

'How did you know that the churches here were open?'

'I don't remember. Maybe my missus remembered, but she went and died.'

'You came here looking for salvation together with your wife, I take it?'

'Sure.'

'Why did you talk about Peter and hell before?'

'I was afraid I'd be sent back to Russia.'

'So you went and made hell out of Russia?'

'I guess so.'

The officer rubbed his hands complacently, thought for a minute, and said:

'Well, well, things are looking up, aren't they? You spoke quite like a human being just now. There's one more thing I'd like to know – is the name in your faked certificate your real name?'

'It says Jürka, doesn't it?'

'That's right. And when in Russia were you also called Jürka?'

'I don't remember. My missus would remember.'

'Do you know Russian?'

'I don't remember.'

The officer asked something in Russian, and Jürka did not reply.

'What language did you speak in Russia?'

'You know what.'

'Your mother tongue, you mean?'

'I guess so.'

By questioning and cross-questioning Jürka the officer learnt enough about his case to present the following information to his superiors: the man had crossed the border with a faked passport. Just one detail was not quite clear, though: if Jürka had really lived in Russia, could he be so entirely ignorant of the Russian language? Or, if he knew it once, could he have forgotten it altogether as a result of being mauled by a bear or being hit over the head with a hard and heavy object?

The first question was unhesitatingly answered in the affirmative: look at all the Russians who lived here all their lives and did not know a word of the local language. So why shouldn't one of our countrymen manage to live in Russia without knowing a word of *their* language? A man, moreover, whose name was Jürka and who was so strong that he could take on a bear?

The officer's second question proved harder to answer. No one dared to attempt a solution without first asking the opinion of American specialists. It might be thought rather strange that Jürka's case should merit such worldwide interest, but there was good reason for it: America was known for a country where it was the thing to hit strong men over the head and go on hitting them until they went quite out of their mind. Even Europe despatched the stronger of her sons there to be stunned, if she couldn't handle them herself. All things considered, it was America where they should know best: could amnesia be a consequence of dementia?

The American specialists, however, asked their colleagues in England by cable to find out what kind of object Jürka had been hit over the head with – sharp or blunt? If it was the former, they had no experience to go by because the practice in America was to use blunt objects on their own citizens and also any foreigners who agreed to it of their own free will. So there was nothing for it but turn to our own specialists.

The doctors who examined Jürka thought that the object used to hit him with must have been solid anyway, and he was either hit twice with the same object and with the same force, or once with a forked solid object which explained the two identical bumps on the top of his head. Whether the blow had merely caused concussion or damage to the cranium was a moot point. There were, however, the twin bumps, the two calluses like those formed sometimes on horses' legs.

The layman could easily mistake these bumps for horns. When Jürka was asked if these bumps caused him any discomfort he replied that they sort of itched before rain or storm. From this it was concluded that the bumps had an unnatural origin, otherwise why should they itch before a natural phenomenon like rain?

These findings were passed on to England whence a cable was sent to America. The American specialists agreed with ours as regards the origin of the bumps. Jürka must have been hit with a sharp object because in America, where men were knocked out with blunt objects, the appearance of calluses on the top of a head, the jaw or the chin had never been observed. The American specialists informed their colleagues in England that the matter was outside their competence, and suggested that perhaps Europe, with her cultural seniority, was better qualified to diagnose cranial damages.

As a result of this correspondence and exchange of cables it was decided that there were no better specialists in the world than our own in the matter of cranial damages. Although a loss of memory like Jürka's (completely forgetting Russian, provided he had known it once and that there had been anything to forget) had never been observed before, the fact itself was recognised as possible and plausible. In drawing up their conclusion the specialists expressed the hope that such science-promoting cases would be repeated, confirming the hypothesis that has been voiced.

The case attracted the attention not only of specialists. Many of the public figures also had something to say on the matter. According to one opinion, of which special mention must be made here, the case presented a remarkable example of how strong a mother tongue is in a man's blood. He might forget everything, even his name, but his mother tongue will glow in his heart like a Fire Bird. This view was all the more valid because it came from a man who spoke nothing but a foreign language to his wife and children.

And so, the story accepted as the most plausible and probable of all was that Jürka arrived from Russia where he was hit over the head with some hard object, and that he wanted to save his soul. The officer took Jürka's faked certificate away, and issued him a new one with the entries copied word for word, as new data were unobtainable. Jürka had lost his memory, nobody knew anything about him, and his wife who might have known was dead.

'This closes the matter,' the officer said with satisfaction, handing Jürka his new certificate. 'You have a real identity now.'

'Is my name still the same – Jürka?'

'Naturally.'

'I thought... maybe if something's wrong, then...'

'Ah, Jürka, do you imagine it's always easy to tell right from wrong, and does it really matter?'

'I guess not.'

'I think so too. When you see Ants thank him for teaching you sense. If he hadn't you'd be hounded to death with all that questioning.'

CHAPTER EIGHT

Jürka had not seen his wife and children in all this time, and when he went home at last there he hoped to find peace from problems of public import.

But things turned out differently to his expectations, because Juula had a surprise ready, which she presented at the first opportunity.

'Old man,' Juula dropped her voice mysteriously. 'Something strange is happening to our twins: they're growing horns on their heads!'

'Don't talk rubbish,' Jürka said quite calmly, as if he had been expecting it or already knew what had happened.

'It's the honest truth,' Juula insisted. 'They're like little knobs.'

'Maybe it's something else?'

'What? They're horns, that's what they are. The boys tell me they itch.'

'Oh well, never mind the horns so long as their papers are in order,' Jürka said judiciously.

But as the days passed Juula grew more and more puzzled by the boys' horns. Finally, she went to see the midwife. This woman was as much in the dark, and so Juula went to see the doctor's assistant who had a wooden leg and only one eye, and that all but blind.

The doctor's assistant said that he had to see one or both of the boys and feel their horns with his own fingers before he could say anything. Juula brought one of the boys, and then the doctor's assistant decided he had to examine the other one as well to avoid making a mistake. Juula took the boy home, and hurried back with the other one, but the doctor's assistant, after thoroughly examining his head, declared that he had to have both boys there together to compare their horns and thus arrive at the truth which, of course, was learnt only through comparison. And so Juula trudged home again, and returned with both boys, so that all the four sprouting horns could be examined at the same time. The doctor's assistant carefully compared the boys' heads, asked Juula how old they were, had she other children, boys or girls, and how old they were.

'The matter is still obscure – I mean the horns,' he told Juula. 'We'll have to wait until your other children and those yet to be born will reach the age of your twins. That's when we'll be able to say something definite, because your other children may have no knobs at all, and then it will be clear that what the twins have are not horns but simply an anomaly frequently observable in firstborns, the more so if they're twins.'

'What can we do about this anomaly thing?' Juula asked.

'It's hard to say,' the doctor's assistant replied. 'Recently, an unfailing remedy has been devised: not to have firstborn children at all.'

'But how will they come into the world?'

'They won't.'

'Well I never!' said Juula testily. 'What happens to the baby then?'

'That I don't know. Ask the midwife or the doctor. About those horns, too, you ought to see the doctor. He'll tell you the right thing, if no one else will.'

'I was thinking – maybe I should go and see the pastor?'

'You might do that too, but better see the doctor first. The pastor is usually left till the last. We start on the soul when the flesh is already beyond help.'

Juula liked these wise words, and acted on them at once. Luck was with her this time and, without meaning to, she killed two birds with one stone, so to say. The doctor, as it turned out, had studied theology first and had shifted to medicine some time later, when he had learnt enough to start doubting everything. Still, the seed planted in his soul by the Holy Writ sprouted just the same and when he experienced doubt in medicine he sought comfort in theology which seemed to him to be more perfect than the other sciences because it rested on faith alone and owed its existence to belief only.

It was an algebra of the soul, a counterpoint in music which needed neither proof nor substantiation. It existed, and that was that! To the doctor's mind, the weakness of the natural sciences lay precisely in their attempt to prove and explain phenomena. The human mind was frail, and man himself was mortal, and therefore he usually lacked the qualities required, or else his life span was not long enough to do the explaining and the substantiating.

Evolution interested him especially, but it did not take him long to become disappointed in it as well, finding in it a great multitude of inexplicable questions and contradictory opinions. Reflecting on these opinions, he finally arrived at the conclusion – with the help of theology – that obviously the problem was approached from the wrong end: it was not the ape that had developed into man, but man who had developed into ape. God had created man in his image – that was a truth not to be questioned. But the human soul loses the image of its creator, and likewise the flesh of a mortal departs from its divine model and sprouts a tail or horns, develops into arachnids or crustaceans, fish or reptiles, a flower or a tree.

The doctor was working on his new teaching on evolution when Juula brought the twins to show him their horns and ask him what to do. He examined the boys and found their vitality extraordinary.

'There's nothing wrong with your boys,' he told Juula, smiling and rubbing his hands with a happy look on his face.

'But what if their horns grow big?' Juula asked anxiously.

'Let them grow, the bigger the better.'

'But what if they grow so big that the boys won't be able to wear hats?'

'They'll go without hats, it's the fashion.'

'But people will see that they have horns!'

'Let them see.'

'Why, they won't be allowed into school, or into church either!' Juula gasped.

'My dear woman, there's no cause for worry, because schools have gone out of fashion, and anyone is allowed into church, horns or no horns, so long as you've paid what's due.'

'I wish it were so, but...'

'Be happy and proud of your boys if they really grow horns. Just as Adam was truly the first man, so your sons will truly be the first born horned men. Oh, you'll naturally have no end of trouble with them, but that can't be helped.'

'What trouble? Tell me please, so I'll know.'

'It's hard to tell, my good woman.'

'Try anyway, only so I'll know.'

'Well, let's put it this way: everyone believes that the more he has the happier he'll be, isn't that so? Now, supposing every man had ten wives, and every woman had ten husbands, would they be happier than if they had one wife and one husband?'

'Heaven preserve me from having several husbands! I'm in and out of childbed all the time with just the one man I have.'

'Good. Think then what will happen to your boys if they grow horns? Believe me, my good woman, they'll have no less than ten females hanging on to each of their horns, for a husband born with horns will be a prize they'll all want to grab for themselves. Nothing captivates a woman as surely as horns on a man's head. They'll tear your boys to pieces because of those horns alone.'

'Oh, the poor darlings,' Juula broke into a wail. 'Those women will be the death of you!'

'But there is an alternative,' the doctor said.

'What?' Juula clutched at this straw eagerly.

'That your boys won't have horns.'

'How can that be when they have them already?'

'They have or have not – it's a very trickly question.'

'I don't get it, doctor.'

'How shall I explain it to you... Well, I'll try it like this: every creature has its soul and...'

'It's immortal like ours, yes?'

'We'll leave that question open for the moment. Let's simply say that every creature has its soul, and every soul has its peculiar features – the beasts of prey have fangs, the eagle has claws, the sheep has horns, and so forth. Therefore, we can assume that horns represent the soul of a sheep, can we not? Incidentally, people also have a soul and a brain – smaller in some, larger in others. In some, the brain is too big for their head even.'

'The human soul, you know, is in the heart and not in the head, seeing that blood is in the heart, and the soul is in the blood,' Juula said.

'Quite right, my good woman, the soul is in the heart, and the brain is in the head. When there's more brain than the head can hold it protrudes in sort of swellings, like sprouting horns. Consequently, horns are the outcroppings of brain, in which case they form little knobs and are quite a different thing from real horns. We'll have to wait and see what the lumps on your boys' heads develop into – outcroppings of the brain or real horns. Nothing definite can be said at present.'

'What will happen to my boys if their horns are not real but this other kind? Will they come to a bad end?'

'People with an excess of brain, protruding in hornlike swellings, are crucified, made to drink poison, stabbed, starved and otherwise murdered from sheer ignorance, mind you, and not in anger.'

'Oh, my poor twins, may the horns God has sent them be real, dying from too many women is better than starving anyway,' Juula moaned.

'There is yet a third possibility,' the doctor said.

'It's all so awful, I don't want to hear any more,' Juula protested.

'Hear me out first, and then decide if it's awful or not.'

'All right, but I refuse to listen to more horrors after this.'

'Good. The third possibility is that your boys will grow real horns and at the same time their skulls will become so strong that butting a sheep will be child's play.'

'It may well be. Their father, you know, is so strong that he killed two bears with his own hands,' Juula put in.

'There, you see, that gives us all the more hope! And if, moreover, your boys harden their skulls with constant training they'll be so good at butting that they'll easily knock out anyone, not just some Black, and travelling from one country to another they'll challenge any ram to a butting match, a small one or a big one, with or without horns. And if they're capable of doing that, their names will be recorded in heaven and monuments will be erected to them on earth. And girls in white will lay red roses at the foot of these monuments, piling them right to the top, and old ladies will be moved to tears. The feet of your boys will tread on gold, and their names will be immortalised, even if they are brainless and heartless.'

'You talk so beautifully!' Juula sighed admiringly. 'If only it all came true!'

'Let us trust in God that your boys will develop the horns and skulls of rams, and then it shall come true.'

'Thanks to you, doctor, I feel so much easier in my mind, so happy that...'

'That's the thing, my good woman, there's nothing like an easy mind,' the doctor spoke as he saw Juula and the twins out.

Juula carried the mood home, but here a surprise awaited her: it was Sunday, but Jürka was working away, his shirt drenched in sweat. And what's more Juula couldn't make out what he was working so hard at. Had he gone out of his mind, or had something happened in her absence? What other reason could he have for digging holes all over the place – in front of the house, behind the house, in the gateway, along the road, and just simply everywhere?

'Are you nuts, or what?' Juula asked her furiously digging husband.

'What did you say?' Jürka asked, puffing and grunting.

'I said: have you gone nuts?'

'I guess not.'

'What are you digging those holes for?'

'To make our house look pretty.'

'With those holes?'

'I'll plant trees in them when I have time.'

'And if you don't have time?'

'I'll fill them in again.'

'What's got into you all of a sudden?'

'The police told me to do it when they handed me my new certificate.'

'And you jump to it right away?'

'What have I got to do with it? It's Ants.'

'Ants doesn't live in a forest.'

'The trees here will be chopped down too, Ants said.'

'Why?'

'I don't know. We didn't plant them, that's why.'

'Oh, rubbish!'

'It's the honest truth. Ants wouldn't talk rubbish.'

'What's Ants to us, he's at one with the authorities. Look at his wife and daughters with their fat mugs painted like the face of that clock! Try keeping up with them. And they tried to teach me too – I wasn't cultured enough, if you please, and they themselves live like pigs!'

'Don't insult the pigs, a pig likes to keep its pen clean.'

'That's what I say, and all they do the livelong day is show off their clockfaces – cultured they are, cultured pigs. You're a good one, too! Wasting your Sunday on digging holes, when you might have had a go at the bedbugs instead – the kids wake up in blisters every morning. Think how many you could have killed in a day! Maybe you'd have got rid of the cockroaches too...'

'It's not a man's job to squash bedbugs. They couldn't bite through my hide anyway, they haven't the jaws.'

'They would bite through your hide if you weren't so terribly dirty. A bedbug is scared to crawl over you because it would throw up. Look at your shirt, it's rotting from sweat! And when it dries it's like the bark of a fir. Try washing it! I smashed my roller against it, and still I didn't wash it clean.'

'It doesn't matter if it's washed or not, because it will get dirty again when I put it on clean. The time to wash it is when it's worn enough to give to the ragman, because if it's washed maybe he'll give you a better bowl for it.'

'They way you talk, the bowl needn't be washed either until it breaks? It's all food anyway, different though it be.'

'No, don't wash the bowl, just throw it away. The ragman doesn't collect broken bowls.'

'What about yourself? Maybe you, too, can do without a wash until you're laid out?'

'Me or my shirt, what's the difference? You wash only to get dirty again.'

'And yet you're prettying up the house, of all the crazy things! Like painting those fat faces, eh?' Juula took a stab at her husband before she flounced off.

'I guess so,' Jürka replied calmly, and dug all the harder, almost splitting the skin on his back with the effort. He was thinking as he worked: 'Sure, a man needs a good front and a good document, he can save his soul if he has them, and I do want to save mine.'

When Jürka came into the house in the evening and sat down to cool off a bit after his exertions, Juula sat beside him – the children had been put to bed, and she had a minute to call her own.

'Look, you know what they said?' she whispered, although there were no eavesdroppers to fear as their farm hand and the servant girl had gone off somewhere that Sunday evening.

'Who they?' Jürka asked.

'The midwife, the doctor's assistant, and the doctor.'

'You went to see them?'

'All on account of the boys.'

'What boys?'

'As if it's news to you that our twins have horns on their heads! Everyone says this deformity or some such thing must run in our family.'

'What are you talking about?'

'Good heavens above, their horns, what else! The boys have horns – haven't you got that through your thick skull yet?'

'Sure, but why call it a deformity...'

'When human children have horns?'

'But supposing they weren't fathered by a human?'

'Did I produce lambs or children, tell me that? And you've no horns that I can see!'

'I have, though.'

'You're a great one for a joke, aren't you!' Juula gave him an angry nudge between the ribs with her elbow.

'It's no joke.'

'So you have horns now. Where?'

'Feel in my hair.'

Juula stood up and started feeling through his hair for horns. And great was her surprise when she discovered two bumps, slightly bigger than the boys'.

'But you told me that's where you were hit over the head with something?'

'It's others who said so, not me.'

'What others, I'd like to know?'

'Specialists.'

'You mean no one hit you over the head?'

'Never in my life.'

'You mean they're really horns?'

'Horns they are.'

'Go on with you! Next thing you'll be telling me you're Satan!'

'That's right.'

'You mean my children were fathered by Satan himself?'

'That's right.'

Juula felt his horns once again, then lowered herself on the grass before him, all but falling on her knees, folded her hands as in prayer and, raising her eyes to her husband, uttered ecstatically:

'So you come from an ancient and noble race!'

'Yes, a noble one, Ants says so.'

'A great and noble race! Do I belong to it too now, and the children?'

'And the children.'

'Then Ants is nothing compared to us?'

'Nothing.'

'Why does he put on airs then and brag of his family?'

'He doesn't believe and doesn't understand. The police don't believe it or understand it either. Nobody has any faith or understanding. Those specialists, you know, also said I had calluses on my head, like on a horse's leg.'

'But why didn't you tell me before, and you made me drag those kids to all those doctor people?'

'I was afraid you wouldn't believe me.'

'But I do!'

'If you do you'll understand.'

'What's there to understand, I'm not a halfwit.'

Still, it was a pity that the doctor's prophecy would never come true now. Her boys would never grow real horns, nor skulls hard enough for them to go travelling about the world and winning butting matches with Blacks and rams. Never would their feet tread gold, and dozens of girls would not hang on to their horns. Ah, that was beautiful talk! Oh well, it was just too bad. There was no grabbing all the good things there were in the world. If a person was decent he was bound to be stupid, and if he was clever there was no decency in him, and that's the way it went!

But that day was the happiest yet at the Pit. Never mind that people didn't believe in their happiness and failed to understand it: they themselves believed in it, so what more did a body want? Juula was the one who did most of the rejoicing actually, because Jürka had long lived with it and so he was rather less ebullient than his wife. What really pleased him was that he could work in peace at last – for his own family and for Ants. It was a strange thing, but for all his trying he could never quite settle his debt: no sooner did he square his old account, than something new came up and he was in debt again. There seemed no end to it. And this convinced Jürka that if you were Satan and wanted to save your soul like a plain mortal you had to be someone's debtor all your life and slave for him, whether you liked it or not.

Occasionally, some pious book-peddlers, selling edifying literature, strayed to the Pit. Juula knew the alphabet and could make out some words, but she never bought anything. And Jürka always told them that he had no need of pious reading seeing that he was earning the salvation of his soul by working for Ants. And if some sins were left over he'd redeem them by toiling for his family at home.

Travelling salesmen of other wares also disturbed Jürka's peaceful toil sometimes. They praised to the skies the bicycles, sewing machines, gramophones or whatever fashionable junk they were selling, they would give it away for a song, on an instalment basis, anything! Jürka was talked into buying a bicycle once, and squashed it when he tried to ride it. He had to pay for it just the same, and it cost him a calf. Luckily for him the travelling salesman and the butcher happened to arrive at the Pit at the same time, and so the money simply changed hands. What's more, the salesman turned out to be such an obliging gentleman that he agreed to whip on the calf from behind as the butcher led it way by a rope. The two men went off with the good calf, and Jürka was left with the wreck of a bicycle. After that he showed all travelling salesmen the door immediately, and any who lingered he threw out bodily.

'Better not use violence!' the evicted usually screamed.

'I'm the master here,' Jürka growled. 'Violence is what masters use, what else?'

'I'll bring the police, then you'll know who's the master!'

'Go ahead, I'll show you the police!'

But none of the salesmen he threw out ever brought the police. And there was only one man among them whom Jürka favoured as an exception: this peddler carried a bale on his back and a box on his stomach, worn on shoulder straps. When Jürka threw him over the fence together with his bale and box and strode back to the house, the man suddenly shouted:

'Are you afraid of my wares, master? You needn't buy if you're afraid, but a look you can have for free. I've thread and needles, pins and buttons, ribbons, kerchiefs, socks and stockings, just name the thing you need and I am sure to have it!'

Jürka stopped and, turning round, asked:

'No bicycles?'

'Huh, I'm my own bicycle,' the peddler replied.

'No gramophones?'

'There's a gramophone playing in my belly.'

'No instalments, nothing for a song?'

'Who wants to starve, I don't,' the peddler sang out.

'Come in then,' Jürka said, throwing open the gate.

Tht was the only salesman who could call at the Pit without fear of getting thrown out.

The years came and went, and Jürka's household grew, increasing in livestock and in the size of his family. Before he knew it, the twins were old enough to go herding – first pigs, then sheep, and finally cows. Jürka was forced to send one of them to Ants, however. Once upon a time he dreamed that both boys would work on their own farm, but things turned out differently. True, this did not worry Jürka much as he was more concerned with his own salvation. The twin who worked for Ants came home sometimes and told his brother what he had learnt away from home: to spit through his teeth, trip up his opponent in a wrestling game, poke his thumb into the enemy's eye in a fight, do a handstand, tell lies, and do a little stealing.

'It's what every boy should know,' he told the brother who lived at home.

CHAPTER NINE

One day Ants asked Jürka, 'Why don't you buy the Pit?'

'I haven't the money,' he replied.

'Anyone could do it with money, try doing it without,' Ants said.

'I bought a bicycle that way, and when I got on it it fell to pieces, but I had to pay for it just the same.'

'The Pit is not a bicycle, it won't fall to pieces. Besides you don't have to pay cash for it, it'll pay its own way,' Ants said.

'How do you mean?' asked Jürka

Ants then explained how Jürka could buy the Pit without paying any cash at all or for a trifling sum which he, Ants, would lend him if Jürka didn't have even that much. After this conversation, Ants went on pestering Jürka until he finally agreed to buy the Pit. He wanted to make sure about one thing first: was it easier for an owner than for a tenant of a farm to earn salvation?

'I should say so!' Ants assured him. 'As a well-to-do farmer you'll be elected churchwarden and your soul's as good as saved.'

'All right then, I'll buy the Pit,' Jürka said, but another thought had begun to worry him and he asked: 'Who is it even easier for to earn salvation?'

'That's hard to say, very hard.'

'Maybe for those who make out the real documents for people?'

'No, Jürka, those who write and talk couldn't have it worse. It's the priests of mammon and executioners who run everything nowadays. For another thing, the spirit used to influence power, and now it's all the other way about. Just think, how can anyone

111

save his soul with the help of the spirit when it's mammon that's taken control over power, and power has taken control over the spirit?'

Jürka didn't understand a word, but he was impressed by the tone of Ants's speech, and ventured to ask timidly:

'You mean that digging in the earth and carting manure is more pleasing to God?'

'Even more pleasing than forgiving men their sins, because the main thing in this business of forgiving is not what the sinners are being forgiven for, but the ritual itself, with the prayers, gilded cross and everything.'

'I guess, you're right,' Jürka said.

As Jürka did not have the money to pay for the Pit he had to borrow it from Ants, and was again up to his neck in debt. Ants tried to cheer him up, saying that Jürka was his own master now, he was making the effort for himself and his family, for his own farm. The Pit, he reminded Jürka, was to be the home of his children and their children for now and forever. To be sure, owning property was not the same as leasing it, and Jürka had to live up to his new status of proprietor by taking better care of the land, tilling it, digging ditches, laying pipes, and suchlike. This meant that he and his family had to work twice as hard as before. Ants suggested that farm hands could do the bulk of the work if one had the money to hire them, and there was always money to be found in the world. And Ants also knew where a farm owner could lay his hands on some money: the bank granted loans at a very small interest to farmers for the express purpose of improving their land. And so Jürka did as Ants told him, accustomed as he was to blindly following his advice ever since that time it had freed him from the clutches of the police.

No sooner was the loan granted, than Ants came up with a new idea.

'Look, Jürka,' he said. 'D'you think you ought to sink all that money into the Pit?'

'Where else?'

'That needs thinking about. Maybe you could put it into something more profitable. What about building a new house?'

'At the Pit?'

'Why there?' Ants asked.

'But where else?'

'Let's think. Land improvement is what you got the loan for, you must bear that in mind.'

'So it can't be used for building a house, you mean?' Jürka asked.

'Generally speaking, no. But if you're set on building a new house, you'll have to do it in someone else's name, see? For instance, in mine. You'll have to sleep on it first, of course, before you decide. Although I've pulled you out of many a hole, you'll have to think hard anyway, because building a house in someone else's name is not a trifling matter. It's all above board, of course, because the house will bring an income and the income can be invested in the land, and the end result will be land improvement, see?'

'But what if...' Jürka faltered.

'Don't worry. If the house is in my name I'll keep you out of trouble. It's a sure business: the house will start bringing in an income, you'll grow richer with every day, and before long you'll be able to leave the Pit for good.'

'Why should I? I like it here.'

'Please yourself. A rich man will live well anywhere, even at the Pit.'

'There's just one thing: the missus is always nagging me about the bedbugs biting the kids.'

'Forget it,' Ants dismissed the matter. 'They're domestic creatures, they haven't gnawed anybody's bones away yet.'

'That's what I say, too,' Jürka agreed.

They put their heads together and worked out a cunning plan: with the loan they'd build a house with premises for a store on the ground floor right at the intersection of two busy roads. And so that Jürka could not be accused of misapplying the money, the house would be built in Ants's name. And on Ants's land too, to make the scheme appear all the more legitimate, as Ants was known as a rich and enterprising person.

The loan did not go very far because Ants had devised the

house on a very ambitious scale, and so willy-nilly he was compelled to put money into it himself: after all, construction could not be abandoned half-way, could it?

'I've had to make a loan, too, you see,' Ants told Jürka. 'We're building your house on borrowed money, and all the profit I get from it is that it's in my name.'

When the house was ready and tenanted and Jürka wanted to collect rent from the tenants, he discovered that Ants had already pocketed the money.

'Why did you, it's my house, isn't it?' Jürka asked him in dismay.

'It's yours, that's the whole trouble,' Ants told him. 'If it were mine, it would be a different thing altogether. The house is yours, that's a fact, but the money you had did not cover the building costs, and so I had to borrow the sum you were short of, because if I hadn't your house would have remained unfinished and your land-improvement loan would have gone for nothing. And now I have to pay back the money I'd borrowed for your house. Where am I supposed to take it from? And why should I get it from anywhere, seeing it went into *your* house? Let the house pay it back – both the loan and the interest. Got my point?'

Jürka understood well enough that it was up to the house to pay back the money invested in it. What he wanted to know was who'd give *him* the money to pay back the loan?

'The house, naturally, who else?' Ants explained. 'Only first it will pay *me* the money I'd borrowed plus the interest on it, and after that it will pay *you*. It's your house, after all, you can wait. You have the house and I have nothing, so it's easier on you.'

And so Jürka settled down to wait. Months passed and even years, and still he waited because Ants continued to pocket the rent and what was left over went towards repairs.

'A house wants tending, just as land does,' Ants would say. 'You're lucky that you have me to take care of your house, because if you had the maintenance of it you'd only get into more debt. Actually, owning a house is both difficult and expensive, and so it won't surprise me in the least if you and I go broke.'

'How can we? You told me yourself that it was going to bring in a profit, and that...'

'I told you. Of course, I told you. But at the time I didn't own a single house. However, don't worry, I'll settle everything, just leave it to me.'

Jürka stopped worrying and left everything to Ants. And then the bank demanded repayment of the loan. He was asked to account for the money as very little land-improving work had been done. Jürka replied that he didn't remember, as Ants had instructed him to reply. But, finally, driven into a corner he blurted out the truth about the house, only so they'd leave him alone.

'I built the house with a loan.'

'Where?'

'At the crossroads, on land belonging to Ants.'

The statement was checked, and it was established that the house belonged to Ants, not Jürka.

'It is my house,' Jürka persisted. 'I built it in Ants's name, that's all.'

'If it's in Ants's name, how can it be yours?'

'It is mine, only in Ants's name.'

Ants was then interviewed.

'He's a great story-teller, he is,' Ants said with a chuckle. 'He goes around telling people that he's Satan who has come down to earth to earn his soul's salvation, and that it was Apostle Peter himself who gave him his credentials. And when Jürka's wife died and her body vanished, he told everyone that she went straight to hell. His farm hand perished in a fire that broke out in the hay-filled barn he was asleep in, and Jürka swore that he had burnt the fellow alive himself for chasing his old woman. Why didn't you take all that talk of his seriously? Anyone can see that Jürka is not quite like other people, he's obviously not all there. Far from receiving anything from him, all I've been doing was giving him this, that and the other, without any profit to myself, mind you, but simple because I want salvation too. I receive the eucharist twice a year, and I have my own pew in the church.'

That was all Ants could say, and it was obvious to everyone that there was nothing more to talk about. Jürka, however, persisted that the house at the crossroads was his and that he built it with his land-improvement loan. And now Ants sued him for slander. Jürka happened to be working at Ants's place when the court summons was brought to him.

'What does it say?' Jürka asked the man who delivered the subpoena.

'You're to come to court, that's what,' the man replied.

'What for?'

'For slandering Ants, that's what for.'

'That's not true.'

'It has to be since it's written here.'

'I'm sure it's been faked.'

'That could never happen,' said the messenger.

'Why not? I did have a faked certificate, didn't I?'

'But this is just a summons, so why fake it?'

'I never slandered Ants. He's my friend,' Jürka said.

'That's for Ants to tell the court.'

'He'll be there too?' Jürka asked eagerly.

'Naturally.'

'Oh, then it's all right. Ants won't let me down.'

Jürka tried to see Ants before the trial, but Ants was either not at home, or he was too busy, or he had gone away on some business of his own, or else on some business concerning Jürka's house. He didn't see him in court either – Ants was represented by his solicitor. This roused Jürka's suspicions, but since Ants wasn't there, he wasn't. And anyway nothing bad could happen here because he was certain in his own mind that he had not slandered or swindled anyone. The trial itself began very simply and politely, no one yelled at Jürka or bullied him. Not like at the police. The judge read something in a quiet voice, and when he had finished reading he asked softly: 'Defendant, do you plead guilty?'

Jürka looked round to see who the judge was speaking to. Why, it was to himself! The person called a defendant was himself, and Ants was called a plaintiff, of all things. The judge now told Jürka what he was accused of, and in conclusion asked him if he pleaded guilty, to which Jürka replied tersely: 'No.'

'Do you still insist that the house built on Ants's land at the crossroads is your property?'

'It's mine.'

'Why do you call that house yours when it stands on Ants's land and is registered in Ants's name?'

'I built it with my land-improvement loan.'

'Who can confirm this statement?'

'Ants can, he got the money.'

'Have you no other witnesses?'

'No.'

'Ants says that you are slandering him, and wants you to be punished.'

'It's a lie. Ants is my friend, so why should he want me to be punished for building that house?'

'You were granted a loan for land improvement and misapplied the money, did you not?'

'Ants advised me to build a house instead, it was more profitable, he said, and I'd grow rich.'

'Why did you build it on Ants's land?'

'Where else? At the Pit?'

'Why not?'

'Not a soul comes near the place.'

'People would come for the summer.'

'They'd be scared of bears. My missus is, she doesn't go berrying or mushrooming in the forest any more.'

'Ants states that the house is his property and that it was built with his money.'

'The house is mine, built in Ants's name.'

'But why in Ants's name? Will you explain it to me?'

'Ants said on account of the loan.'

'Do I understand that you built the house for him because you had taken the loan?'

'Not for Ants, only in Ants's name.'

'Isn't it the same thing?'

'Not at all. It's *my* house built in Ants's name, and that's not the same thing as Ants's house built in Ants's name.'

'Why did you trust your money to Ants so simply?'

'Because he is my friend.'

'What has he done for you as a friend?'

'He freed me from the police.'

'What did he do?'

'He taught me to tell good lies.'

'Good lies?' exclaimed the judge.

'He told me to say that I ran away from Russia.'

'You mean you did not?'

'Why from Russia when I am Satan?'

The case was taking an interesting turn. The story already heard by the police and the pastor, of Satan coming to earth as a human to gain salvation, was once more confirmed in court.

Ants's solicitor had little trouble proving that they had before them a case of slander. There was no need to call witnesses as the defendant himself had admitted the facts of slander, albeit he did not consider himself guilty.

'The reason for this,' explained Ants's solicitor, 'is that it is difficult for the defendant to associate a criminal fact with a sense of guilt. A poor understanding of honour and honesty is, in fact, observable in the defendant. While he is a Christian and goes to church, he still believes that he is Satan. This is a little more and, at the same time, a little less than what an ordinary mortal will permit himself. Something has gone awry in this man's intelligence and morality. The plaintiff, on the other hand, is a man who is well-known and esteemed, a citizen of means, a prominent public figure and a loyal son of the state, a church warden, a bridge player of long standing, and the first owner of a gramophone in the parish. He is a friend of the defendant who has himself confirmed this before the court, which fact, however, does not prevent the defendant from slinging mud at his friend. All this leads one to suspect that the defendant is unanswerable for his actions in general. But, on the other hand, we know that he owns property and has a large family; we also know that to protect his wife and children he attacked a bear with his bare hands. The conclusion to be drawn from these facts is that he does have a sense of responsibility in some, though not in full, measure. Consequently, according to the law, the court should impress it upon the defendant with some light punishment that while protecting his children from a bear he cannot at the same time cast aspersions on the honest name of his friend – the father of a family.'

Jürka listened so strenuously that sweat poured down his face, but he did not understand a word. These gentlemen talked at such length and so beautifully, but what did they talk about, he wondered? It couldn't have anything to do with his case, of course. Because what was there to talk about? He took a loan, Ants built the house, and that was all there was to it. Why Ants? Because Ants was his friend. Those who didn't believe it wouldn't understand anything anyway.

The judge re-entered. Everyone was ordered to stand up. Jürka stood up too, because he didn't want to disobey orders although more often than not he saw no sense in orders generally. The judge read something out quickly. Jürka's ears only caught the concluding words which the judge read out more slowly, clearly and loudly: '...two days' detention and a year on probation.'

'Who? What?' Jürka mumbled in confusion, and suddenly Ants appeared from somewhere together with his solicitor and both of them, smiling happily, started congratulating him.

'Well, I managed to get you out of a hole again,' Ants said. 'You did right today to tell them you were Satan, this made the judge take a different view of the case.'

Jürka's mind was still befuddled, but when Ants took him by the arm, led him to his trap and told him to get in, he understood that everything was all right. And if so, did it matter how or why?

They were already driving across open country when Jürka broke the silence.

'That judge is a good man,' he said. 'He addressed me so nicely, and...'

'The judge may be a nice man, but the law is stern, it can't take a joke. It was a pretty close shave,' Ants said.

'What do you mean?' Jürka asked, uncomprehending.

'I mean that you'd be in the soup if it were proved that you'd used the loan to build that house.'

'But I did tell the judge that.'

'He didn't believe you.'

'How funny! He asked me and I told him, and still he didn't believe me, so what did he ask me for?' Jürka was getting more and more confused.

'The law demands it. A judge has to act according to the law.'

'Oh, I see. And the law says the judge mustn't believe what he's told?'

'That's right.'

'But who invented such a law?' Jürka asked.

'People did. The law says that you must have a witness to confirm what you're stating in court.'

'Then why didn't they call you?'

'You think I'd tell them anything? You think I'd confirm that you'd used the land-improvement loan to build that house, and so make you out an embezzler, a thief? Oh no, my friend, you can't know me very well if you imagine I'd do that. Get this into your head: small fry like you and I must not dip our hands into the state coffers. It's the privilege of those who are in power. Wre must rest content with swindling one another, if we're lucky enough to find a simpleton to swindle. And so I'd never tell, even if an axe hung over me, that you pocketed the land-improvement loan and built a house with it.'

'What you mean – pocketed?'

'You misapplied it, didn't you? And in the view of the law it's a punishable crime.'

'But I wasn't punished, you know,' Jürka said innocently.

'You weren't because I didn't give evidence against you. And I got out of giving evidence against you by suing you for slander.'

'I never slandered you, you know.'

'Of course you didn't. Why should a friend slander his good friend. But I had to sue you for slander otherwise I'd never convince the judge that you did not misapply the money.'

'You mean you lied?'

'They wouldn't believe me otherwise, so I had no choice. It's the way people are: tell them a pack of lies and they'll believe you at once, and try telling them the truth and they'll start doubting you, probing and prying, interrogating you as a suspect and demanding witnesses. This time, thank God, you got off lightly enough – what's two days behind bars, and even then it's a suspended sentence.'

'I can't get the meaning of this for the life of me,' Jürka said, shaking his head.

'It's very simple, really. I told the judge that you had slandered me, and because it's a lie and the judge found witnesses, he believed me. Slandering someone is not allowed, it's punishable. But seeing that this was your first offence, the judge gave you a light punishment – two days under arrest. And, considering that you and I are friends, he gave you a suspended sentence which means that you'll go to jail only if you slander me once more in the course of the year. Simple, isn't it?'

'Sure, but I didn't slander you.'

'Of course you didn't, and that's why you won't be jailed. Everything's all right, and we can go home with an easy mind.'

'Why did we have to go to court then?' Jürka asked.

'To prove that you didn't steal that money.'

'Does the judge believe it now?'

'He does now.'

'Oh well, if he believes it he must understand something, too.'

CHAPTER TEN

True, the trial ended well for Jürka, but the noose round his neck became tighter and tighter with every day. For all his back-breaking toil he simply could not make enough money to repay the loan. He told Ants his troubles and asked him for advice. Where would he go with his wife and children if he was evicted from the Pit? Ants heard him out, pondered deeply, and said:

'As a worker you're first class. I won't let you come to grief, we'll find a way out.'

In the meantime things went from bad to worse for Jürka, until there was no hope left of repaying the loan. Like many other farms, the Pit came under the hammer, and as there were few buyers Ants bought it for a song, as he himself was wont to brag.

'See, Jürka,' he said. 'I told you I'd get you out of this hole too, and I have! You can stay on at the Pit now until you die. No one will touch you, don't be afraid. Just be your own hard-working self, that's all.'

'I'm hard-working all right, I always was.'

'That's fine then, let's hope you stay that way.'

'I guess so.'

'There's just one little matter we have to clear up,' Ants went on.

'What little matter?' Jürka asked with a sinking heart.

'Concerning that house which we built on my crossroads with your loan. You see, Jürka, this house is, so to say, part of the Pit, in as much as it was built with that land-improvement money, and during the time you were the owner of the Pit. And now it's I who am the owner of the Pit, while you have become the tenant as before. But when you were merely the tenant you wouldn't have received the loan, and you only got it when you became a property owner. I don't know what you think about it, but the way I see it is like this: if you're only a tenant and not the owner could the house which is part of the Pit belong to you? To make my meaning clear, here's an example: supposing you have an axe and you sell it, would you say that the handle belongs to you after the deal has been made and the money for the axe has been paid you?'

'I guess not.'

'The handle, therefore, belongs to the chap who bought the axe, doesn't it?'

'I guess so.'

'We've got it all clear then. The Pit is the axe, and the house on the crossroads is the handle, and since I've bought the Pit – the axe, in other words, the handle that came with it, meaning the house at the crossroads, also belongs to me.'

'I see. The Pit was there before the house, of course.'

'That's what I say too,' Ants said in agreement. 'There was the Pit and then the house appeared – no Pit, no house, because what good is a handle if there's no axe? And so, to settle the matter once and for all let's agree to close all our old accounts: I've nothing to receive from you, you've nothing to pay me, all that's done and finished with. I make you a gift of whatever's left over because you've more than enough difficulties to cope with. You've a large family, and it's no joke feeding so many mouths. You and I are friends, so don't mind my saying what I'm going to say now. I had a look once, and I had a look a second time at your home life at the Pit, I saw how and where you lived, and what you ate. Believe me, my good man, my pigs and my dogs have better things to eat than do your wife and your children. We'll try to remedy matters, the times have changed. You were the owner and you lived as you pleased, but you're no longer the owner because I am, and so it's my business now to keep an eye on things here and do as I see fit.'

'Sure, why not,' Jürka mumbled obligingly, too confused to say anything else. Life was moving faster than Jürka's mind, and he could not keep up with events.

'Well then, we'll make a new beginning from today,' Ants told him. 'You will be the tenant of the Pit as before, and we'll see what can be done there. I've been thinking about it and here is the idea I have hatched: why not begin with improving the land? After all, nothing has changed, has it? Nothing at all. The Pit is still the Pit, you are the same Jürka and I am the same man as before, and the house we built hasn't changed.'

'Nothing's changed except that you're the owner now,' Jürka said.

'That's the only change, and everything else remains the way it was,' Ants said quickly before Jürka could continue. 'And that's really a speck, a drop in the ocean, no more! It's a small matter actually: once you were the owner, and that's over and done with, and the same thing might happen to me. I'm the owner now, but for how long? You never can tell, you know. But never mind. The Pit will remain, and the house will remain, and we're equally attached to them. You are attached to the Pit, aren't you?'

'Sure,' Jürka grunted.

'Well, that's the main thing. You're the owner today, someone else is the owner tomorrow, but true love doesn't change hands, it's forever – our love for the Pit.'

'I guess so.'

'And when we love something we go out of our way to make things better for whatever we love. You see, I look after the house, and you look after the Pit. Its welfare always came first with you. Together with your wife and children you lived on the swill you made for your pigs, and yet you made improvements on the farm because what you're after is salvation.'

'Can you hope for salvation without a bellyful of swill?' Jürka asked.

'You can,' Ants assured him. 'But you have to work hard, very hard. If you don't you'll succumb to wicked thoughts and temptation.'

'Do you also want to save your soul?' Jürka asked.

'Of course I do, naturally,' Ants readily replied.

'But you don't work, you know.'

'That's my bad luck, and that's why it's so hard for me to save my soul. Oh well, everyone has to his cross to bear. My health is pretty poor, you know, and it's been like that since I was a child, the Lord must have cursed me with it. The only thing He did give me in place of health is my big, generous heart. Here you are, striving for salvation with toil, and I – with my good deeds. I'd never bother with the Pit if I didn't long to do you a good turn and give you a chance to live in peace in the place you love best. Anyone else would have thrown you out, together with your wife and kiddies, and moved in himself, but I don't want to do that, I have a place to live, and it's not a bad little place, as you very well know.'

'I guess I do.'

'So, you see, I bought the Pit simply from the kindness of my heart, guided by one wish only: that your family should continue to grow and prosper. There's just one thing that I could never understand: why are you so stuck on salvation?'

'But I'm Satan, aren't I?'

'Does Satan really need to save his soul?' Ants asked.

'If he doesn't no more people will come to hell.'

'Do people live in hell?'

'Where else?'

'In the world.'

'For how long? And before they know it they go to hell...'

'As for me, I'll go to heaven,' Ants said.

'Supposing Peter doesn't let you in?'

'Why shouldn't he? I believe in redemption.'

'Peter told me that doesn't count any more.'

'Did you say that to the pastor?'

'Sure.'

'And how did he take it?'

'He turned chalk-white.'

Ants suddenly felt faint, and it worried him that Jürka would notice his pallor and tell everyone about it as though it were the natural thing to happen, and telling it as casually as he'd just told him about the pastor. Was it true the pastor had turned chalk-white, or was it Jürka's imagination? If only Ants could know. Had the pastor felt the same shock of horror, the same inexplicable, vague fear that stabbed Ants in his heart and his innards every time Jürka declared so confidently and simply that he was Satan who had taken the shape of man in order to pack all the people off to hell by means of attaining salvation for himself? It was all quite fantastic and impossible, of course. Surely the Lord, having allowed His son to be crucified, would not fling mankind, redeemed by this sacrifice, into the hands of Satan to do with as he pleased? Surely a man's going to heaven or to hell could not depend on whether this devil would earn salvation or not like an ordinary mortal on the earth? And yet, who could have foreknowledge of mankind's destinies and the ways of Our Lord, and who'd have the audacity to say definitely what was and what was not possible? What if Jürka were really Satan, what if he understood what was happening about him and with him, what if he was just acting the simpleton in order to see where Ants and the rest of mankind were heading with their deeds? Supposing on the Day of Judgment he tried to get into heaven, and suddenly Jürka would appear and ask: tell the judge all about the land-improvement loan and the house we built with the money, tell the judge about my slave labour and the food which my wife and children had to live on. Why did your dogs and your pigs have better things to eat than my wife and my kids?

These thoughts flashed across Ants's mind and evaporated as quickly as they arose. For a brief moment he fancied that he was in church, kneeling before the altar, waiting to partake of the consecrated bread and wine. And then everything vanished, and he became so much his usual self that he asked Jürka, with a smirk:

'What will you do if the pastor himself is sent down to you in hell?'

'The same as with everyone else.'

'And if it's me?'

'It's all the same – you or the pastor.'

Jürka said this so simply as though it was the kind of thing one naturally took in one's stride, and Ants again felt a chill run down his spine, from one vertebra to the next. How very strange! Until now he had regarded Jürka as something of a beast of burden, whom he drove like a slave, and robbed him as soon as he had acquired something by dint of truly supernatural strength and doggedness. And here Ants suddenly knew – and he could not suppress this feeling – that Jürka did not care one way or the other, you could shower gold on him or fleece him, he did not care, because he was not the draught animal Ants treated him as, but God

126

alone knew who and what he was. Still, Ants made another attempt
and, smirking, asked:

'I wonder what you'd do with me in hell, push me into the fire?'

'There's no fire in hell,' Jürka replied.

'What is there, if there's no fire?'

'You'll see when you come there.'

Once again a chill ran down Ants's vertebrae, but he could not
stop now.

'Why won't you tell me what happens in hell if there's no fire
there?' he asked.

'I can't.'

'Why can't you?'

'I am a human being. That's why.'

'But you've just said that you're Satan!'

'I came down in the shape of man for the salvation of my soul.'

They were back in the vicious circle again: Satan, mortal,
salvation, hell; Satan – mortal, salvation – hell. There was no point
in continuing this argument for it defied human logic. Even so, one
could imagine that an inhabitant of the nether world could not think
like a human being, just as a human being, endowed with the power
of speech, could not describe the nether world. Just how things
moved round this vicious circle was unknown but obviously they
did move somehow or other. Jürka's replies best proved that there
really was something out of the ordinary in this vicious circle. His
replies were very simple, clear and brief, though at times they were
inaccurate and not easy to understand. However, it could be that he
acted as he did because he had knowledge of something else,
besides our earthly life? Would a comparison between electricity
and man be apt here? To a man, a metal wire is a solid object, and
to electricity it's simply a hole in the air. The air in its turn tastes so
divine that men call the weight of air above them – heaven. From
the point of view of electricity, air is as hard as rock, and electricity
is obliged to shatter it with a terrible noise in order to get through.

And does anyone know why electricity must cleave the air with
such a terrible noise? Does it not pursue the same, clear and
understandable aim as a man who blows up rocks? And while the
purpose of electricity's destructive activity remains obscure to man,

electricity for its part will never appreciate man's effort to shatter rocks. And that's how they live side by side, they *live*. For who can prove that electricity is not as animate a creature as man? Because we use electricity, while electricity does not use us. Is that really so? Perhaps it is, in fact, electricity that compels us to do what we do. Is there anyone who wants war? Perhaps it's electricity, indulging its passion for playing with people that makes them fight wars? Is it not electricity, perhaps, that compels man, that poor dumb creature, to study his own self and everything else, to build huge houses and bridges, design automobiles and furniture, paint pictures and mould statues, write books and compose music, and then, a moment later, to destroy all this? Our entire thousand-year-long endeavour is collapsing like a house of cards, built by a child, and very possibly simply because we do not understand electricity, thinking it is heavens knows what. Whereas it is only a living creature playing a silly joke on man with his imagined greatness and wisdom, quite possibly believing mankind to be an inanimate body, which is what we think of electricity. And it isn't as absurd as it sounds, for if we review the history of mankind, noting the rise and fall of nations and cultures, shall we not have the feeling that man acts like the wind and the water which pile up mountains and erode valleys, or like the heat and the frost which distend bodies and destroy them, unable to explain why they do it and what for.

But what if a being as powerful and eternal as electricity was watching all human activity in its entirety? Leaping high on the northern lights, it could see all the doings of people and even all the layers and caves of the world, for it has no need to dig or shovel earth in order to explore its bowels. In the eyes of such a creature, man must seem to have less sense than a grasshopper, than the wind, than fire or water. Because one could understand someone who destroys and only destroys, or someone who creates and only creates, but it is impossible to understand a creature who builds something today, smashes it tomorrow, and rebuilds the same thing all over again the day after tomorrow. Anyone who acts in this fashion must be as lacking in sense as the nature surrounding him, but if he does possess any sense notwithstanding, it must be akin to that of alternating electric current.

CHAPTER ELEVEN

These abstract reflections made Ants probe deeper into the phenomenon confronting him. After all, knowing so little about inanimate nature, as it was called, could man know a great deal about the life of Satan? Satan was a living thing, Ants had no doubt about it. To make quite sure and to stimulate his thinking, Ants took to reading books – big books and small ones. Lately, our literature has been developing so vigorously that it seemed the obvious thing to start with. But he did not find anything even remotely satanic in these books. Nothing like his reckless boldness and extravagant absurdity. Everything here was beautiful and noble, majestic and heroic, ideally realistic or realistically ideal – depending on how the authors perceived, felt and saw things. This last was most important, because everything in the world depends on how you look at it, and from what angle. Take a table: it's a narrow strip if you look at it from the side; a stick is just a dot if you look at it from one end. And who can say with any certainty precisely when a wide table-top becomes a narrow strip, a long stick becomes a dot, and vice versa?

There were two writers among the lot whom Ants thought worthy of attention. One of them fashioned epic novels from lyrical poems, then he transformed the epic novels into romantic stories, and the romantic stories into dramas, or else did it the other way about. It was slightly reminiscent of Jürka and his vicious circle: Satan, mortal, salvation, or again: salvation, mortal, Satan. To be sure the resemblance was very slight, but it was there, and again it made Ants think of alternating current. The other writer actually spoke of Satan, but not a word about his hurrying back to hell once he had attained salvation here on earth. After that, Ants wanted to try foreign literature, but he was talked out of it by people who knew, because, they alleged, foreign literature had lately become wholly influenced by our literature. Perhaps if Ants made a study of the very, very ancient books, he'd glean something from them. But the idea did not appeal to him at all, he liked everything modern best. History did not have any task comparable in grandeur to that of making an Ants who was afraid of Satan.

He need only ask the pastor if he wanted to know for certain whether there was anything of interest about Satan in books. Who, if not the pastor, should be familiar with ancient writings? And so Ants went to see the pastor and, needless to say, he trod with caution, asking him in a roundabout way if Jürka's unshakable conviction that he was Satan might be based in some sort of reality?

'What do you mean by reality, dear Ants?' the pastor asked. 'Which reality do you have in mind – the reality of faith or the reality of life?'

'Can't the two be somehow combined?'

'Hardly, dear Ants. People are always trying to combine the two, that's all they do, you know. But it's about as easy as starting a fire in water. You may have heard that some ancient Greek or other once invented liquid fire, but I've never read about anyone in Greece discovering a way of combining the reality of faith with the reality of life. Even if a combination like that has ever been observed, it was certainly not the real thing, for in those days people did not yet know what real faith was. It was in consequence of Greece's downfall, liquid fire and all, that true faith emerged. By simple tracing the development of faith and life from that time on, you will see that the closer faith comes to truth and purity, the closer it comes to dispensing salvation, and the farther it is from life. Blessedness which is inherent in faith and consequent on it has nothing to do with life, for blessedness is in heaven, and life is here on earth. If there were no promise of blessedness, there'd be no sense in having faith. Life claims everything that can be tasted, felt, measured and weighed, while faith has that which cannot be grasped with either the mind or the senses, and therefore the blessedness of faith remains on the outside of life. Now if you ask us – this is strictly between us – whether we are certain that the blessedness promised by faith really exists, we shall be compelled to reply: in order to believe firmly in blessedness it has to be found, and consequently it must exist on earth. But this is a religion of contradictions, according to which blessedness is a thing of heaven and never of the earth, and only the dead are entitled to it, never the living.'

'Forgive me for interrupting you,' Ants said, 'but I have to ask you something before I forget. You've just said that blessedness is very difficult to believe in, you've got to find it first and then you'll believe in it. Is that right?'

'Almost, but not quite, dear Ants.'

'But it's almost right anyway?'

'I dare say.'

'It's good enough for me, it's all I wanted to know. In other words, if someone believes that he is a human being, he must have been a human being before, if only for the briefest spell.'

'That, at least.'

'Now, can a dog or a horse believe that it's a human being?' Ants asked.

'There's no faith in animals, dear Ants.'

'Why not?'

'Faith only dwells in the living and immortal soul,' the pastor replied.

'Don't animals have an immmortal soul?'

'No, dear Ants.'

'Are you sure?'

'I am sure. We believe in redemption, in salvation.'

'But in that case Jürka is really Satan who has donned the guise of a human being in order to save his soul here on earth.'

'What do you mean?' the pastor, bewildered by Ants's giddy logic, asked in a shocked voice.

'But it's obvious!' Ants cried. 'If neither a dog nor a horse can believe that it is a human being, can a human being believe that he is Satan? But Jürka does believe in it, he believes in it so firmly, so obsessively that he really must be Satan.'

'No, my dear Ants. You are wrong.'

'You mean it's harder for a horse to believe itself a human being than for a human being to believe himself to be Satan?'

'Unquestionably.'

'But we've been rubbing shoulders with horses for such a long time, whereas...'

'It makes no difference, dear Ants.'

'...whereas few people have seen Satan.'

'That's the whole point: people believe in what they haven't seen, and they don't believe in what they do see,' the pastor said. 'Besides, you're forgetting that we have a far greater spiritual kinship with Satan than with animals, because Satan, like us, has an immmortal soul, the only difference being that his soul cannot be saved.'

'But what if he comes to believe in redemption like we do?'

'He doesn't believe in it,' the pastor said. 'Jürka says that redemption doesn't count any more.'

'I take it Jürka won't find salvation either?'

'Not unless he believes in redemption.'

'You mean there's no chance even if he really is Satan who's come down to earth for it?'

'No, not a chance.'

That was what Ants wanted to know. If there was no salvation for Jürka, people would go to heaven anyway because they believed in redemption, and even if Jürka were Satan ten times over Ants couldn't care less. Now that he was his tenant at the Pit, that was the main thing. Nor did he worry overmuch about redeeming his sins, which one was supposed to believe in if one didn't want to go to Jürka's hell. He wasn't too devout, of course, but he had the wits to give the matter serious thought shortly before the end. What counted was whether you believed or not just before you died.

And so it was with an easy mind that Ants left the pastor, and already on the way home he got busy devising ways and means of exploiting Jürka's extraordinary capacity for work to his very best advantage. Should he keep him wholly engaged at the Pit which was now his property, or should he use him for different jobs, sending him wherever he was most needed? He went to see Jürka, and in the course of conversation tried to find out how long he intended to stay on at the Pit.

'Until I find salvation,' Jürka told him.

'And supposing you never do?' Ants asked with his taunting chuckle.

'I will,' Jürka replied with unruffled confidence.

'And go back to hell? Right?'

'Of course.'

'Supposing it transpires, once you're in hell, that you didn't really find salvation, what then?'

'I'll return to earth.'

'Here, to the Pit?'

'No, not to the Pit if there's no salvation to be found here.'

'Where will you go?'

'Where Peter sends me. Maybe to the place owned by Cunning Ants.'

'But I'm there, you know,' Ants protested.

'You'll be dead by then.'

'How do you know?'

'Men die before Satan does.'

'Men may die, but they're immortal.'

'Sure they're immortal, otherwise they couldn't get into hell.'

'Look here,' Ants cried. 'Surely it wasn't to people hell that God created man?'

'Why else?'

'I don't know, but surely...'

'Try believing, then you'll know.'

'Only those who will save their souls will truly believe...'

'Believe, and you'll be saved,' Jürka said.

'And once I'm saved I'll go to hell, is that it?' Ants asked with rising irritation.

'It's all the same to the person being saved,' Jürka replied

133

placidly.

'How can going to heaven or hell be all the same?'

'It can, if you believe.'

'What's the sense of believing then?'

'No sense, because you'll go to hell just the same.'

'Why hell, I'd like to know?'

'Because I'm going to find my salvation.'

'And if you don't?'

'I will.'

The way Jürka harped on about his salvation was nightmarish enough, but what frightened Ants even more was that the more he talked with Jürka the more he caught himself thinking and feeling like Jürka. To break this spell, Ants tried to shake Jürka's faith, but to no avail. He had a store of arguments, yet lost every one. The question of redemption worried him most, and the thought preyed on his mind more and more insistently: did it count, or not? Who was right – the pastor or Jürka (that is, Satan, if Jürka was really Satan)? Which of the two had a better knowledge of the mysterious working of heaven?

In the meantime, everyday life ran its usual course. Ants's job was to scold, lecture, order and forbid, and Jürka's was to slave all day and well into the night. Ants always used the same argument, simply varying the approach, to goad Jürka to even greater effort.

'Do as you know best, but I'm thinking only of your own good,' Ants said. 'You keep saying that you long for salvation, and the pastor says that easiest way to earn it is by working hard. The other day, we wondered if your life couldn't be made a bit easier. The pastor thinks it can, but that might jeopardise your salvation, you see. And if you're absolutely set on it, then...'

'I am set on it,' Jürka confirmed quickly.

'Then there's nothing anyone can do. The pastor thinks you'll have to go on toiling as before, and toil will pull your stocky body into heaven even if the entrance is no bigger than the eye of a needle.'

'I'm going to hell.'

'It's all the same for the one who's saved,' Ants repeated what Jürka had told him once.

'It's all the same?' Jürka said, but after a moment's thought asked: 'You mean the harder the work the sooner I'll earn salvation?'

'The harder the work and the more of it,' Ants replied. 'Toil takes the place of redemption, since redemption doesn't count any more.'

And Jürka toiled. He dug ditches, uprooted tree stumps, levelled hummocks, carried and crushed stone, ploughed up virgin soil, handled the second crop alone, and did everything Ants told him. In Jürka's own household there were more sheep and pigs now, and more children were born to him and Juula. Some of them died from illness or accident, like that three-year-old little boy who was bitten by a snake. Maybe he could have been saved, if more attention were paid to him. Jürka was busy clearing the field and levelling hummocks, and he thought the kid was asleep in the grass. No one had really mourned him either: the parents had no time to weep, and while the dead boy's brothers and sisters had the time they had no idea how to mourn.

Jürka grieved over the living, older children more than he did over the dead little boy. Young Jürka, the twin who worked for Ants, did well enough at first. He was quick on the uptake and so Ants gave him a job at the store in the new house at the crossroads, and here everything went wrong for the lad as though a curse hung over that house. Ants's daughter Eleonoore came into the store during her school holidays, saw Jürka there and spoke to him. Young Ants, the firstborn of Ants, resented her chatting with Jürka so much that he let fly at him right there in the store.

'Leave my sister alone, or else...' he said and raised a stick.

'You better tell your sister to leave *me* alone,' young Jürka replied.

'Shut your mouth, you dirty devil,' young Ants shouted at Jürka, and stalked out.

Eleonoore came to the store again on the following day, and insisted that young Jürka and none other should serve her.

'You told my brother yesterday that I pestered you,' Eleonoore said to him.

'Miss Eleonoore's brother told me that I should not pester Miss Eleonoore,' Jürka replied.

'He said that?'

'Yes, he said: 'Leave my sister alone, or else...''

'Or else what?'

'I don't know. But the young master had a stick in his hand.'

'Was he going to hit you with it?'

'I'd like to see him try.'

'Are you threatening my brother?'

'No, but I'm not afraid of him.'

'He's very strong, you know. No one could beat him.'

'I can.'

'You don't know how really strong he is.'

'Never mind his strength, I have horns on my head.'

Eleonoore gave a loud peal of laughter. This was something she very seldom permitted herself even in the company of her equals, let alone with her father's employees.

'What's makong you laugh, Miss?' Jürka asked.

'You. You're so funny!' Eleonoore said, and laughed.

'I'm not funny at all.'

'Do you really have horns?'

'Really.'

Eleonoore looked at him gravely, and her clear eyes seemed to become clouded for a fraction of a second, but long enough for young Jürka to notice. She remembered there was something else she wanted to buy and while Jürka wrapped her purchase and tied it with string, feeling his fingers trembling involuntarily, she said to him in a low voice, keeping an expression of complete indifference on her face:

'Tonight, on the forest edge, beside the rye field.'

Holding her head high, she said goodbye to everyone there except Jürka, as if he did not exist all. The words she had whispered to him rang in his ears. The meaning did not penetrate at once, and then suddenly he understood.

That night Jürka went to the rye field. He had a long wait. Eleonoore did not come. It was young Ants, armed with a club, who kept the date instead of her.

'What are you doing here in the middle of the night?' he yelled at Jürka. 'No wonder you're half-asleep all day! Go home, you hear me?'

'I'm not going,' Jürka told him.

Young Ants swung his club, but Jürka was the quicker: he caught the young master by the arm, and wrenched the club out of his hand. Ants, who was taught boxing in town, went for Jürka with his fists, but before he knew it he was lying on his back, in the rye. He lept to his feet and went for Jürka again, but once more he landed on his back. Cursing savagely, he went home.

It was several days before Eleonoore appeared at the store again – this time she wanted a chocolate bar.

'Why didn't you come that time?' she asked young Jürka.

'I came.'

'Only to have a fight with my brother! For shame!'

'It was he who started the fight.'

'And the fight was more important than meeting me, I suppose.'

'But you didn't come.'

'I like that! Be there tonight.'

Young Jürka was in two minds about going, he wasn't sure if Eleonoore meant it or if she was playing him for a sucker. In the end he decided to go, throwing caution to the winds.

This time young Ants came with two accomplices, both hefty fellows. The moment Ants saw Jürka, he shouted: 'You here again? Get going, and make the going fast!'

Before Jürka could answer or make a move, the three of them attacked him. Jürka saw red: three against one! He struck back, and gave the three fellows such a beating that they couldn't run away quickly enough. To be sure, Jürka himself was black-and-blue all over.

Early next morning, young Jürka was ordered into the

137

presence of the master.

'Why did you beat up your young master, you dirty dog?' Ants demanded.

'It's he who beat me up.'

'Serves you right for trampling the rye at night. You've done bodily injury to your young master, and you'll have to answer for that.'

'But there were three of them, and they attacked me,' Jürka protested.

'No, it's you who attacked them, all three swear to it.'

'They're lying.'

'We'll soon find out who's lying. What were you doing at night in the rye field?'

'Young Miss told me to come.'

'What young miss?'

'Miss Eleonoore.'

'You foul-mouthed brat!' Ants screamed, and ordered his only daughter to be called for a confrontation with young Jürka.

Eleonoore tossed back her head haughtily, and said:

'You surprise me, Father! Calling me in to disprove such a silly lie! I haven't gone out of my senses, have I?'

'You heard her?' Ants asked when Eleonoore left the room, without vouchsafing Jürka a single glance.

'I heard her,' Jürka said.

'To think that my daughter would...'

'Miss Eleonoore wanted to see if I had horns growing on my head.'

'And for that she told you to come to the rye field, at night?'

'Sure, for what else?'

'For giving you a good hiding to teach you manners, that's more like it,' Ants said.

'Everything's all right then. The others got as much as I did.'

'I'll have you locked up for this, you may be sure.'

'If you try to lock me up I'll kill one of those three fellows who attacked me.'

'Are you threatening me?'

'I'm not threatening. I'm simply telling you what I'll do.'

'You're Satan, like your father.'

'Naturally, otherwise I wouldn't have these horns.'

Ants decided to drop the matter.

A few days passed, and Eleonoore came to the store again. She had a proud and haughty air, but tarried there longer than strictly necessary, and when no one was within earshot she asked Jürka:

'Did you tell Father that you're sprouting horns?'

'He wouldn't believe your reason for calling me to the rye field,' Jürka replied.

'And did he believe it when you told him?'

'Sure.'

'What did he say?'

'That Miss Eleonoore made a date with me in the rye field to have me beaten up.'

'Maybe Father was right, and then again perhaps he wasn't.'

'He was not.'

'Don't be so cocksure,' Eleonoore said.

'I know what I know.'

'And what do you know?'

'That Miss Eleonoore likes me a little.'

'The cheek! A little? And why?'

'Because I have horns.'

'Sheep do too.'

'That's different, they're sheep!'

'You're loathsome!'

These words, rising from the depths of her heart, sounded like the hissing of a snake.

Eleonoore left the store at once.

CHAPTER TWELVE

The plans which Ants had spoken of vaguely some years ago became clearer when Jürka, on his master's orders, finished uprooting trees and clearing large tracts of land at the Pit for ploughing and for haying. True, even now he did not disclose all his schemes, and spoke of them in a roundabout way. He began by saying that it wouldn't be a bad idea to build a new dwelling house at the Pit, seeing how times had changed. Next, he went into a lengthy discourse on where these new buildings should best be erected, considering that the old ones could not have been more wrongly situated. Oh, Ants had a hundred arguments to prove his point.

First: the house should be located at the hub of the farm's activities. That was how it was before, but when new fields and meadows were added to the property the centre naturally shifted nearer the forest. And that was the best site for the new construction, the more so in view of Ants's intention to enlarge his holdings by clearing more forest and shrubbery.

Second: it was a pity to build on good soil, which was where the old house stood now. Everything must be considered with a view to profit, and if a sound judgment was made at the right moment, two birds could be killed with one stone – new buildings erected and good soil released for grain production.

Third: the proximity of the forest suited Jürka's temperament. He liked the quiet, the singing of birds, the sounds of animals. There were those trees he had planted round the old house to show for it. But why plant trees when they grew all around in abundance? It was far simpler moving the house nearer the forest than moving the forest closer to home. It would be different if there were no forest anywhere. Ants had no doubt that this would be so before long, because people were much fonder of chocks, poles, logs, beams, laths, stakes, sleepers, switches, wattle fences and Christmas trees than they were of the forest. This was essentially because living forests were harder to do business in than dead timber. It went without saying that people loved the living forest too, appreciating the protection it offered from the sun and the wind, but there was no comparing it with the value of timber.

Therein lay the difference between forest and man. A living man brought in much more profit than a dead one, although business could also be made on the dead by helping them on their way to heaven with caskets, graveyard plots, wreaths, tombs, embalming, and touching obituaries. But the worth of the dead was piffling compared to that of the living man. To see it in its proper perspective, take war, for instance, that greatest enterprise of the modern age. Try harnessing a dead man into a chariot! It's as impossible as digging trenches with a living tree. And so we have a dead tree and a living man – herein lies harmony. But since there are still some isolated instances of living men loving living forest – like Jürka, the Old Nick from the Pit – they must be given a chance, before it is too late, to build their homes close to the forest and enjoy it.

Four: there was a fourth point, and a fifth, and a sixth, but there is no sense in repeating everything Ants said, because it all boiled down to one thing: the new buildings had to be set up on the edge of the forest.

And that is where they were set. Jürka was ordered to pull down the old structures, clear and level the ground on which they stood, and make it ready for ploughing. He was only to till this land for a couple of years, however, because Ants decided that the farm had grown too large for Jürka to cope with, and some change had to be made. Jürka tried to protest, saying that with his growing family there'd be an increase in manpower with every year, but Ants was not to be persuaded. The long and short of it was that Ants deprived Jürka of that part of the Pit where the old house once stood, which was all the more natural and understandable because he had been buying more plots of land over the years between his own farm and the Pit, until the two had merged into one.

'The Pit is not what is used to be,' Ants told Jürka. 'Besides, you have all these new buildings now. Actually I should redouble your rent and your other dues, but you couldn't afford it.'

'But you already raised the rent several times,' Jürka made a feeble protest.

'Quite naturally. Everything grows and so rents have to grow as well. Thank you lucky stars that it's me you have to deal with, you'd have it ten times worse if it were someone else. To make it easier on you I'll take over part of the Pit, and...'

'And knock off a bit of the rent and my debt?' Jürka asked hopefully.

'I would very gladly, but I simply can't. Just think what those new buildings cost me! Look how much you stand to gain, Jürka: by clearing the forest and the shrubbery you'll get more arable land than you can want. And it's good land, I give you my word.'

And so Jürka got down to clearing the forest, and the land turned out to be so good that before long Ants raised the rent again. When Jürka grumbled, Ants feigned astonishment and cried:

'You sure are a strange one! Everyone the world over is glad that life is on the up, but you're forever grumbling and complaining! Remember this well: if the whole world prospers, our nation will prosper too, and the Pit with it, and working against the tide all by yourself you cannot prevent it. Or, perhaps, in your opinion we're so wretched that we can't keep in step? Where's your national pride then, and your precious salvation?'

'Will the proud be saved?' Jürka asked, submitting that Ants had every right to talk about prosperity.

'Not the proud, but the meek and the dedicated who are fighting for the glory and prosperity of their nation.'

Jürka would have liked to give Ants a fitting rejoinder, but he was at a loss for words and let it pass.

When he told Juula about the new rent increase, she looked at him gravely and said:

'It's as though the forces of Heaven were driving him on, the way he keeps raising the rent on the Pit.'

'He says if he doesn't our nation won't be great and proud,'

Jürka told her.

'And for that the rent has to be raised? The nation can't do without the Pit, is that it?'

'I guess so.'

'It must be some new trick. We know that great-and-proud-nation stuff alright. You can't put it in a pot and cook it, nor can you put it on your back and wear it. One thing is true: the higher the rent for the Pit, the prouder and haughtier are Ants and his brood. I bet they're the great and proud nation for whose sake our rent is raised all the time.'

'You're talking nonsense now.'

'But it's you who came and told me that the rent had been raised again!'

'Ants says that everything in the world is going up, and that we're no worse than others,' Jürka said.

'It's always Ants this and Ants that with you! Will you get your salvation through him too?'

'Sure. Who else?'

'Your salvation's in your toil and your cares.'

'And who gives us this toil and these cares?'

'Ants, of course, who else! The way you talk, we're sure to save our souls with his help.'

'That's what I say, too. So don't you curse Ants any more, he is a wonderful friend to have.'

He was, indeed. What with the new machinery and enterprises he was always acquiring, he'd always have jobs enough for Jürka's entire family, even if Juula had twins or triplets every year. True, he did dismiss young Jürka who, after doing time for beating up young Ants, was obviously not fit to serve the customers (Ants was very particular about morals and respectability). Actually, the pugnacious brat should have been thrown out altogether, but Ants kept him on for his old man's sake.

'I do not want to put a smear on your good name,' Ants explained to the Satan of the Pit. 'Besides, it might prevent your salvation. The young people today have gotten quite out of hand, and I sometimes wonder – Where are we heading, our nation and the whole world, for that matter? We are busy erecting new monuments just now, but who shall we erect them to in the future with our present young generation so badly spoilt? What will become of our nation and our art if there's no one left deserving of a monument? How will we bring the young generation back to the fold, and who will set the example for them?'

'We are the example ourselves,' Jürka said.

'Only the dead make a good example, it never works with the living. The young generation should learn to be hard-working, sober, abstinent, simple and honest, and living people are prone to rakery, trickery, larceny, lying and cheating. If a man doesn't do any of this he thinks he is not a living person, but more like an animal, a plant, or a stone.'

'I guess so,' Jürka uttered quite as though he had grasped Ants's thoughts, and added after a pause, 'This earthly life, if it's really like you say it is, seems to be chockful of trouble.'

'What did you think?' said Ants with conviction. 'You're living in clover at the Pit, compared to life elsewhere – You're not bothered with any monuments or anything, you just live as you please. If you imagine that life is softer and easier anywhere else, forget it. How could it be if it's worse all over the world?'

'That's what I keep telling my missus. But Juula thinks that you're after salvation yourself, and that's why you raise the rent every couple of years.'

'No, Jürka, she has it all wrong,' Ants replied. 'Raising the rent won't open the gates of heaven for me. It's more likely to land me in hell.'

'How come?'

'Raising the rent too high is a sin, and sins take people to hell. And so, every time I raise the rent I have to think hard first: am I acting fairly, or am I committing a sin which will land me in hell. I won't raise the rent if I have the slightest doubt. I'm not that big a fool to risk going to hell for it. So don't worry your head about it. Before I made this raise I gave it plenty of thought, so there's nothing you or anybody else have to talk about.'

'That's how it goes then,' Jürka voiced his thoughts aloud. 'Charging too high a rent is a sin, and for his sins a man goes to hell.'

'That's right, hell it is,' Ants said. 'Only don't take advantage of this.'

'I don't get you,' Jürka said.

'It's very simple: supposing you start paying me more than I charge you, or more than is fair, and foolishly I'll take the money, thus committing a sin and going to hell.'

'To my place, you mean.'

'If you're already there. If not, I'll have to wait for you to come.'

Ants's talk on rent, sin and hell took some puzzling out. How could anyone be expected to understand all these tangled earthly considerations? Even raising the rent could not be done simply, but had to be tangled up with sin and hell. Obviously Ants wouldn't let himself be lured to hell with a rent raise, he was too cunning for that, Jürka well knew. But then Jürka wasn't born yesterday either, he'd seen enough and learnt something. He'd find some other way to hoodwink Ants. And, true enough, Jürka's chance came sooner than he could hope. After two years of bother with the meadows and fields Ants had dispossessed Jürka of, he decided to give up the effort and offered these meadows and fields to Jürka for a third or two-thirds of the yield, depending on the fertility of the given plot. And this was Jürka's chance to get the better of Ants. For Ants's share of the crop he selected the largest grains, keeping the lighter and smaller ones for himself, and when making hay for Ants he cut the best grass there was.

'Nothing's too good for Ants, eh?' Juula said, watching her husband's effort to please.

'I'm paving his way to hell,' Jürka replied with a sly smile.

'That's all you have on the brain – hell and heaven.'

'But that's what I'm here on earth for.'

'You'd better worry about your own hell, Ants will take care of his himself.'

Oh no! It was up to Jürka make sure that Ants went to hell. And so he exerted himself to inveigle Ants in sin: each bundle of firewood was thicker than necessary, when he cut stakes for Ants he delivered more than was bargained for, and he tilled larger plots of virgin land than Ants expected.

The days and years rolled on like water into the sea. And then came tragedy, stirring up the placid flow of life. Young Jürka got his hand caught in the machine he was operating at the factory, and it was torn off at the wrist. The doctor at the hospital dressed and bandaged the stump for him, and a few days later Eleonoore came to see the patient. Visitors were not allowed, as a rule, because Jürka was restless, turning quite violent at times, although he was not running a very high temperature. An exception was made for Miss Eleonoore in the hope that her coming would calm him.

'Still spoiling for a fight?' Eleonoore said to young Jürka.

'I'm not, it's people who want to pick a fight with me.'

'Why do you try to get up then?'

'What's the use of just lying here?'

'But you're ill, you know.'

'I'm not ill, it's just that my right hand has been ripped away.'

'Isn't that bad enough?'

'It isn't. Let them rip away my other hand too, and chop my head off for good measure. If they refuse, I'll do it myself.'

'You can't blame anyone, it's the machine that ripped your hand away.'

'Very well, let the machine take my other hand together with my head.'

'One hand is better than none.'

'And no head is better still.'

'Aren't you sorry to lose a head like yours, it's sprouting horns, I believe, isn't that so?'

Jürka made no answer, taking her words as a nasty gibe to which a cripple could only respond with silence. His taciturnity was misinterpreted by Eleonoore and everyone else there to mean that the patient had calmed down. On order to mollify him even more, Eleonoore promised to come and see him on the morrow. That night, when everyone had gone to sleep, Jürka hanged himself on a hook in the wall of his room. There were whispered rumours that when he was discovered in the morning the rope was hanging slackly, and everyone marvelled how anyone could have killed himself like that. There was something fishy here. The devil himself or his henchmen must have had a hand in this. As sure as eggs is eggs. And proof was not long in forthcoming. The nurse fainted straight away when she found Jürka in the morning, and on coming to she heard something flapping its wings over the hanging boy, just like a rooster before he starts crowing. What else could it be if not Satan himself? Satan, as everyone knew, usually came for the soul of a suicide in the guise of a rooster who flapped its wings in glee before taking off for the nether world.

'Good God, how could that be?' Juula gasped, on hearing the talk. 'We slept under the same quilt all night, and anyway would a father go hunting after the soul of his own child?'

Still, doubt gnawed at her heart, and once, in conversation with her husband, she mentioned in passing the story people spread about a rooster flapping its wings over young Jürka, hanging with a rope round his neck. She wondered who did the flapping – her old man, or some other Satan? Jürka heard her out attentively.

'I'm not the Satan I was before, so how could I flap a rooster's wings?' he asked.

'Who was it then?' asked Juula.

'How do I know?'

'Who knows, if you don't?'

'No idea.'

'But you are Satan, aren't you?'

'Sure.'

'Then it was you, there's no other,' Juula said.

'But I'm a human being now, how could I have a rooster's wings?'

'That, I don't know.'

'Neither do I.'

The death of their son grieved both Juula and Jürka. He was a smart boy, quick and sharp, not at all like his twin brother who had been kept at home – a slowpoke who pottered with something all day. Young Jürka would have made good. Troubles never come singly, and Ants's annoyance was yet another one.

'You and your son are a smear on my good name,' he said to Jürka. 'Listen to what people are saying! They say that Satan appeared on my property and flapped his wings like a rooster! And everybody blames the machine. And what I say is it's his own fault

– he should have used his common sense, the machine doesn't have any.'

'I guess not,' Jürka mumbled, as though in acquiescence.

'He shouldn't have come so close to the machine, he shouldn't have poked his fingers into it, he shouldn't have...'

'Sure, he shouldn't have,' Jürka repeated.

'In all justice you should pay me damages seeing that it was your son who messed up my machine because of his carelessness. But what could you pay me? No one wants to come near the machine now, saying that it tears off people's hands and legs. Some even think it would chop a person's head off if it got a chance. What have legs and heads got to do with it, I ask them. One single hand was all it ripped away, and that only because the gawk was careless and didn't watch his step. But there's no reasoning with them, it'll tear their legs and heads off, first chance it gets! What am I supposed to do with everyone refusing to operate that machine? Perhaps I should operate it myself, eh? I have enough work to do as it is. I can't put my son on the job, because he's badly needed in town. The Minister himself said that if young Ants, that is my son, left town to live here, everything would come to a standstill because there's no one to replace him. Which means that he's indispensable. That's what the Minister's wife told her friends at the café, repeating what her husband said. The Minister himself hasn't the time to go about repeating what he said to people. And so it occurred to me that inasmuch as all this upset was caused by your son's carelessness, how about putting your other son on the job? Only you'll have to hammer it into his head in a fatherly way that he must be more careful than that other one, young Jürka, was. Well, what do you say, what about your other son?'

'He's a dawdler, you know, he'll mess up your machine again.'

'The boy I had in mind wasn't the twin brother, it was the younger boy I meant, Kusta – is that his name?'

'But he's only a stripling.'

'Never mind. The earlier he starts working the sooner he'll learn the job. Operating a machine does not take strength. These aren't the old days when a man bust his guts working, machines do all the work nowadays, it doesn't take effort – just diligence. And younger boys are more diligent than older ones. Had your Jürka been a few years younger he wouldn't have stuck his head into a noose for no better reason than merely losing one hand, and doing it on the sly too, in the dead of night, like a sneak thief...'

This lengthy conversation with Ants ended in Jürka promising to let him have Kusta. True, the boy was under age and was useful at home, but there it was: Ants was in trouble and had to be helped. Jürka was not forgetting the times Ants came to his rescue. Before seeing the boy off to work, Juula and Jürka told him again and again to be careful with the machine, or else there'd be no end of trouble from Ants again. But what he must never do, no matter what, was stick his head into a noose like his brother had done, because a man could live with one hand or one leg, the thing was to get used to it. Look at the cripples that come back from war – no arms or legs at all – and yet they got along somehow, and lived. Was that reason enough not to fight a war? Apart from everything else, Jürka, being the firstborn, was unduly obstinate; but Kusta was not the firstborn and so he needn't follow in his brother's footsteps.

'You're wasting your breath,' Kusta said to his anxious parents. 'I won't be the first machine operator there. Machines don't attack people so long as you keep a safe distance.'

'That's what Ants says too,' Jürka said.

Kusta left the house to take his dead brother's place at the machine, and everyone thought he seemed pleasantly upbeat at the prospect. His leaving, rather than frighten the remaining children, made them eager to follow his example. Maia, the eldest girl, was dying to leave the nest more than the others.

'Girls are supposed to stay at home,' Juula preached. 'A daughter only leaves home with her husband.'

'And if I've no husband?' the girl parried.

'If you're a good girl, there'll be one.'

'I'm not a child any more, I've been to Confirmation.'

'What has that got to do with it, when you're not yet twenty?'

CHAPTER THIRTEEN

Maia was set on leaving home, and nothing her mother said could dissuade her. She nagged and nagged about it all the time.

'Has someone put the evil eye on you, or bewitched you?' her mother asked.

'I don't know. Maybe,' the girl replied.

'Listen to me, wench, who have you been talking to, who have you been seeing?' the mother demanded with a sinking heart.

'No one,' replied her daughter. 'You don't really need me in the house, and besides Juula's grown up too, time she went to Confirmation.'

'That's silly talk. You are needed, and Juula is needed, and all the others, too.'

'And young Ants said that...'

'Heavens, where did you see him?' the mother asked in alarm.

'It's he who saw me.'

'Where, I'd like to know?'

'In the potato field.'

'And what business had he there?'

'He told me he was looking for a hare that was hiding in a furrow.'

'Out hunting, was he?'

'Why, of course! He had a gun and everything.'

'And what were you doing there?'

'Digging up potatoes for soup. You sent me yourself and told me to dig on the forest edge, and so I...'

'Did he come up to you?'

'He come up, stopped, and started talking so nicely, saying such funny things... He did not put on airs at all, for all that he is

150

the young master and everything.'

'I see now why you can't wait to go and work for Ants. What a silly fool you are, child! Just because a young fellow talked to you nicely and joked, you're ready to run away from home.'

'That's not why, Mother.'

'Did he put these ideas into your head?'

'No. He only said that the girls at their place were dressed quite differently. They wore high-heeled shoes, and tripped lightly, tap-tap, he said. And I go barefoot, my feet are all black and grimy, like clods of earth.'

Maia's words touched her mother to the quick. She remembered her own girlhood on Ants's farm, her own feet also like huge clots of earth as she plied between the barn and the cattle yard, envying the housemaids who flitted about the rooms wearing a white apron and pretty shoes. Lord, how she longed to be one of them! Alas, she was too dull-witted, clumsy and slow for that, and hard, menial labour was all she was fit for. Maia was different, she didn't take after either her mother or her father. Maybe she'd be taken on as parlour-maid in Ants's house, and would trip about the rooms like those girls Juula had envied so in her youth? Would Juula's old dream come true for Maia?

These reflections made Juula take a kinder view of her daughter's ambitions. Really, why should she forbid her child to do what she herself had once dreamed of so passionately? If anything, she should help the girl to make her mother's dream come true. And so, fortune smiled upon Maia – if her mother did not mind her leaving home, her father would not object either. All Maia had to wait for now was the right moment which, luckily, was not long in coming.

In the autumn, when harvesting was almost done, Ants came to the house to say that he needed a housemaid, and that Maia seemed to be made for the job.

'You have to be diligent and quick, and not talk back, that's all,' Ants told Maia.

'She wouldn't talk back, heaven forbid!' said Juula.

'There's one other condition, because of which I had to dismiss some of my domestics,' Ants began loftily. 'Good behaviour comes first with me. And look at our modern young girls: before they've been in service a day they start putting on airs and playing the fine ladies. And it always comes to the same thing: a good girl grows morally slack and has to be dismissed, because, as my wife always says and I quite agree with her, my home and I myself must serve Jehovah. If anyone wants to earn their daily bread in my house, they have to have good manners and an impeccable moral character. We are very pleased with Kusta, and so it occurred to me that if his sister is like him she would shape up well. And what is more, Jürka and I are people of the old school, we bring our children up in obedience and piety. And what is even more, we teach our children to work, and love their work. Such is the basis of our upbringing. The man who walks behind the plough is always on the right path. Well then, how about Maia?'

'If you need her, why not? We've got to help each other out,' Jürka uttered, impressed by Ants's wise speech.

'She's a hard-working girl, have no fear,' Juula put in. 'She'll try hard without your prompting or urgings, she's been like that from birth.'

'I guess she has,' Jürka confirmed his wife's words.

'I noticed it too, and that's why I came here first,' Ants said. 'Hard-working girls have the best chance of employment, hard-working girls whose conduct is good and who want to save their soul.'

It might have been not Ants who said this but Juula and Jürka who strove for salvation more than anything else in life, as the parish clerk and the parson also noted.

'Good conduct – that's our daughter,' Juula said boastfully. 'Her one fault is that she's terribly fond of washing and prettying herself up. What the soap alone costs! But her neatness will go well with your home, it's not like our Pit here, folks live quite differently there.'

'I dare say,' Ants agreed with a smug chuckle.

'Why, even your cows look cleaner than my kids,' Juula said.

'That's the breed they are – Dutch and Finnish,' Ants explained.

'They low differently too,' Juula said.

'I guess they do,' Jürka grunted, simply to contribute something to the conversation.

And so, the matter was settled, and Maia was engaged to work in Ants's house. No one knew at first what she'd have to do there, but since Ants was hiring the girl he'd surely find work enough for her. Juula couldn't help daydreaming about her: wouldn't it be wonderful if Maia married someone there, a factory hand or someone! All kinds of men worked for Ants or came to his place.

When Maia was ready to set off, her mother had a word with her.

'Take care of yourself, daughter, don't let anything happen to you...'

'You're so funny, Mother,' interposed Maia. 'What could happen to me? I wasn't born yesterday, you know.'

'That's just what worries me, because at home you were always wanting to sleep together with the boys, and so...'

'And did anything happen? Nothing did. And what's so special about Ants?'

'There is something, daughter dear. When Ants was younger he never let even the cattleyard girls alone, to say nothing of the housemaids.'

'He's too old for that now.'

'But his son's young enough. He takes after his father, people say, ravishes the wenches, he does. If you don't take good care of yourself, he'll ravish you too.'

'What, that sprig?' Maia gave a hearty laugh. 'A man, is he? Why, I'll beat him up with one hand.'

'If you feel like it, of course.'

'Why won't I feel like it?'

'It's all right then. What I'm saying this for is so you'd know what's what. I grew up there, you know, and saw everything with my own eyes. It's no better now, it's always the same routine: the men stuff themselves with rich food, and don't know what they want and what they're doing. That's how it is in that place. If the fodder's good and there's nothing to do even the bull will start roaring, and the stallion will neigh...'

'The way you talk, Mother, we might be animals.'

'I don't know what we are, I'm just telling you what I saw with my own eyes and heard with my own ears.'

'Times have changed,' Maia said in an attempt to refute her mother's arguments.

'Times have, but men have not,' Juula replied.

And on this Maia left.

'Did she say when she'd be coming to see us?' Jürka asked his wife when Maia was gone.

'She didn't say. I didn't ask her – what was the point? If she's miserable she'll come soon, if she's happy she won't come for all your inviting. That's the way it goes with people. It's only cows who come home, no matter how good it was somewhere else.'

However, Maia did come home very soon, driven not by misery but by a desire to tell the family how happy she was in Ants's home, where the work she did was so easy and clean. She gushed about the marvellous food, the lovely, soft bed she slept in, the splendour of the rooms in which she moved, and the ladylike conversations she had with people!

Evidently she wasn't making up these stories, and her happiness was sincere. She had new clothes on to show for it, they were smarter and lighter than the things she left home in.

'You'll get spoilt there, and no good will come of you,' Juula said, giving her daughter a sharp look.

'They'll make a fine lady out of this wench,' Jürka added.

The next time Maia came home, her mood wasn't quite as joyous as before, and nothing seemed to please her, as though she had a grudge against the Pit itself. When her mother took down a cracked bowl to serve the potatoes in, Maia suddenly snatched it from Juula's hands and flung it into a corner. The bowl was smashed to pieces.

'That's what we do with cracked crockery,' Maia said.

'Oh, for shame,' her mother exclaimed, close to tears, as she picked up the pieces. 'What's come over you – smashing things?'

'It was broken anyway.'

'That's not true, because didn't we eat porridge and potatoes from it? True, it couldn't be used for milk or soup.'

'You live here as in the days of Noah. When I left home this cracked bowl was standing on the table, and here I'm back after all that time and the same bowl is still there! I couldn't stand the sight of that broken old bowl any longer.'

'Why didn't you say so, I would have set out another one, I have a bowl that hasn't a scratch on it. This bowl here, the cat knocked off the bench the day I got it from the ragman. It cracked, but it served us till now, crack and all, and would have gone on being useful if you hadn't gone and smashed it. That time I scolded the cat for stupidly knocking over the bowl, and now it turns out that our own child is stupid – smashing bowls with her own hands. That time, the cat had kittens when she knocked over the newest bowl we had, and what's eating you, Maia, what made you let fly like that?'

'What might be eating me, d'you think?'

'How should I know. But if you're such a great lady now that you think you can come home and smash things, then better don't come.'

'But I want to come,' Maia said.

'Why throw things if you're homesick?'

'I can't help it, I hate that cracked bowl.'

'Then don't come here, we've lots of chipped and cracked things.'

Maia stayed away. She left that day, and never came home again in her life. Jürka had to go and bring her himself, because Juula wanted her eldest daughter to start on her last journey from her father's home, over her own threshold, through the gates where she ran about and played as a child. So Maia had to come from the church first, and only then back to the cemetery again. There were just the two of them – Maia and her father. She lay stretched out in the cart, and he strode beside the cart, muttering his thoughts aloud.

'That's human life for you! I had a cart with wooden wheels before, and now I've iron wheels, but I wouldn't think twice about exchanging them for my old wooden ones only so my daughter would be sitting up in the cart.'

This was, in fact, the only lucid thought he had as he strode

155

home beside the cart, wiping his tears when they flowed over. Juula was waiting for them at home. She wanted to know all the particulars, she had to know what had really been the matter with Maia, her eldest daughter. But all she could gather from what Jürka said was that nothing seemed to be the matter – Maia had bled to death, that's all, she crawled into the straw in the hayloft, and never got up again.

'Why should her blood flow so that there's no stemming it?' Juula asked.

'You know why – she was a wench, you know...'

'Good Lord!' Juula screamed. 'Who was the man?'

'Try asking her. It's all over now, she won't answer.'

'Don't the others know?'

'Think they'd tell us even if they were in the know?'

'Of course not, it's always like that with Ants: no one knows a thing, it's as though everyone's mouth has been stopped. And if that's how it is, it must have been Ants himself, or young Ants. If it were someone else they wouldn't keep mum.'

'If I could find out who it was, I'd twist the gander's neck into a knot,' Jürka said.

'You're crazy, throw the thought out of your head! Think what would become of us,' Juula begged him in fright.

'I'll twist it so his eyes face backwards,' Jürka growled.

'What happened anyway? Did she want to get rid of the baby, or what?'

'I guess so.'

'She didn't do it herself, did she?'

'That's what they say.'

'A likely story! I'll bet Kupu-Kai had a hand in it.'

'Oh, well, if it was Kai – this is the end of her,' Jürka said.

'Silly daughter, she could have brought the baby to us, I'd have reared it, on sow's if not its mother's milk,' Juula said.

'I guess you would.'

'Everything's different nowadays, it's not like in the old days.'

'I guess not.'

Juula went to see Ants, but came back none the wiser. Even Kusta refused to talk, as though someone had a strangle-hold on his throat. All he kept saying was that Maia was secretive and didn't confide in anyone, so no one had any idea where she went and what she did. He didn't even come to his sister's funeral – he was that busy doing an urgent job of work.

There was more trouble over the funeral. At first the pastor would not have Maia buried in consecrated ground.

'Why?' Jürka cried, startled to hear it.

'Because, my beloved son, she may have taken her own life,' the pastor explained.

'Not her, she didn't.'

'How can one know? In any case, the name of her accomplice has not been ascertained. Someone may have told her in secret what to do, but whether anyone actually helped her is something we cannot know.'

'But she didn't hang herself...'

'There are different ways of taking one's own life, but in the sight of God it's all the same, the main thing is that...'

'It wasn't herself she tried to kill, you know!'

'So much the worse. She killed in her body that which the Lord had granted her as a blessing. That is a heinous crime in the sight of men, and in the sight of God.'

'In other words...' Jürka faltered.

'In other words, we have before us a most difficult case.'

Jürka sat down on a chair and stared stonily at the floor. The pastor watched him from across the table. He had not forgotten the fright this peasant gave him the first time he came years ago, calling himself Satan who had come down to earth to save his soul. 'The blessedness of madness,' the pastor said to himself. The peasant who sat before him now was crushed by grief. Did he still think he was Satan? The pastor did not venture to ask him, stifling his curiousity as the moment was far too grave.

'Why don't you want to have your daughter buried outside the graveyard wall?' he asked. 'She'd be next to her brother there.'

'I don't want it.'

'But why not, beloved brother?'

'From there she'll go to hell.'

'How can you know? Or can it be that you'll be there

157

yourself?'

    'Sure. Where else?'

    'Why will you?'

    'I'm Satan, aren't I.'

    'My beloved borther, do you still believe in this?'

    'Sure.'

    'If your children come there to you, it will be wonderful, won't it?'

    'No. I want Maia to go to heaven.'

    'How can she, being your daughter, and you being Satan?'

    'On earth, I'm a human being, and Maia is a human child, and when a human earns salvation he goes to heaven. Oh, good, kind Reverend, help Maia to go to heaven, she's a human being!'

    Jürka raised his head, and looked at the pastor. Tears welled from his eyes, and trickled down his cheeks into his matted beard.

    The pastor had seen so many rivers of tears in his lifetime that he was no longer moved by them. Over the years he had arrived at the conclusion that life needed watering, much like the soil needed rain for seeds to sprout. It was not tears that touched him, but the happy smiles that sometimes lit up the faces of young mothers or brides. He often wept in response to these smiles, but no one knew what he was feeling in his heart of hearts. People said that he had some secret grief to nurse, and therefore could not bear to see the happiness and joy of others. The truth was that the pastor simply knew how quickly joy turned into grief and happiness into misfortune, and the knowledge made him display such inappropriate distress.

    But what came over the pastor now was indeed amazing: his own eyes brimmed over when he saw Jürka's tears! The thought flashed through his mind that the man sitting before him was not a human being but Satan, as Jürka himself had believed for decades. Supposing his faith was so strong that it would continue unshaken for thousands and millions of years, for now and forevermore, while there was life on earth? What then? Could a faith so strong perform miracles? Was it capable of transforming this ordinary peasant into the real Satan? And if it was, and sitting before him was the real Satan in the shape of a peasant with a shaggy mane of hair and a matted beard, begging the pastor to help Maia, Satan's daughter, to go to heaven, what then? What must a pastor do if he believed in salvation, in life eternal, and preached it to his flock?

'Do you truly believe that I can help your daughter go to heaven?' the pastor asked at last.

'I do,' Jürka replied fervently.

'Is your faith firm, beloved brother?' the pastor adjured Jürka, for he was beginning to doubt his own power.

Over the years the pastor had granted people absolution times without number, opening the gates of heaven before them, so to speak, but he did it as an official, empowered by his superiors. This was the first time he felt that he was acting on his own behalf, as a man who had his own private conscience and an ability to make his own decisions. He needed such unassailable faith, and he sought support in a man who believed he was Satan.

'My faith is firm,' Jürka replied so simply, that if the pastor still had some lingering doubts they were dissolved.

'You may bury your daughter in the churchyard, may the Lord have mercy on her soul.'

'I guess He will,' Jürka said.

CHAPTER FOURTEEN

A little later, when time had begun to heal the pain caused by
Maia's death, Kusta came home and told his mother that the
man responsible for his sister's tragedy was young Ants. As
soon as Maia knew that she was in trouble, Ants told her to get
rid of the baby or else she'd be kicked out of their house. Maia
asked where she could go in her condition. Go back where you
came from, Ants told her. 'But you promised to marry me,'
Maia said, and Ants replied: 'The way you are now I wouldn't
marry you for the world. If you get rid of the child it'll be
another matter.' And so Maia agreed to do it.

'Surely she didn't do it herself?' Juula asked.

'I should say not! Ants had it all fixed for her, but when
things went wrong, they spread the rumour that Maia had done
it herself. It couldn't be simpler – the girl did the thing alone, in
the dead of night, where and how no one knew, and by morning
she was cold. Young Ants left for town the day before as if he
had nothing to do with it. So it must have been agreed between
them, and he'd probably told Maia that she wouldn't see him
until she was through with that business.'

'She called young Ants a sprig, you know. That's what she
told me just before she left home. And now, you see, she died
for that sprig,' Juula said.

'And to me Maia was always talking about his gold watch
and the charms jingling on the chain, that's what got her,' Kusta
said.

'She must have been joking,' Juula said in Maia's defence.

'Maybe she was, but anyway that's what she said.'

'Not a word of this must come to your father, God forbid. He

160

swore he'd wring young Ants's neck if it was his fault.'

'He won't,' Kusta said. 'You can talk freely, he might as well know it too. Young Ants, you know, is abroad. He hopped across as soon as he heard about Maia. He wants to sit it out there, and see how the case goes: will it be hushed up or will it stink to high heaven.'

'But he'll have to come home one day anyway.'

'Everything will be forgotten by then.'

'It better be, because Maia can't be resurrected, can she?'

'No, Mother, I'm not going to forget, and I want you to know it. I'll get him by the short hairs no matter how much time will have passed. It's all to the good if he stays away for several years, it'll give me time to grow bigger and stronger. Listen, Ma, it's only you I'm telling this to, so you'd know how I loved Maia. I won't let her death go unavenged, not for anything in the world. And so, if you ever hear that something's happened to young Ants, you'll know it was my doing. They may be smart and cunning, covering up their dirty doings so cleverly, but I, too, will know how to go about it the right way, and so if you die before then, you can die in the certainty that I'll do what I promised.'

'Son, my darling boy, how will you save your soul if you're scheming such horrors?' Juula asked.

'Let God decide whether to let me into heaven, or send me to hell. Why must I worry about salvation, if others don't give a hoot for it?'

'Others may, but what are they to you? They have protectors in all the high places, and you have none. Ants can twist anyone round his finger, and what can you do?'

'Don't worry, Mother. If Ants and I go to hell together – and he'll be despatched there top speed, you may be sure – of the two of us I'm certain to be made a stoker, because loafers like Ants would never be given a job like that. Ants will sit in the pot, and I'll get the fire going under the pot.'

'Son, what's happened to you?' Juula wailed. 'Who put this evil into you, it couldn't be the machines, could it?'

'No one's put any evil into me, Mother, at Ants's place we

161

are all like that. We have no fear of God or of the Devil, our only worry is not to get our hand caught in the machine. The machine is both our God and our Devil.'

'I guess the end of the world is near,' Juula sighed. 'Who'd ever believe that this was my own child talking!'

All at once, she felt old and tired – her children had aged and tired her. Maybe it was time for her to fold her hands on her breast and rest. But her baby daughter, the family's pet, was too young to be left, and so she couldn't lay down her load yet.

Juula, too, grew up and worked on Ants's farm, but unlike her children she never lost faith. Was it because she tended dumb animals, and not people and machines? It probably was. In those days, whenever she felt restless and sick at heart as though she were losing faith, she went into the cowshed and watched the animals that seemed to be so strong in spirit, so full of faith and hope. They fed, slept, did their other business, calved, and butted one another in the belly. The sight was so soothing, that were Juula to understand it properly she would have said that faith and hope were to be sought in animals and not in people. Young people, the present generation, would hardly go to the cowshed for it, they huddled together like a flock of sheep, and fussed over their machines all day.

This thought of Juula's was confirmed by what Ants said in conversation with Jürka upon his return from town. Old Ants left home together with his son the day before Maia met her untimely end.

'I'd have managed my affairs differently were I to know that a misfortune like that was going to happen at home. I couldn't know, of course, and since I had to go, I went. A dog show had just been opened in town, to show off the breeds and the families who owned them, you know. Well, my son also wanted to exhibit his hounds – let the townsfolk see what kind of people we were, and the kind of life we led here. You know how it is, it's difficult to see through a man and know what he's like, you've first got to find out what he owns. That's why the wise and the educated thought of arranging these shows. When you see what's shown, you understand the person who's showing it.

And every reasonable person craves understanding – you do, and I do. And so we took our dogs there, so that people might form an opinion about us. Dear Jürka, you simply couldn't imagine the noise at that show, where all hell seemed to break loose. We've lived to a ripe old age never knowing what it was like when hundreds of dogs were gathered together! Thank God, I'm much wiser now than I was before. And if there's ever another show as instructive as that one was, I promise to take you along, so you might also see and hear...'

'What for?' Jürka muttered.

'Well, to learn the dogs' family names.'

'I don't even know people's names.'

'You don't need to, if you know their dogs you'll know the owners.'

'What's there to know – dogs have four legs, and people have two.'

'Ah no! Two legs is what they have.'

'How come?'

'You'd know if you went to a dog show. There was a posh lady sitting there with two or three silver foxes on her shoulders, and next to her – a little black dog with fluffy fur that sat up on its hind legs, a perfect mannequin! Even its face was like a human's, except that it wore no make up or false eyelashes, but otherwise it was the spit and image of its owner, you might hang those silver foxes on it by mistake.'

'How did a dog become so learned?' Jürka asked.

'The lady trained it herself, I heard her telling another lady. And was that little dog clever! When the lady had those silver foxes on, the dog sat up, when she took them off – down it went on all fours! I couldn't understand what the trick was though I tried hard to puzzle it out, and finally I went up to the lady and said: 'Madam,' I said. 'Forgive my asking, but seeing that your dog sits up before three silver foxes I suppose that if there were four or five it would stand up on one leg?' The lady didn't like it, she thought I was needling her. 'Heaven forbid,' I said. 'I wanted to learn some tricks from your learned dog.''

'Why does she want to teach tricks to a dog, has that lady no children?'

'Oh, Jürka, of course not! I was told that nowadays it's dogs and not children who are taught manners. As it is, we're the foremost nation in the world, so we don't need schools or any stuff like that any more! And that posh lady, I was told, was a most obliging midwife. She used to help women before – one way or another, as they wanted it – and now she helps bitches to whelp for the simple reason that women have stopped this child-bearing business, and even if they do conceive they won't have the child anyway. So, there's no more work for a midwife, because if something happens it's the doctors who take charge. And occasionally something happens the way it did with your Maia. In a case like that no one knows who did what, where, how and when.'

'I guess so,' Jürka uttered.

'You see what it ended in – death, just that. It's a pity because I think the story might have had a different ending. But no, life was too good for the wench here, she didn't want to lose her soft job. Afterwards I often felt sorry that I was such a stickler for moral conduct, but I had to be! Think what would happen if all the servant girls began to fornicate in my large house where I have so many men coming to see me. I could never permit it, if I wanted to save my soul. And the pastor has warned me time and again that I must not allow any looseness in my house. And so I had no choice but to tell the girl to take care, or else... Evidently, she took it so close to heart that she... I don't have to tell you what happened, you were here at the time, and I was in town, looking at that two-legged bitch.'

'I was here, true enough.'

'So you were! And so... Do our children give us, their old parents, a thought? What do they care? Even death doesn't scare them because they won't have to suffer after it. It's those who remain that suffer, we their old parents, and the dead – they couldn't care less. I thought I had to be on the lookout, watching them day and night, for we have to stand answer for what the young people do. But you can't be vigilant enough. And that dog show coinciding so unfortunately too! As a matter of fact, I did have something like a premonition, I felt sick at heart and wondered why? And you see what happened! Still, if you were to see with your own eyes all those dogs there, you'd be comforted because you'd realise that the death of one wretched human being couldn't matter when there were so many living dogs belonging to famous and noble breeds. By and large, Jürka, you know what I sometimes feel, pondering on how we and our children live? I begin to wonder if life wouldn't be better and easier to live if we walked on all fours and not our two legs. Just picture it if your children were born pups and had some posh lady wearing three silver foxes taking care of them, wouldn't they have a softer life than they have now? Eh?'

'Dogs can't attain salvation,' Jürka replied.

'Are you quite sure?'

'Quite.'

'You ought to have seen that little dog sitting up before those three silver foxes. Maybe it would rather stand on all four legs, and sitting up was a trial for the dog – did you think of that?'

'It wouldn't help the dog any,' Jürka insisted.

'And if a man drops on all fours and wags his tail, will that earn him salvation?'

'Maybe yes and maybe no.'

'Therefore a dog may also earn salvation, especially if it sits up before silver foxes, and so respectfully too, as if it were a human being.'

'No, it can't.'

'How do you know all this so well?'

'What's there to know? There's not a single dog in hell.'

Ants shuddered involuntarily, re-living the fear of many years ago when he almost believed that Jürka was really Satan. The pastor had convinced him that it could not be, and now Ants was sorry he had. All these years he had treated Jürka as someone of no account. If it hadn't been for the pastor, he would have acted differently and gone in fear of Jürka, even if this fear was insincere and hypocritical sometimes, like people's fear of God.

He presumed that the same thing went on in heaven as on

earth: you don't mean what you say, you don't do what you promise, for there are always plenty of fools who can't read your thoughts and will believe in your promises. The pastor himself, Ants believed, was one of their number. To secure his salvation, however, Ants made a point of going to confession once, twice or even three times a year, and invariably after committing some dastardly act, such as misappropriating Jürka's house, ruining Jürka, and conniving at the death of his daughter.

True, this last sin had not yet been redeemed, and after this talk with Jürka, who again made it clear enough that he was Satan, Ants fretted until at last he went to the pastor to confess all his sins and plead indulgence. One sin he kept back, though. He did not confess that all his 'God-fearing' life, he had played the pastor for a fool who took what people said at face value, a fool who believed promises and was blind to deeds. However, for reasons of his own he painted the story of Maia in the most lurid colours, confessing how he extorted the promise of silence from people, where and how much he gave to the officials to remain blind and deaf to the truth.

'Why don't you tell this to Jürka?' the pastor asked. 'Go and tell him and beg his forgiveness, for if he forgives you God will too.'

'I'm afraid,' Ants replied.

'Really? You're not afraid of God, yet you are of a mere man.'

'I'm afraid that Jürka is not a mere man.'

'What is he then?'

'Satan. You will perhaps remember that we had a talk about it once.'

'In all these years you believed in an empty rumour and not in the word of God?'

'You see, Jürka believes so strongly...'

'Yes, Ants, you are right. Jürka's faith is indeed strong.'

'Because it is, you see, I'm beginning to believe him in spite of myself.'

'But, Ants, if you believe Jürka more than me, your pastor,

why don't you confess your sins to him? Why come to me?'

'I'm afraid Jürka will kill me if he hears the whole truth.'

'But maybe it is good to kill people like you? What do you think?'

'I don't think it would do much good.'

'Why not?'

'Someone else, perhaps a sight worse than me, would take my place.'

'I like you today, Ants,' the pastor went on. 'You pass judgment upon yourself saying that you ought to be killed, and then you concede the senselessness of it, for someone even less worthy might take your place. But if even murder is not a solution, what is?'

'I came to you for absolution,' Ants said.

'How can I grant you absolution if you have no faith?'

'Today I do have faith.'

'No, Ants, you're lying as you have always lied. You came to me in search of consolation, while your faith is in Jürka. You came seeking help from God, though you are devil-fearing and not God-fearing, as though your salvation were in the hands of Satan.'

'It's not quite so simple.'

'Tell me then.'

'I do not have a clear aim in striving for salvation.'

'What more of an aim do you need? It's an aim in itself.'

'Not so with Jürka, that's why his faith is so strong, perhaps. If you ask him why he wants salvation, he'll promptly reply: 'To keep hell going.' Now, he does have a clear aim, and I do not, because the moment I leave the church I forget all about my soul's salvation. And to make it easier for people to forget, a tavern has been opened most considerately right next to the church. That's how it is with me, you see. If my salvation was tied up with an enterprise as profitable as Jürka's hell, then I...'

'Dear Ants, who told you that hell was a profitable enterprise?'

'Why else would Jürka's faith be so strong?'

'You have gone out of your senses, you and your Jürka,' the

167

pastor said, getting to his feet and nervously pacing the floor.

However, his calm was soon restored. He thought of the tears flowing from Jürka's eyes when he pleaded with him for his child's soul. Jürka was easier to help because he sincerely believed that if his daughter was buried in consecrated ground she would go to heaven. What was he to do with Ants, the crafty villain? Was there any hope that he would mend his ways in his old age with the pastor's help? No. Ants has been proved a hopeless case. Even so, a happy thought occurred to the pastor, and he said:

'You see, dear Ants, you are afraid that Jürka might really turn out to be Satan sent down to earth in the shape of man. Wouldn't you like to fix things in such a way that you'd have nothing to fear, even if Jürka were really Satan?'

'What must I do?' Ants asked, brightening up.

'Try balancing the evil you have done Jürka with good deeds. But you must go about it very, very carefully, so Jürka himself will not notice.'

'No, it won't work,' Ants said hopelessly.

'Why not? Good deeds always work one way or another.'

'It won't work, I've already thought about it. Because, if Jürka is indeed Satan, he'll have seen through me long ago, and my feeble attempt to save my hide would only make him laugh. On the other hand, if Jürka is simply Jürka, then there's nothing to worry about at all.'

'Except that he might kill you,' the pastor said.

'Except that he might kill me,' Ants repeated.

'And you fear that less than you do Satan?' the pastor asked.

'Of course. I'll have to die one day anyway.'

'Well, in that case, nothing can save you.'

'Jürka also says that.'

'Did you speak to him about it?'

'I did. And he said: 'No matter what a man does, he'll never escape hell.' And I asked: 'Me too?' Jürka said: 'You too.' I asked him about you, and he said: 'The pastor too. If I, Satan, attain salvation no one will escape.''

The pastor did not speak. He sat down again. He was

overcome by a beautiful, touching emotion that seemed to wash over him in gentle ripples... 'Here is a man who is convinced that he is Satan. He has hell in store for me, yet he comes to me, begging me to help his daughter go to heaven,' he mused. 'What must I, his pastor, tell him, and how will our merciful God judge him? He has to be forgiven, that is clear. But what must I do about Cunning Ants, this hardened sinner who has no fear even of being killed? Send him packing until he reforms? But he never will. Or perhaps he should be handed over to the police and punished according to the law?' Alas, the pastor was too old to believe in the lawfulness of the authorities or the fairness of the law – Ants himself made the law, and then took advantage of it. Besides, the pastor was not a servant of the authorities nor was he a lawyer – he was a preacher of charity and mercy.

'Well, dear Ants,' he said in conclusion of his meditations. 'It would not matter if Jürka alone thought so, but I'm afraid everybody does, including you.'

'I don't.'

'You do, Ants, whatever you say. You and all the others come to me with your sins to be consoled by me as if I were a friend and accomplice of villains. Why don't you go to those who'll judge you according to the law? Oh no, you come here because you are convinced that I shall reconcile myself to any crime, however enormous and heinous. Christ did that, and he was crucified, and the mob shouted that it was just, that he got what he deserved. By consoling such as you I have long earned my banishment to hell. Believe me, beloved soul, it is all very painful and hopeless.'

'I believe you.'

'You don't, that's the whole trouble. You only say you do. And though you're an unbeliever I still have to support you with faith.'

'We all have our duties to perform,' Ants sighed, as though symphatising with the pastor.

'Yes, we have, we have, beloved soul,' the pastor repeated.

When Sunday came Ants sat in the front pew, literally

hanging on the pastor's words. He sang at the top of his senile warble, as though hoping to be heard by the congregation, by the pastor, and by God Himself in high heaven. Afterwards, he received the eucharist, and at that moment he fancied that he truly believed in absolution. As he walked home from church, his heart sang for joy. Even the question of whether Jürka was just simply Jürka or Satan did not worry him, for his sins had been forgiven!

And the pastor, smoking his after-dinner pipe with the long stem – the only one of all God's blessings that still roused a desire in him and gave him pleasure – mused: 'One blindly believes that he is Satan but lives like a human being, while another believes that he is a human being and lives like Satan. Ah yes, such is the lot of mortals on earth – they either believe wrong, or they live wrong. How can people be taught to believe what is right and live righteously? Is it within the Lord's power? If it is, why hasn't the Lord seen to it long ago?'

Before he could find the answer to these questions, the pastor succumbed to his after-dinner sleep which with the years grew sweeter and sweeter.

CHAPTER FIFTEEN

And so Ants had no more sins on his conscience, and this knowledge aroused in him a fresh lust for action. Jürka and Juula noticed that building materials were being delivered to the old site of the Pit, but they were stacked not where the house once stood, but some distance away, nearer the fields.

'Ants is up to something again,' Juula observed.

'I guess so,' Jürka said. 'Maybe he wants to move us back to the old place.'

'You think it's us?'

'Who else?'

'We'll see.'

'I guess so.'

When Jürka tried to find out what was afoot, Ants merely smiled into his beard and said:

'Time will show.'

'I guess it will.'

And time did show. The foundations of the future buildings were laid in the autumn, and in the early spring, even before the snow had melted, a team of workers arrived and very quickly built up the walls and roofed the houses.

'I can't believe my own eyes,' Jürka gasped.

'It is indeed a wonder,' agreed Juula.

A couple of weeks later, tenants moved in. They weren't local people, and appeared well-to-do, judging by the goods and chattels, including livestock, which they brought with them. They settled in just in time to start ploughing and sowing.

'I've brought you some neighbours for company,' Ants told Jürka. 'Before you become even more of a boor.'

171

'I've no use for them,' Jürka said sullenly.

'They won't bother you,' Ants assured him. 'I'll fix the boundaries between you, drive in stakes, and you'll be able to live like bears, each in his own lair. If you want to make friends – go ahead, if you don't – you needn't. You'll naturally have to give up some of your fields and meadows, because your neighbours are also entitled to a plot of their own. But you can afford it, you have a sizeable chunk, and what with the acres of forest you clear every year...'

Ants let the sentence trail, leaving what he really had in mind unsaid. But it all came out when shortly afterwards Ants called Jürka to be present when he divided the land up and drove in the stakes. The new tenants got all the best fields and meadows, while Jürka had to console himself with the prospect of clearing more forest for himself.

'Mind you,' Ants told Jürka, 'the land you're going to clear is the finest for miles around. It's as black as soot, and so sticky that you'll want to oil your plough before tilling it, otherwise you'll never get it clean. That's how rich that soil is!'

'Water is a bother there,' Jürka attempted to protest.

'Why, that's nothing, my dear man! All you have to do is dig a few ditches. Rest assured that when this new land, virgin land as it is called, virgin, you understand...'

'I guess do.'

'Well then, in a year or two when this good, virgin land has been properly drained, broken up and loosened, it will be the best anyone has ever had,' Ants concluded his paean to virgin soil.

'For a start, you must reduce the rent,' Jürka ventured to say.

'We'll see,' Ants said complaisantly. 'I'll either reduce the rent or let you pay part of it at some later date. It isn't so very important, we're friends, aren't we? It's not our first deal, we always arrived at an agreement, so there's no reason why we shouldn't this time. It's different with total strangers, but there aren't enough local people, so one simply has to bring in people from outside.'

A new chapter began in Jürka's life. He wasn't on his own at the Pit now, he had neighbours. Not that he noticed them particularly – they didn't come to his house, and he didn't go to theirs. The forest attracted him more than people did, and he'd be perfectly happy if his house were shifted closer to the forest edge. With time, he got used to having neighbours, and life rolled on as before. There was no reduction in the rent, however, but Ants explained it away with his usual glibness.

'On paper, let everything remain as before, or we'll get confused and there'll be a complete muddle. Let's see if the next few years are good or bad, let's see what the yield is like, and we'll always be able to subtract whatever you have overpaid.'

'I guess so,' Jürka said thoughtfully, and went on toiling. Besides his everyday work he dug ditches and cleared land. He did everything Ants told him to do, knowing that Ants was concerned for his welfare not only here on earth, but also in the hereafter.

Though completely engrossed in his work, Jürka was able to notice that much in life was changing. Even the weather, heaven-sent as it was.

'What's going on? I don't get it,' he once said to Juula.

'It's old age, what else,' Juula told him. 'We haven't had any babies for years, so what more proof do you want?'

'It's true, we haven't had any more children,' Jürka said.

'That's the whole trouble. If our flesh is denied blessing, there'll be no blessing in anything else. And what's the good of everything else if the flesh is weak?' Juula reasoned.

'I guess you're right.'

'It's time we gave some thought to death.'

'And save our souls.'

'We'll depart from this vale of tears, and enter the kingdom of heaven.'

'Myself, I'm going to hell,' Jürka said.

'Then I'll go there with you.'

'Oh no, you and the children will go to heaven.'

'I don't want to if you're not coming with us,' Juula said.

'But I have to go to hell, you know that as well as I do.'

'Sure, but still...'

'I have to keep hell going, haven't I?'

'Have you?'

'I guess so.'

'Let someone else take over. Why must it be you?'

'Because I'm Satan.'

'That's true, of course, but...'

'And for another thing I want to see Ants's face when he shows up in hell.'

'You think he will?'

'And how!'

'What about the pastor?' Juula asked.

'I guess he won't.'

'You mean he'll go to heaven?'

'I guess so.'

'Even though he sides with Ants here?'

'There's only one road for him and Maia – to heaven.'

'Maia will go to heaven too?'

'She will.'

'Together with the pastor?'

'Hand in hand with him.'

'Ah, if it only came true!' Juula sighed.

'It will if you have faith.'

'Oh, I do, but still...'

'The pastor says strong faith does it.'

'Is your faith strong?'

'I guess so.'

'Then mine is too,' Juula said.

Both firmly believed that Maia would enter heaven hand in hand with the pastor. Joy burst into flower in their souls, and their hearts overflowed with gratitude to the Almighty for His great mercies. Although their bodies were worn out, they continued their strenuous toil uncomplainingly, for they firmly believed that the ultimate reward was salvation.

And suddenly, out of the blue, they were struck a shattering blow: Joosu, their eldest son and young Jürka's twin brother, came down with some terrible illness. He tossed and raved in fever, and by the third day he was still and cold already. The parents were stunned by this shattering blow. It was not until later, when they had recovered somewhat, that it occurred to them that Joosu might have lived if his tongue had not become so horribly swollen, filling his whole mouth and suffocating him.

'Even a beast dies when it can't breathe, so what chance has a man?' Juula said.

'None, I guess.'

Others died too, but no one died as frightening a death as Joosu. Neither Juula, nor Jürka, nor anyone else could understand why a man should be doomed to such a horrible end. 'Why couldn't he die like all of us mortals die, and why couldn't he live longer?' people wondered. Besides, Joosu was so perfectly suited to a backwoods like the Pit! He was placid and reticent, modest and shy, and he loved work more than anything else in the world. Now, why did God want to recall a soul like Joosu at such an early age? Neither Jürka nor Juula doubted for a moment that their boy went straight to heaven, because if a meek and quiet person like Joosu didn't, who did? It took them a long time to find a satisfactory explanation of their son's untimely death.

'It was divine grace, that's what,' Juula said.

'I guess so,' Jürka agreed.

Divine grace had to be submitted to, there was nothing for it. But what made it all the harder on the parents was that none of their remaining children resembled Joosu. All of them were forever hankering after something. Joosu alone had been content with what the Pit had to offer. His parents would never have recovered from the shock of his death, had not other disturbing news diverted their attention and thus mitigated their grief.

Young Ants had returned from abroad where, his father said, he had mastered all the wisdom of the world. He brought two school friends home with him. They passed the time in hunting, fishing and catching crayfish. They enjoyed catching crayfish best, perhaps, because it was done at night. The three friends would sit round a fire, talking, fooling, laughing and singing songs mostly in some foreign language which lent spice to their fun. Judging by their yells, whoops and revolver shots, the revellers were not convinced teetotallers.

The merrymaking did not go on for long. All of a sudden there was no more hunting, no shots were fired in the forest, and the river no longer resounded with the yells and shouting of men catching crayfish. And then the news reached the Pit: young Ants had drowned when he was catching crayfish, and with him a certain young lady.

'It's a pack of lies,' Jürka said. 'There's only enough water in that river for frogs to swim in...'

'Oh no, it's deep in places, people have drowned there before,' Juula told him.

'On a dark night maybe, or drunk.'

'That's what I say too,' Juula said.

'What were his friends about?'

'They were drunk too.'

'Then maybe it is true.'

Later it transpired that the accident occurred on that very night when Kusta, after a long interval, came home to see how the family were getting on at the Pit. He told them at great length all about the homecoming of young Ants, describing the friends he had brought along and the way they passed the time.

The more Juula thought about it, the heavier grew her heart, and at last, to lighten her burden, she said to Jürka:

'How lucky that Kusta was with us that time young Ants got drowned.'

'Why lucky?'

'Because you never know, he might have...'

'What?' asked Jürka with mounting bewilderment.

'Well, they might have suspected...'

'What?'

'That Kusta had done him in.'

'Mind what you're saying, woman!'

'I mind it all right. When Maia died didn't you tell me you'd wring the man's neck if only you knew who it was. Why couldn't Kusta do it?'

'Did he tell you he would?'

'I know what I'm talking about, don't you worry.'

'So it was young Ants Maia had it with...' Jürka said reflectively.

'Seems so. He had a gold watch and charms on the chain, that's why. He promised to marry her if she got rid of the baby.'

'And I had no idea!'

'I was afraid to tell you. You wouldn't be past wringing old Ants's neck if you couldn't get at the young one.'

'I'd do it too.'

'You see how clever it was of me to keep my tongue! That young fellow got what was coming to him, thank God, and I feel so much easier in my mind now – it has been taken out of your hands, yours and Kusta's.'

'I guess it has.'

So Jürka and Juula took the news of young Ants's death with a feeling of gratification. The fact that a young woman had drowned with him left them unmoved: she was a stranger, and this was the first and probably the last time they'd hear of her. Any number of strange people had drowned or died some other death, and you surely couldn't care about all of them, could you?

However, there were people who were upset by the death of the strange young woman as well. A double drowning – just think of it! To some it signified that the end of the world was nigh. It was a sign of warning to both men and women that the eternally great and unknowable from which there was no escape for anyone was approaching. And be you a man or a woman, young or old, rich or poor – God could always drown you at will like a kitten in the slops pail. And, in point of fact, the spot where Ants and his lady friend were drowned was no deeper for a man than a slops-pail was for a kitten.

The pious read a special meaning in the fact that the drowned woman was young and beautiful. Why did she have to be young and beautiful? Because the Lord wanted to show how little youth and beauty meant to Him. What was more, beauty was displeasing to the Lord, for it incited lust. Young men should therefore avoid beauty for danger of drowning with it like that young Ants had done. Some of the older God-fearing people were convinced that it was still possible to reform the world and ward off the young from sinfulness, even though their teachers and parents were sunk in sin. These old people folded their hands devoutly and thanked the Lord for once again showing the mortals where a man's arrogance – that weakness common to the young – might lead him, and also beauty if it was devoid of meekness. Hope was ignited in some that no one would want to look beautiful after this, and, with business going downhill, aestheticians would turn to God.

When Blind Mari heard about the accident, she said that in a vision she had it was not a mortal woman who had her arms round Ants's neck, but a river nymph who did not want people to catch crayfish in her waters. That often happened in the world: a man would imagine he was embracing the wife of his best friend, and lo! she'd really be a nymph pulling her victim down to the river bottom, deep under the broad leaves of the water lilies, her hands locked so fast round his neck that he could never get away.

At the inquest it was asked if young Ants had any enemies, but everyone averred that he was a wonderful person and no one could bear him malice. This sounded all the more plausible because no signs of violence were found on the bodies. Had Ants and the lady been lovers? Heavens no, she was the wife of his best friend! And so presumably it was an accident. In all likelihood the woman fell into the river in the dark, and when young Ants rushed to the rescue she clutched him by the neck and pulled both of them down to the bottom. Did not the friends sitting round the fire hear anything? No, they were shouting and singing, and heard nothing. Why did Ants and his friend's wife go off together to see if there was anything in the landing-nets? They all went in turns, alone or with someone else for company. What time did they leave the fire? Everyone named a different time, within a range of hours. How long did they stay away? When did their absence begin to worry their friends? There was an even greater divergence of opinion on this point. The only thing the witnesses agreed upon was that it was already light when they went to look for Ants and the young lady. What prompted them to go to the very spot where the two bodies were later found? One landing-net was afloat there, while all the rest were stuck into the bank.

Everything seemed straight and above board, and the police had no grounds for pursuing the investigation further.

All that remained to be done was to bury the victims of the accident – either separately, or in each other's arms as found. But that was a private matter, concerning only the families involved. The pastor, as it later transpired, was also involved inasmuch as he was the person old Ants came to for solace and support immediately after the occurrence. They had a very long talk. It remained a secret what the two old friends had talked about, but something did leak out: apparently, they had in the main debated how to bury the two – in one coffin and locked in a fond embrace the way they were found, or each in a separate coffin. The pastor objected to the double coffin on the grounds that the deceased were neither single nor married to each other. The man was single, but the woman was married. And so, burying the two embracing bodies in one coffin in consecrated ground would give people food for idle talk. Aspersions would be cast on the Church for encouraging adultery, which it absolutely forbade, of course, although this did not deter the Christians from violating the sanctity of holy wedlock whenever they had the chance. Now, if the couple were to be buried beyond the graveyard wall, the pastor would raise no objections to even a double coffin.

Ants would not even hear of it. His son wasn't a wretched suicide to be buried beyond the graveyard wall! He was simply a victim of his own gentlemanliness or of accident, as the official investigation had confirmed. Apparently the lady fell into the water in the darkness, Ants hastened to the rescue, and she clutched at him so awkwardly that both of them went down. A death such as this was all the sadder occurring as it did to a young man who had travelled over the world, and had safely sailed the seas and oceans in hurricane and storm. To think that a young man like Ants should drown in a puddle only large enough for pigs to wallow in, perishing in the heroic act of

179

rescuing the wife of his best friend!

'Even if my son had sinned with that woman, the dead do not sin, you know,' Ants pronounced in conclusion.

'They do, through the living,' the pastor said. 'If we were to bury the embracing lovers in consecrated ground, the living would immediately want to live as sinfully, for there is no greater temptation than a beautiful sin.'

The pastor stood firm, but Ants was more than a match for him, and overruled his prejudices. In the presence of the entire community he had his son, locked in a fond embrace with another man's wife, buried on a knoll, not far from his house, having first had the ground consecrated. In due course he erected a stone monument over the grave and surrounded it with a solid wrought-iron railing, thus immortalising his son and the beautiful young woman clutching his neck. However, the more old Ants adorned his son's grave, the more people believed in what Blind Mari said: it was a river nymph, none other, who had pulled Ants down with her. She had first bewitched the son, and now that he was dead she was after the father. When asked what she meant by that, Blind Mari replied prophetically: 'You'll see.' Those who knew how to interpret mysterious signs, whispered among themselves, convinced that if they could peep into the coffin now they'd find young Ants lying there all alone. Poor boy, he thought it was a loving woman who embraced him, whereas his sinful soul had been seduced by a coldblooded thing with a fish tail and webbed toes. And with every day, more and more people gave an ever wider berth to the grave of young Ants, especially at night when it was pitch-dark or if the moon shed its sickly light on the knoll.

CHAPTER SIXTEEN

While the death of young Ants gave Jürka and Juula a certain
amount of satisfaction and tangible proof that the doings of the
rich on earth were also recorded up in heaven, their own life
seemed to be approaching its natural end. The worst thing of all
was that Juula's strength was giving out. Was it old age, or was it
something else – who could know! What didn't she do to be well
again! She drank fresh milk, brewed all sorts of concoctions from
forest herbs which once cured any ailment, either taken by mouth
or rubbed in, she refrained from hard physical labour, pampering
herself, as she said – but nothing helped. She grew weaker by the
day, she lost her appetite, and found it more and more difficult to
breathe. Finally, Jürka put her in his cart with the wooden wheels,
and took her to the doctor. For someone who was very ill, he
honestly believed it was more comfortable travelling in a cart like
this, for the wooden axle allowed the wheels to turn this way and
that, sparing the passenger the jolts and bumps of the deeply rutted
road.

'You'll murder me before my time,' Juula reproached her
husband.

'Don't worry, you won't die before God calls you, no matter
what you do,' Jürka said. 'And death won't miss its time once God
does send it down. These wooden axles are as good as steel
springs, the going is smooth. It won't kill you.'

'I guess not,' Juula said.

'That's what I've been telling you.'

'Perhaps we should go to the pastor, not the doctor?' Juula
wondered aloud.

'Let's go to the pastor, if you like.'

181

The cart clattered on, stopping first at the doctor's and then going on to the pastor's – seeking human aid, and then God's mercy. They did not stay long at the doctor's, for he was of the opinion that no remedy has been found yet to cure an illness that was a visitation of God.

'A visitation of God did you call it?' Juula asked, wanting to make sure that she had heard right.

'A visitation it is,' the doctor confirmed.

'Now, what did I tell you?' Juula said to her husband. 'There was no need to jolt me in that cart. Something told me it was a visitation, otherwise my own remedies would have surely helped.'

'I'll give you some powders anyway,' the doctor told her. 'But you're to take them only if you're in great pain.'

'If the pain's a visitation, never mind,' Juula said.

'No, you see, God sends people illness and death, but pain – that's from the Devil,' the doctor explained.

'In that case we'll take the powders,' Jürka said decisively.

'Of course, we'll take the powders,' Juula echoed her husband.

They stayed much longer at the pastor's, because it turned out that healing an immortal soul was a far more complicated business than treating the mortal body. To save the pastor a walk to the cart, Juula had to enter his house herself. The long ride, however, had exhausted her and she had not the strength to stand up. What was to be done? And here Jürka hit upon a bright idea.

'I'll carry you in,' he said.

'You think you can?' Juula asked.

'Sure. Only you'll have to put your arms round my neck.'

'The idea! With death staring me in the face,' Juula demurred.

'Never mind...'

Jürka lifted his wife out of the cart, and she put her bony arms round his shaggy red neck. This was the first time in their long married life that he held her so, and Juula felt that there was more tenderness in him than ever before. She was sorry she was going to die soon, and the end must be near, judging by his gentleness. Juula was moved to tears and she entered the pastor's house weeping in her husband's arms. Her emotional state affected her confession, and she told the pastor more than she would have

182

ordinarily. In conclusion she blurted out the true story of Maia and young Ants, and all about Kusta swearing that he'd do the young master in the first chance he had. Was it a sin to feel glad that he was dead, Juula wanted to know?

'But why does it make you feel glad, beloved sister?' the pastor asked.

'Because Kusta did not have to take this sin upon his soul,' Juula replied.

'And young Ants drowning so strangely was no sin of Kusta's, was it?'

'Oh no. Kusta was at home at the Pit the night the young master got drowned. That's why I was so glad to hear it, because it meant my son didn't have to take that sin upon his soul.'

'I am pleased to hear this, beloved sister.'

'Will young Ants go to heaven?'

'Great are the Lord's mercies.'

'You mean, he and Maia might meet in heaven?'

'If that is God's will.'

'Look, what if I don't want young Ants to go to heaven and meet Maia, is that a sin too?' Juula asked.

'It is, my beloved sister, for we must not judge our neighbour.'

'And what if I don't want to go to heaven either because of young Ants, is that a sin?'

'But why because of young Ants, my beloved sister?'

'Because even here on earth I have no truck with cheats, so surely I don't have to in heaven?'

'Is Ants a cheat?'

'Huh! He wore a gold watch and promised to marry Maia and didn't.'

'In the heavenly kingdom evil shall be forgiven and forgotten.'

'Well, I can't either forgive or forget.'

'Put your faith in God's mercy and in your soul's salvation, and then you'll forget and forgive. But where do you intend to go, my beloved sister, if not to heaven?'

'I'd sooner go to hell to be with my old man.'

'Is hell where he is going?' the pastor asked.

'Where else? He's Satan, isn't he, so where else...'

'Very true, very true, my beloved sister,' the pastor said, recalling everything Jürka once told him about himself and also what Ants had said about him. 'There is one thing you must not forget, though: your husband has another wife in hell, the one who went there when you had your twins. Seeing that you two did not get along here on earth, will it be any different in hell, where you intend going to join her? Do you imagine, perhaps, that she'll have forgotten all her mundane grievances, your twins, and everything else?'

It took the pastor a long time to persuade Juula to settle for heaven with young Ants, so that he could give her the Holy Communion. When Jürka had carried his wife out and laid her in the cart, the pastor lit his long-stemmed pipe and sat down in his rocking chair to meditate on the things that went on in the world. The longer he lived, the more he marvelled.

One man would rob his neighbour all his life, legally or illegally; another would become a professional crook, a thief and a liar; a third one would commit rape, and a fourth – murder, and yet towards the end they all came to him in the hope that he'd help them gain admission to heaven, where they'd all be dumped together – the robber and the robbed, the swindler and the swindled, the liar and the deceived, the murderer and the murdered, the ravisher and the ravished. And what could he, a servant of God, do? Was it not his duty to carry out the behest of the Lord and comfort man in this vale of tears, not heeding the voice of his own conscience? What made his profession holy was that it forbade him to heed his own conscience. He was not to judge men, right or wrong, he was to bestow the grace of God upon them all, and with it both the righteous and the unrighteous acquired salvation.

It was a pity that people did not always appreciate the munificence of God's grace. And this lack of appreciation led them to all sorts of quandaries like this Juula woman's with her reluctance to go to heaven because the young man who had ravished her elder daughter and was morally responsible for her death would be there too. But what could he, the shepherd and slave of these sinners, do if such was God's will? Surely it was time people stopped being so difficult, and would be considerate enough not to balk when he flung open the gates of heaven before them? If the unscrutable ways of the Lord had taken a different course – if Ants's drowning had been not an accident but the work of Kusta or Jürka – and if these two had appealed to him, the servant of God, at the death hour, he would have also sent them to heaven. And would it have been any easier for young Ants to meet his murderers face to face, than it was going to be for Juula to encounter the ravisher of her daughter?

While the pastor sat meditating on his duty and Providence, Jürka's wooden-wheeled cart clattered on its way to the Pit. Juula, who felt she had been bumping along for hours on her bed of straw, was seized by doubt once again, despite the confession and the Holy Communion. And finally, unable to keep her thoughts to herself any longer, she told Jürka everything and asked him if, in his opinion, young Ants would go to heaven or hell.

'To hell,' Jürka replied promptly.

'You really think so?'

'I do.'

'And the Saviour won't redeem his sins?'

'Redemption has nothing to do with this.'

'You have lifted a weight from my heart,' Juula gave a sigh of relief. 'You ought to have been a pastor, giving people real comfort.'

'Believe and you'll be comforted.'

'How can I when the pastor wants to send me to heaven together with young Ants?'

'Don't worry, Ants won't be there.'

'Oh well, I can die in peace then.'

'You can, if young Ants is all that worries you.'

Poor Juula, however, was not to die as peacefully as she hoped. Kusta came to see his mother on her death-bed, picking an hour when his father was certain to be out.

'You've been to see the doctor and the pastor, I hear, and that's why I came,' Kusta said to her.

'Yes, Kusta, your father wanted us to go and that's why we went. It's a good thing we went, because my soul is at peace now.

185

I told the pastor about you too, to die with a clear conscience.

'What about me?'

'You and young Ants, I mean.'

'What do you know about it?'

'You told me yourself.'

'I never told you.'

'Are you telling your mother she's a liar? You told me that Maia came to her ruin through young Ants, and that if you ever got your hands on him you'd...'

'So I did get my hands on him, but I never told you about it.'

'Kusta, merciful heavens!' Juula cried. 'Was it you?'

'Sure, who else?'

'But everybody thought they were drunk, that's why...'

'It was me,' Kusta said, so simply that his mother believed him at once, and was too shocked to utter a word. 'I swore to you that I'd avenge Maia, and I came here today to tell you I'd kept my word, and you can die with an easy mind.'

'In other words I lied to the pastor,' Juula said.

'Rubbish. You didn't know you were lying.'

'I didn't know, but still...'

'Oh, mother, don't let such a small lie upset you. You should feel glad that Ants went soon after Maia.'

'The pastor says that Ants will go to heaven.'

'Let him. We're quits now, so I don't care.'

'I didn't want him to go to heaven.'

'Of course you didn't because you didn't know how he died. And if you meet him in heaven now you'll have no bone to pick with him.'

'You're right, Kusta, now that I know, I won't mind if he does go to heaven.'

'That's why I came, to make peace between you, like I've made peace with him.'

'What about her, son?'

'Who do you mean?'

'The woman who was with Ants...'

'I had to take that sin upon my soul, too, there was no helping it, Mother.'

186

'Oh, why did you, son?'

'At that moment they were in each other's arms, the woman clinging to Ants's neck, under the willows. I took off my clothes, hung them on a tree some distance away, and lay in wait behind some shrubs, stark naked except for the jacket draped over my shoulders. I'd watched their doings for several nights in a row, and I knew exactly where they caught the crayfish and what they were about. I decided to carry out my plan that night. The spot suited me fine: the people sitting round the fire couldn't make out anything in the darkness beyond, and it was all of a hundred steps to the landing nets. So what risk was I running? I thought he'd go into the water alone, but that woman stuck to him like a leech. I almost didn't go through with it, but then I thought of Maia who may have also hugged him like that, and my mind was made up. As soon as they went into a clinch under those willows there, I shrugged off my jacket, dashed to them, grabbed Ants round the middle from behind and, walking backwards, hauled him into the water, with the woman clutching him fast. Never mind if I drowned together with them, I was thinking, so long as Ants didn't get away. And that woman, she ought to have released her hold on him, but no, she hung on tighter than ever. True, Ants struggled to break my hold for all he was worth, but what a hope, when I was the stronger! Besides, they had their clothes on and I was naked, they swallowed water from fright, and I held my breath. It was all over very quickly, I climbed out of the water, grabbed my jacket, ran to where the rest of my clothes were, pulled them on, and ran straight here through the forest...'

'How can you talk about it!'

'I'm only telling you so you'd know that I have kept my word and so you could die in peace. Remember, Mother, God was on our side that night. He sent us a dark night with lowering clouds, and no dew fell, so there were no footprints on the grass. And if there were any they were washed away by the rain that started in the morning. And there was one more thing that God willed: While we were thrashing about in the water, the people sitting round the fire made such a row, hollering songs and yelling, that none of them ever knew when the thing happened.'

Juula and Kusta remained silent for a long time, thinking their secret thoughts.

'Mummy,' Kusta now mumbled timidly.

'Yes, son?'

'You're not going to die, surely?'

'My days are numbered.'

'Do you believe you'll go to heaven?'

'I do, son.'

'Does Father believe it too?'

'He does.'

'And the pastor?'

'The pastor, too.'

'I also believe it, Mummy, and so...' The words stuck in Kusta's throat, not from fear but from some emotion he could not have explained.

'What did you want to tell me, son?'

'When you're in heaven, Mummy...' again words failed him.

'Speak up, son.'

'You see, Mummy, when I was dragging them under, I had a feeling that the woman's arms were helping me to drown Ants. I can't get it out of my head. She clutched him so tight because she was sort of on my side. And so I wondered if you couldn't speak to God about her when you're in heaven... She's not to blame, you know, she only hugged Ants like our Maia had before her...'

'I'll speak to the Saviour about it if I go to heaven.'

'Do that, Mummy.'

'And with the Virgin too, son.'

'With the Virgin too, if you've the chance, Mummy.'

They fell silent again, and then Kusta asked:

'Is your soul at peace now, Mummy?'

'It is, son.'

'It's just between you and me, Mummy.'

'Yes, son, between you and me.'

'I'll tell Father when the time comes, so he, too, could die in peace.'

'Do that, son, tell your father when the time comes.'

CHAPTER SEVENTEEN

Juula had long been ready for death, and still death did not come. At moments she believed she was drawing her last breath, the family thought so too, but one day followed another and life still flickered in her body. This gave Jürka plenty of time to think things over and get used to the thought that soon he'd be left to live by his own lonesome self. Juula herself had become quite accustomed to the thought of leaving this world soon.

'I wish you'd make the coffin for me, I'd like to see what it'll be like,' she once said to Jürka.

'I've picked out the boards already,' Jürka told her.

'Why didn't you get down to it then?'

'I was afraid you'd go imagining things...'

'What's there to imagine now?'

'Maybe you'd think I couldn't wait for you to die...'

'I can't wait for it myself, so it's all right.'

'I can't do it, wife.'

'You've got to.'

'I guess so.'

And so Jürka brought the boards into the room and started sawing, planing, measuring, and hammering. This went on for such a long time, that Juula grew sick and tired of the noise and bustle to which she now greatly preferred peace and quiet.

'Why d'you take such hours over the planing?' she asked Jürka at length.

'I want the boards to be smooth.'

'Do the outside only to make it easy on people's eyes.'

'I'll do the inside as well, you'll sleep better.'

'I'll sleep like a log anyway, once you lay me in it.'
Jürka went on planing.
'Come here, husband,' she called him after a while.
'What d'you want?'
'Come closer.'
He laid his work aside and came to the bed.
'Sit down,' Juula indicated the edge of her bed.
Jürka sat down.
'Old man,' Juula began again.
'Mm?'
'Listen, do you remember that she-bear who had twins?'
'We also had twins.'
'That she-bear you killed with your knife...'
'It was you who stuck that knife into her...'
'And she struck the handle with her paw...'
'What's it all about?' Jürka asked, puzzled by his wife's long silence.
'What was there on the ground?' she asked.
'Moss.'
'Such lovely, green moss!'
'I guess it was.'
Again there was a silence.
'D'you remember us making love in the forest?' Juula asked.
'I sort of remember at times.'
'And what was there on the ground?'
'Moss.'
'And wasn't it even softer and lovelier than where we met that she-bear with the twin cubs?'
'I guess so.'
'I wish you'd lay me out on moss like that.'
'Can be done.'
'Oh, do that, do! Then you won't need to plane the boards on the inside.'
'Nothing doing. I'll plane the boards, and fetch the moss too, so everything will be right and proper.'
'Fetch plenty of moss, soft, green moss like it was that time we killed the she-bear, or the time we got the twins started.'

'Look, wife, you must really be dying.'

'Why?'

'Otherwise you wouldn't talk like that.'

'No, it's not that. As I listened to you planing the boards for my coffin, I remembered things and how happily we have lived.'

'Without sin, mind you.'

'Happily and without sin. Our children, it is true...'

'Too bad about the children.'

It cost Juula quite an effort not to tell Jürka about Kusta and young Ants. Let Kusta tell him himself when the time comes, as he promised. But the longing to tell Jürka before Kusta did devoured her like a flame, and quite possibly she would not have been able to resist the temptation had not Jürka's prophesy come true – Juula was now really dying.. She was in great pain, as the doctor predicted, and the time came to give her his powders. But before she had taken the lot, she gave up the ghost. And as the powders had cost money, and quite a lot of money, Jürka took what remained himself. If they were good for a dying person they could do no harm to a healthy one, could they?

And indeed, the powders did not do Jürka any harm at all. He fell fast asleep after taking them, and did not even snore as usual. Riia, his youngest daughter, noticed this and said:

'Father, you're scared of our dead mother!'

'Mm?'

'You don't even dare snore when you sleep!'

He would gladly have given Riia some of her mother's medicine so she'd fall as fast asleep and not notice these things about him. But, alas, there was only one powder left, and Jürka decided to take it himself. Of course, he might have divided this last remaining powder in two, but it never occurred to him, and how could he when he had never done it before? And so Riia wasn't to know if her mother's medicine would have given her sweet dreams or not. And again she noticed that once the funeral was over, her father started snoring as usual.

'How strange!' thought Riia. 'Father has stopped being

191

scared of Mother now that all that earth's been heaped over her.'

She did not say another word about it to her father, but she went on wondering about the strangeness of everything in the world: when a person was alive no one was afraid of him, when he died people shrank in fear, and once he was buried this fear went away. As if the dead, until they were buried, could do anything to you. As for Riia herself, it was only her living mother she was afraid of sometimes, and her dead mother – never, not a bit, before or after burial. And father was afraid. Why else would he have made such a handsome coffin for her, the only beautiful thing she'd ever had in her life? And that bedding of moss, too, on which her mother lay down so comfortably? She lay down on it, Riia insisted in her thoughts, she lay down herself. Riia liked that moss bedding so much that she'd gladly lie down on it beside her mother and be buried together with her. If Mother was going to heaven, Riia would have to follow her as she'd followed her about all her life, so why not go together now? Riia tried to find consolation in running to the coppice behind the field where the moss was thickest and greenest and stretching out on it, the way her mother had done in the coffin. But it was a terrible bore lying so still, and Riia was glad she wasn't sharing her mother's new bed. Imagine lying stretched out like this without moving for days and nights, many days and nights! It was the hardest thing in the world for Riia to keep still and not run about. Now, her black, yellow-eyed cat, her best and only friend, liked keeping still, and then only when it was warm and sunny. And how could it be sunny in the coffin with the lid nailed down, and tons of earth heaped over it? What a hope. The cat was no example then. Pussy loved warmth, and Mother was ice cold. Riia had touched her. She had never been so cold, not even when she came home drenched through in the autumn rain, her teeth chattering. Anyway, they were both lying on soft, green moss now, the only difference being that Riia had the sun shining down on her.

Riia made another discovery that had a direct bearing on her mother's death. When her mother was living, her father seemed almost a stranger to Riia, and all she felt for him was fear. What made her afraid of him was mainly her mother's attitude to him, for even she was afraid of Father. And so there was no room for any other emotions except fear. When her mother was living, her father never asked Riia if she'd had anything to eat. He'd come home, take a bite of whatever he could find, and then either lie down for a snooze or go back to work. Most of the time he seemed like a total stranger who lived with them for some unknown reason. And that's why Riia was rather reluctant to call him Father, as her mother bade her do, much preferring to call him Jürka like people did. She rarely ventured to approach him, and even more rarely heard some endearment from him. And Mother was always telling her not to bother him when he came home tired from work.

With Mother gone, Father seemed to become a different person. He even found time for Riia. He'd ask her several times a day if she had eaten, and if she so much as hinted that she was hungry he'd always find something to give her. Very soon Riia began to notice that he would drop whatever he was doing, and however urgent the job, if she was in need of anything. He talked to her, too. Not like Mother, of course, but it was talking all the same. The memory of her mother's manner of speaking was growing fainter and fainter with every day, and only the sound of her voice still echoed in Riia's ears. The things her father called her puzzled Riia at first, and she wasn't sure if he was teasing her or meaning them kindly.

'Now then, dirty-face, come here, come to Father,' he'd say, and if she hesitated or wanted to run away, he'd repeat: 'Come to Father, snotty!' And if this failed, he'd say: 'Well, why don't you come, you little sloven?'

In time Riia got used to these and some even less pretty names, and when he called her to him she gladly went because he always had something for her in his pocket: a berry, a whistle, a reed pipe, a tiny horse he had carved from wood, a wilted flower, a sedum leaf, some sorrel, or something else. Once he brought home some bumblebee honeycombs in a

193

birch-bark basket, and seating Riia on his knee taught her how to suck out the honey.

It was then that the thought first struck her that perhaps, like Mother, her father also loved her and just never said so and instead called her a nitwit, a flea, or dirty-face. Before long she started running to him herself, without waiting to be called, especially if he came home in the cart. There was always the chance of a ride in the cart or on horseback. Riding was the most exciting thing in the world, it was so wonderful that after her first ride Riia dreamt of it for two nights in a row, and in her dream the horse had her father's face and eyes and had turned to look at her.

'Why did the horse have your face?' she asked her father in the morning.

'What horse?'

'The one in my dream.'

'Look at the brat! The horse, you say, looked like me?'

'It kept turning round when I was riding it.'

'Means the horse liked you.'

'Why, do you think?'

'You're light, the horse couldn't feel any weight on its back.'

'And it's nice for the horse?'

'I guess so.'

Riia was perfectly satisfied with Jürka's interpretation of her dream, all the more so because the dream didn't come back though she wanted to go galloping on horseback more and more. Sometimes, when there was no horse to ride she'd climb on to her father's back and sit astride his shoulders while he held her by her sunburnt legs and jumped around. Riding a real horse was more fun, though, because she could hold on to its mane, but when she clutched at her father's hair he roared at her straight away:

'Hey, brambles, let go, don't touch my mop!'

One thing she resented was that her father did not spend enough time at home with her, and she often felt terribly lonely. Sometimes she'd whimper and beg him to stay a little longer, but he'd simply get up and go, turning a deaf ear to her pleas.

He hardly ever took her along with him, unlike Mother who always let her tag behind. There was this difference between her mother and her father – Mother was always there, you could touch her, see her and hear her, while Father only appeared now and again, as though he'd come from the other end of the world, and the waiting for him to come home was long and tedious. After her mother's death Riia's entire life seemed to be compounded of waiting and loneliness.

'Riia doesn't want to stay alone,' she sometimes told her father plaintively.

'But you're the mistress of the house, you know,' he would say.

'And does the mistress have to stay at home all alone?'

'I guess so.'

'Then I don't want to be the mistress.'

'But where can we get another?'

'I don't want to be the mistress anyway.'

'Just for a little longer, all right? And then...'

'Then what?'

'We'll see.'

The days went by, and finally Riia got used to staying alone in the house without her parents. And then a stranger appeared who was to replace them for her. She no longer complained of loneliness, she did not beg her father to take her along, and all she did was ask:

'Will you be going far today?'

'Very far.'

'Through the forest?'

'Yes.'

'Across the big field?'

'Yes, across the field too.'

'And you'll go into the next forest?'

'That, too.'

'And walk through it?'

'I will.'

'And then what?'

'Nothing.'

'And after nothing?'

'I'll return home.'

'What will you bring me from far away?'

'Whatever I happen upon.'

'Bring plenty.'

'I'll bring enough.'

'Bring enough to eat all we want and also leave some for later.'

'I will, I guess.'

Here, Riia's thoughts slightly changed direction, and she asked:

'If you bring a lot, shall we keep some for Mother?'

'Sure, we'll do that.'

'When is she coming back?'

'We'll go to fetch her.'

'May I go with you?'

'We'll see if we go together or separately.'

'When?'

'You'll have to wait a bit.'

'Riia wants to go now!'

'First I'll go and bring whatever we'll need to take along with us.'

'All right, Riia will wait for you to bring a lot of everything.'

'A great big lot.'

There were moments when, left all by himself, Jürka seemed to ruminate or grieve, but no one ever discovered what went on in his mind and his heart. One thing that was noticed about him was that his gaze invariably rested on the church whenever he sat brooding alone. Was he about to go there, or was he expecting someone to come from there? However that may be, the habit of staring at the church remained with him until the end of his days. Even when talking with Riia, he would involuntarily look at the church.

CHAPTER EIGHTEEN

Time passed and, in spite of all his misfortunes and cares, Jürka felt a fresh surge of energy: he worked with a will, and despondency released its hold upon his spirits. He joked more and more with Riia, predicting that she would one day be the mistress of the Pit. The joke enchanted him, and together with the child he began to take it seriously. The fact that Ants had long been the owner of the Pit never seemed to enter his head. He plunged into the work with new vigour, as if he were toiling on his own property; he dug new ditches, repaired the old ones, stubbed and cleared new meadows, and tended the fields for the generations to come. The neighbour Peeter, who was a tenant like Jürka, came over one day.

'Keeping the hell fire going for us, are you?' he said.

'Not yet, but the time will come,' Jürka replied.

'It will come, all right.'

'First, I have to save my soul,' Jürka told him.

'Is there salvation for someone who slaves for another?' the neighbour asked, uncertain what Jürka meant.

'I slave for myself.'

'Aren't you digging these ditches for Ants?'

'No. For myself.'

'The Pit belongs to Ants, and not to you and not to me.'

'But we live here, don't we?'

'Ants can refuse to renew the lease. Mine's for two years only.'

'And I've lived here for years.'

'How long is your lease for?'

'What lease? I have no lease.'

197

'Too bad for you. Ants can throw you out any day.'

'But Ants is my friend!'

'Some friend,' the neighbour said with a sneer. 'He's your friend while he needs you, and once he has no more need of you he'll become your enemy.'

'Enemies have to be killed.'

The neighbour laughed, thinking that Jürka was joking, and then he said:

'It's simpler profiting where you can than killing Ants.'

'Profiting won't save the soul.'

'And murder?'

'It does sometimes.'

The neighbour took it to be another of Jürka's jokes, and brought the conversation back to normal.

'I still can't understand why you want to work so hard on land that's not yours.'

'Because I want to earn salvation.'

'I didn't know it was earned through hard work.'

'What else?'

The neighbour had no ready argument, and after a moment's thought he said:

'Maybe it'll earn you your salvation, but you're certainly making it hot for others, it's as hot as in hell.'

'How d'you mean?' Jürka asked, puzzled.

'Listen to this: this spring Ants renewed my lease and raised the rent. I tried to make him see reason, it wasn't fair, I told him, because I wasn't getting a bigger or better plot of land, so why raise the rent? D'you know what he said to that? I'll repeat it word for word. He said: "Work hard like Jürka, and your plot will be bigger and better."'

'That shows you that Ants really is my friend,' Jürka said proudly.

'What does?' cried the neighbour in exasperation, unable to follow Jürka's logic. 'And anyway why should we improve his land for him?'

'Why not?'

'And all he does for the land is raise the rent, is that it?'

'I guess so.'

'But then there is no sense in improving the land.'

'The rent will still go up whether we do or not.'

The neighbour was thunderstruck. Indeed, what were they to do? If you improved the land you paid more rent, and if you didn't you'd never raise enough to pay what you owed Ants, and he'd simply kick you out. And where could you go? Ants had friends and connections all over the world, their reach was boundless. Supposing you wanted to give up farming and earn your living in some other way, you'd fall into Ants's clutches right away just the same. So, whether you improved the land or not, Ants would pocket the profit, and all you'd get for your pains would be a crust of dry bread.

'No, there's no profit in working hard,' the neighbour said with resignation.

'But work promises salvation,' Jürka intoned his usual litany.

'Supposing I don't want this salvation of yours, what then?'

'But you're a mortal, aren't you?'

'Isn't Ants a mortal too? Why doesn't Ants have to save his soul as well?'

'He's helping us.'

'Helping, my arse!' shouted the neighbour, spitting on the ground in anger.

'Where else can you find work?' Jürka asked him calmly.

'Nowhere, that's the whole trouble,' the neighbour replied.

'So, you see,' Jürka concluded smugly.

'You're so easy to please, you'd live just as happily in hell,' exclaimed the neighbour.

'I will, when the time comes.'

Peeter couldn't make him out at all: here he was working like a horse to save his soul, and at the same time he didn't mind going to hell! It was probably true that he was not all there, as people said. And yet as a worker he had no equal. Could it be that work was meant for the dumb only? But then, if Jürka was not all there while he, Peeter, had his wits about him, why must he work too? Why did God give him a headful of brains if he had to share Jürka's plight?

'If only I could reason like you do, life would be so much easier,' said the neighbour at length.

'Reason about what?' Jürka asked, evidently losing track of the conversation.

'Well, about work.'

'What work?'

'I mean your trying so hard to improve land that's not your own, but Ants's.'

'But if I want to gain salvation...'

'Can't you earn it by toiling on your own land?'

'But I've no land of my own.'

'Why?'

'Because it's owned by Ants.'

'Why Ants?'

'Such was God's will.'

'Do you honestly believe it?'

'Don't you?'

'I don't understand these things.'

'Believe, and you shall understand.'

'How can I believe when I...'

'Then, of course, you can't understand.'

No, it was hopeless talking to Jürka, the neighbour decided. He was either a simpleton or not quite human, for all his faith and his striving for salvation.

Ants, on the contrary, seemed to enjoy talking to Jürka, and often came to see him now, as though seeking solace in his bereavement. He insisted, however, that what brought him was not his own need, but his concern for Jürka.

'Your wife has died, I hear,' he said.

'So she has.'

'Children die too, but it's different with them: one goes, but others are left. It's not the same when a wife goes...'

'I guess it isn't.'

'A man of sober habits usually has one woman, and if she dies he must either live without a woman or get himself another one.'

'I don't want another one,' Jürka said.

'But you've a little daughter, the child needs a mother's care.'

'Her mother's dead.'

'Even a stepmother is better than none.'

'Maybe so, but I don't want a new woman.'

'You won't manage without one, if you want to keep your home going.'

'There are no more women like Juula.'

'Hard-working, was she?'

'She killed that bear when it wanted to savage me.'

'D'you remember that it was I who suggested Juula to you? Well, I've an even better woman for you now.'

'There are no better women.'

'What about Mall? She has legs like pillars, cheeks like the reddest of apples, and no work is too hard for her.'

'I can't be bothered,' Jürka replied.

'Well, if you don't want her for a wife, just take her to keep the house in order.'

'My house is in order.'

'You call that order? Why, my pigs are kept cleaner than your kid!'

'It's my kid, and your pigs.'

The finality of Jürka's tone left Ants at a loss for an argument. He wouldn't put it past Jürka to ask for a reduction in the rent 'so the kid might be kept cleaner', or something like that. Ants, therefore, changed the subject and started praising Jürka to the skies for being a marvellous worker and a thrifty farmer whose every undertaking turned out well.

'That's what I call good management,' Ants continued. 'Everything changing for the better in the world, there's an upsurge in everything, for that's how God meant it to be. But to listen to your neighbour, the world is moving backwards, everything's on the decline, and so the rent should go down too. And to my way of thinking, if the price of land is going up how can the rent go down? And so we go arguing back and forth about it, your neighbour and I.'

'He has no faith, that's why he can't understand,' Jürka

clarified.

'Well said! He has no faith, and there you are. When I tell him that I bought the Pit for so much and that I'd get double that much if I wanted to sell it now, he doubts my word. And yet it's so obvious: the times are different, the Pit is not what it was before, the rent is not the same, and all this goes to show that people are making more and more money. Take the taxes, for instance...'

At this point Ants thought it best to drop the subject so as not to get Jürka's back up. His prosperity was an open secret, but the least said about it the better.

He had grown so rich that he no longer had to confirm his national spirit or his patriotism with any kind of commitments – that's how trustworthy he was! He paid no taxes at all, but as taxes were imposed on him anyway he exercised his right to shift the burden on to those who were not as prosperous and whose national feelings and patriotism were therefore questionable. When Ants held forth on the subject of patriotism, which he was rather fond of doing, his own rights and privileges were uppermost in his mind, and this seemed quite natural to him, and to others too.

'You've been seeing a lot of your neighbour lately,' Ants said. 'What is your honest opinion of him?'

'I don't understand the man.'

'In what way?'

'Well, he says he slaves for you, but he lives like a lord.'

'Yes, doesn't he?' Ants responded eagerly. 'He slaves for me, he says, but it's he who takes the profit.'

'I guess so.'

'When he came here he had two horses, and now he has four. He wants to buy the farm, people say. Did he talk to you about it?'

This was clearly the first Jürka had ever heard of it, and Ants had no further use for him. He started to leave, but thought better of it and stayed on until he had pestered Jürka into consenting to let Mall come.

Mall arrived in due course, and disliked everything about the

202

Pit. Nothing pleased her, and nothing would do until she had changed it to her way. When Jürka was at home, she made a great song and dance about him, and her voice sounded as sweet as a shepherd's pipe made from the bark of an ash. She set the choisest food before the master who had in the meantime made a habit of giving the tidbits to Riia. Usually, Riia and the cat slept with Jürka, but Mall told her to come to her bed instead because the master's sleep was heavy after his heavy toil, and he might overlie the child.

'Like a sow, eh?' Jürka asked.

'Exactly,' Mall replied.

'But men are not sows.'

'They're as bad.'

'How do you know? You've never had a child.'

'I never had because I know.'

Though Jürka did not agree that men were sows, capable of overlying their own child, he had to let Riia and her black cat sleep with Mall who wanted to be a loving stepmother to the girl. It did not take her long to show that she really meant to marry Jürka. Once, in the middle of the night, she left Riia and the cat in her bed, and came to Jürka's.

'I can't sleep with the child tossing about. It'll be more restful with you. I don't suppose you can be bothered to disturb anyone's sleep. Don't mind me, I'll just curl up behind your back.'

Jürka grunted and went on sleeping. All at once he sprang from his bed.

'Where are you going?' Mall asked.

'Where people go when they wake up at night,' Jürka said, and went out into the yard.

Mall waited for him impatiently, but she was in for a cruel disappointment. Jürka did not come back to her, and instead climbed into bed with Riia and the cat. This was more than human flesh could bear. Mall went back to her bed and whispered plaintively:

'Something bit me in your bed, must be bedbugs or fleas.'

'Both, most likely,' Jürka replied.

'Won't you let me back into my bed?'

'I guess so.'

Saying this, Jürka swept up Riia and the cat and carried them to his bed, muttering: 'I won't be bothered now...'

'Why are you taking the child and the cat?'

'They're mine, you know, the child and the cat,' Jürka told her, and settled down to sleep.

But very soon, Mall began to whine.

'You've brought your nasty fleas into my bed...'

'Not me. It's the child the bloodsuckers are after. They couldn't bite through such old hides as yours and mine.'

Mall's first reaction to this matter-of-fact statement was a whimper, and then she became furiously angry. The nerve! Jürka thought her so old that even a bedbug wouldn't be tempted. Mall had heard a lot of nice and nasty things about herself, but never anything so awful. The insult, however, did not make her lose any sleep. Why worry, why hatch any schemes, if even a bedbug found your body undesirable? She was aflame with anger at Jürka because in his matter-of-fact words she heard the truth, and believed it.

That first morning, waking up in her father's bed Riia asked him how she happened to be there.

'Who did you go to bed with last night?' Jürka asked her.

'With Mall.'

'Quite sure?'

'Of course, and I took the cat with me, too.'

'Could the cat have done the mischief, d'you think?'

'When everyone was fast asleep?'

'That's right.'

Riia thought it over for a minute, and then said:

'Can I go to sleep in your bed tonight?'

'Won't you sleep with Mall?'

'I don't want to.'

'Why not?'

'Because she's like that...'

'Like what?'

'Like what I don't like.'

'Oh well, come and sleep in my bed, so the cat won't have to carry you over in the middle of the night.'

Riia giggled delightedly. She liked sleeping behind her father's back, it was like hiding behind a huge rock. His lusty snoring bothered her at first, but very soon she began to feel that she couldn't really sleep without these sounds. If she were old enough to think philosophically, she would certainly arrive at the conclusion that if she wanted to sleep so sweetly all her life she herself had to learn to snore like her father.

CHAPTER NINETEEN

And that's how they lived at the Pit: Jürka and Riia stuck together, and Mall remained the outsider she was. At first she tried to teach Riia to call her Auntie, but it didn't work. Still, she did look after the child, and performed all her other duties so well as to be above reproach.

However, some new circumstances soon arose. In all these years it had never once occurred to Jürka to call on his neighbour, and he knew the man only because he himself had walked across to Jürka's once or twice and spoken to him. But Mall quickly made friends with the family, they were as thick as thieves and this intimacy became an eyesore to Jürka.

'You seem to spend more time at the neighbour's than you do at home,' he said to her one day.

'Is this my home?' Mall sneered. 'Living here in the forest I'd start howling like a wolf if I couldn't run across to the neighbours now and then.'

'I guess you would.'

And another thing that surprised Jürka was that Mall was, for the first time in Jürka's hearing, nagging about the shortage of this or that in the household. There had been harder times, Jürka well knew, but none of the family had ever complained. When they ran out of something, they did with what was left, and only when there was nothing to eat at all they went to Ants for help. So long as there was salt and flour in the house there was no cause to complain of hunger, and even on just potatoes and salt a person could live for quite a long time.

'If cows can live on grass and hay, why can't a man live on potatoes?' Jürka reasoned.

'A cow can live even on straw and chaff,' Mall responded.
'I guess so,' agreed Jürka.
'But a man can't.'
'Whyever not?'
'Because man is not an animal.'
'What is he then?'
Mall didn't know, and the question stumped her.
'Well, a man has two legs, and a cow has four...' she said.
'But you eat with your mouth, not your legs!'

This left Mall at a loss again. It was really hopeless talking to Jürka because he twisted everything around the way normal people never did. And so Mall avoided getting into conversation with her master, and only spoke to him if it was quite inevitable. Jürka couldn't stand empty chatter, and so he was well satisfied. If it were up to him he'd make everyone work and not wag their tongues. If he knew how hard it was on people who studied languages and wrote books, he'd probably pity the poor sinners for being laden with such useless labours. All they did was trace out letters and words, imagining that they'd earn salvation with it! A thousand years, no less, of this nonsense might do it, but even so it was doubtful.

Jürka himself still dwelt in that happy state when he did not have to cudgel his brains over the problems of writers and other such strange folk. His one concern was to see that the cows had enough straw and hay, and the family enough bread and potatoes.

That year, however, there was always a shortage of something in the household, things like meat, butter, herring, sprats, wood, flax, soap and soda. Not that Mall demanded this or that, but she was always reminding the master about the lack of things. To be sure, Mall ran the house for him, it was 'her responsibility' as she liked to say. Funny thing, Jürka had never heard these words in his home before, and there had always been plenty of everything. If responsibility meant the same as shortage, why did Mall insist on making so much of the word? It was all too puzzling for Jürka. The same cows were there, so why were they short of butter and milk? The sheep were sheared as usual, so why wasn't there enough wool? Flax was still scutched and combed, so why the shortage? All these questions worried Jürka so much that he couldn't wait to tell Ants, whom he still thought his good friend. Ants listened to him with his peculiar little smile.

'That's all because there is no mistress in the house,' he pronounced.

'There's Mall, isn't there?'

'Mall's not the mistress, she's a servant.'

'We must go to the pastor, you mean?'

'There's no other way.'

Jürka remained glumly silent for a while, and then said:

'I'd rather go short.'

'Well, that's your business, but if you don't look out you might lose your farm,' Ants told him.

'How's that?'

'That's obvious! Since you're running short of everything you'll soon run short of money, too, and what will you pay your rent with? As it is, you owe me for last year...'

'That's true, of course, but still...'

'Our deals have been always based on friendship, on amicable agreement, shall we say, but this can't go on forever. I have to pay taxes and other expenses, you know that yourself. And so I'm compelled to demand payment from you too. If I were you I'd think it over.'

'I guess so.'

Jürka did think it over, he thought very hard, but he simply could not see himself taking Mall to the pastor. How could he when he didn't feel like sleeping with her in the same bed? With Juula it had all been quite different, they had their twins before there could be any talk of a wedding. Oh well, all he could do was carry on as before, come what may. There was a moment when he almost broached the subject with Mall, but he changed his mind – What was the good of talking if he didn't feel like sleeping with her in the same bed? Besides, Mall was becoming ever closer with the neighbours, evidently preferring their place to the Pit.

'Why does Mall hold her hands under her apron when she goes to see the neighbours?' Riia asked him once.

'M-hm!' replied Jürka, without really listening to what the

child was saying.

'I know why,' Riia said brightly. 'Because she's hiding something under her apron!'

'She's hiding her hands, you just said so,' Jürka bestirred himself to say.

'And what has she in her hands?'

'Alright, what?' Jürka was waking up.

'How do I know, I only know there's something.'

'Nonsense.'

'It's true, it's true, Father! When she comes back her hands lie on the apron, and when she leaves home they're under the apron.'

Jürka discouraged the child to say any more, and pretended that he had not understood a thing. However, he decided to watch Mall's comings and goings, wondering if Riia was right. And to be sure Mall did exactly what Riia said she did: leaving the house, she hid her hands under her apron, and coming back she held them on the apron. Funny, he never noticed it himself. One evening, when Mall was starting on her way to the neighbours, Jürka called out to her:

'I say, Mall, hold out your hands.'

Startled, she first wanted to flee, then turned abruptly and dashed back to the barn from which she had just emerged.

'Hold out your hands!' Jürka roared in his thunderous voice that seemed to come from an empty barrel, and caught hold of her in a couple of leaps.

Under the apron she was hiding a huge ball of red thread, wound round the neck of a goose, stuffed full of peas, and there was also a chunk of bacon fat.

'What's this?' Jürka demanded.

'Viiu is embroidering a pretty blouse for me, I've no time for that, working by the sweat of my brow from dawn till dusk, and so she...'

'Wants bacon fat, right?'

'Well, not necessarily bacon fat, but I have to give her something, haven't I.'

'I guess so.'

'This piece would fry so nicely, I thought...'

209

'Wouldn't it fry as nicely at home?'

'Oh really, master, grudging a tiny piece of bacon...'

'That tiny piece would do us for two or three meals,' Jürka said, taking the ball of thread and the bacon from Mall. 'Pack your things and get out.'

'O Lord, where?'

'That's your worry.'

'I won't go like that.'

'Want me to knock the life out of you first?'

'I want you pay me first.'

'Bring back all you've taken away under your apron, and then I'll pay you.'

'What will you to pay me with, beggar that you are?'

'Get out this minute!' Jürka yelled, and Mall didn't want to tarry any longer.

She left the Pit that night with a bundle on her back. Riia was already asleep.

When she couldn't find Mall the next morning, she asked her father where she was.

'She's gone, and when she left she had her hands lying on the apron.'

'Where did she go?'

'Who knows?'

'When is she coming back?'

'Who asked her?'

'Maybe she won't come back at all!' Riia cried gleefully.

'She won't come back.'

A couple of days later Ants arrived at the Pit to find out what Mall had done and why she had been sent packing.

'She's a thief,' Jürka told him.

'Who? You don't mean Mall, do you?'

'Who else?'

'And what did she steal?'

'How do I know what she's stolen over the weeks.'

'Then how do you know that she stole anything?'

'I told her to hold out her hands, hiding them under her apron, she was. And what she had in them was a chunk of bacon fat and a ball of Juula's thread.'

'Oh come, that's not a big crime,' Ants said in the tone of a peacemaker.

'She was always running over to the neighbours, holding her hands under her apron.'

'I didn't know you'd caught her red-handed several times.'

'Once was enough. Should I let her carry on stealing?'

'Did anyone see you catch her red-handed?'

'Who was there to see it?'

'Something's got to be fixed up,' Ants said gravely. 'Supposing you're both brought before the judge? Mall will say she never stole anything, and you'll say she did. Who is the judge to believe, Mall or you?'

'Does Mall say she carried nothing under her apron – no bacon, no ball of thread?'

'She says she was bringing it home from the barn, she wasn't stealing it.'

'But why did she go out of the gate?'

'The gate was open, she says, she went to close it and see what the weather was like, while she was there... You know, women's business, especially since it was dark and no one could see. You hired her for a year, don't you forget it, and if it's proved that you dismissed her for no good reason...'

'How do you mean, no good reason?'

'You can't prove it...'

'Didn't I catch her with that chunk of bacon and that ball of thread in her hands?'

'That's all very well, but how can you prove that she meant to steal the stuff?'

'She told me herself that she was taking it to that neighbour woman for embroidering a blouse for her.'

'Who heard her?'

'I heard her.'

'Who else?'

'Who else was there to hear?'

'There! No one heard her except you and Mall will naturally deny it. We might ask Viiu the neighbour, if she was embroidering a blouse for Mall, but even if it's true don't expect the woman to admit it. She'll deny it, too. Everyone will deny everything, and you won't be able to prove that Mall wanted to rob you. It will be decided that you want to brand her a thief so you don't have to pay her, because you've no money to pay her the wages she is due.'

'Look, Ants, I always thought you were my friend, and here you are at one with that thief.'

'Jürka, my dear friend, I'm only trying to help you by showing you what Mall might say if it came to a trial.'

'Why should it come to a trial?'

'It will, if Mall sues you for the wages you owe her, plus her wages until the end of the year, as agreed.'

'I like that! Paying her for nothing.'

'That's the way it goes, it's the law,' Ants said.

'Who invented such a law, I'd like to know?'

'Those who have the power – the representatives of the Almighty on earth.'

Jürka digested this statement in silence for a minute.

'You mean, you have to pay wages to someone who's robbed you?' he asked.

'You can't prove anything against Mall, you've no witnesses. Besides, she took many of your cares upon herself: she looked after your house, your child and your livestock. Surely you can't be such a miser, it won't help you to save your soul, you know!'

'And what will happen to Mall's soul, thief that she is?'

'Even the thieves who were crucified with Jesus went to heaven – didn't you know? Look here, Jürka my dear friend, you're living like a bear in his lair here at the Pit, in the lap of the gods, shall I say, so what can you know of thieving, cheating and swindling? If you lived among people you'd see that all those things were as essential in our everyday life as pottage to go with our bread.'

'A body can do without pottage.'

'Apparently not, seeing how everyone loves it. That's why it has become the accepted practice in the world for the strong and stupid to rob, and for the weak and the cunning to steal.'

'I neither rob nor steal!' Jürka declared.

'Don't you gather berries and mushrooms in someone else's forest? Don't you rob the bees of honey, the cows of milk, and the sheep of wool, together with the hide sometimes?'

'Cows and sheep aren't people.'

'We're all God's creatures, my dear Jürka. Those who know how and have the power fleece other mortals; those who can't do it rob the animals and the land, and yet all of them want to go to heaven! You and I have lived like good friends for the greater part of our lives, but you must have heard what people call me? A thief, a villain, a bloodsucker, a usurer, a swindler, a cheat and a scoundrel who has neither heart nor honour. And the things people say about you? And you've lived here like a recluse all your life in the forest wilds, thinking only of salvation.'

'I guess you're right,' Jürka said, believing that he had understood everything.

'Well, and what do people think of you?'

'What people?'

'Everyone and no-one – that's the way opinion is usually formed. People think you a murderer, killing people with senseless toil: a miser who starves his household; a skinflint who won't pay proper wages; a rogue who wants to save his soul so as to keep hell going; a criminal hiding away in the forest; an unbeliever, otherwise you'd go to church more often; and a swellhead because you shun the company of your own kind.'

'If I could get my hands on those foul mouths, I'd kill the lot,' Jürka said.

'It's your right, of course. But don't you think there's a grain of truth in what people say? You're such a fiend for work that it would be suicidal for others to try to keep up with you, and you live on swill which not every pig would eat. You pay people less than I do. You can't afford to pay them more, of course, but if you can't – why hire people at all? Become a hired worker yourself, come and work for me, I'll pay you more than you make from your farm, the work will be easier, and you'll live a better life...'

'I'm staying on at the Pit.'

'Of course you are, I only said that by way of example, speaking of what people thought of you. Or take your striving for salvation: everybody wants it in order to go to heaven, and you want it to keep hell going. It's hardly surprising that all this has caused no little confusion in people's minds, and they curse you for an unbeliever.'

'Let them.'

'I quite agree, but occasionally it does seem to me that you ought to arrange your life differently in your old age.'

'How differently?'

'I don't really know, but the way I see it, it's like this: your wife has died, your children have left home, Mall you've sent packing, and all you've left is one little girl...'

'So what am I supposed to do?'

'There's nothing you can do, that's the whole trouble. You'll get yourself a new housekeeper, and she too might hide things under her apron, or in her pockets, you'll dismiss her and take on someone else, but how long can you go on doing it, and what will it lead to? There are just the two of you now – you and your little girl, and you'll never manage, you know. There was a time when you owned three horses, you've only one left; you had four or five milch cows once, and you've no one to milk even two cows for you now...'

'I'll milk them myself until Riia's big enough to do it.'

'Very well, you'll milk them yourself, but isn't it better to fall in with my plan?'

'First time I heard of any plan.'

'Look here, Jürka, we've been through thick and thin together, I've pulled you out of many a hole, you've worked for me, and so you need not doubt the sincerity and soundness of the advice I'm going to give you out of pure friendship. I've a neat little house with a nice barnyard on the edge of the field, and my advice to you is to move in, forget about your plot of land, put your cow and sheep in my herd, and take it easy in your old age, pottering about without stretching your ancient joints to the utmost. You've done enough clearing and draining and tilling, let the young people carry on the good work now! I'd like to have a faithful friend like you living closer to me. Well, how d'you like my plan?'

'I want to earn my salvation at the Pit.'

'But then Mall will sue you for her wages.'

'Let her.'

'Won't it be unfair to our old friendship if you pay Mall her wages and don't pay me my rent? I'll also have to sue you then, if only not to be outdone by Mall. And what will happen if I do? Where will you find the money? Your last chicken will be sold.'

'Who'll sell it?'

'You should sell it yourself, or others will.'

'What others?'

'The court.'

'What's the court got to do with it?'

'Everything. That is, if Mall sues you for her wages, and then I'm forced to sue you as well...'

Ants let the sentence trail off, and Jürka's stunned silence allowed him to assume that the battle was as good as won.

'Truth to tell, the rent you're paying now is nothing really, just pocket money,' Ants resumed confidently. 'Think of all the newly cultivated fields and meadows! It was only in the name of our friendship that I charged you such trifling rent. However, this can't go on forever, because that would be taking unfair advantage of friendship, don't you agree? There are people who'd gladly pay me double the rent for land as good as mine.'

'What people?'

'Your neighbour, for one. It's the honest truth.He has been pestering the life out of me for the Pit, but I declined his offers because you and I are old friends, so to say, and I...'

'I'm staying on at the Pit.'

'Well, you know best. What about Mall's wages and my back rent then?'

'Something will have to be done,' Jürka said.

'Oh well, let's hope it will,' Ants replied.

CHAPTER TWENTY

Something did turn up, with both Mall's wages and Ants's back rent. But not quite what Jürka meant. Actually, Jürka had not meant anything and in spite of what Ants tried to tell him he had not an inkling of what was happening in reality. Ants mentioned the court, but the only time Jürka was tried was years and years ago, and that left him quite unimpressed. Some sort of verdict was passed, he remembered vaguely, but whether it was carried out or not did not matter to him one way or another. And so if anyone wanted to take him to court again, let them. What was that to Jürka? The main thing was that one got over things better as time passed.

And so Jürka went on living at the Pit without really knowing why or what for. When his work took him away from home, he left the house in the care of his eight-year-old daughter Riia, with only her black cat for company. And when Riia went to tend the cows in the pasture, the farm was deserted except for the rooster and the two hens strolling about the yard.

And then strange things began to happen at the Pit. Once, coming home at the end of the day, Jürka discovered that someone had weeded the cabbage rows.

'Who did that?' Jürka asked Riia.

'I did, Father,' the little girl replied.

Jürka wanted to say something, but the words stuck in his throat. He was very pleased all the same that the child was growing into a helpmate. Another time he found the milk tub cleanly scrubbed. He had meant to do it himself, but did he? For the life of him he could not remember. And then he was struck by the care with which Riia's usually tousled hair was combed.

'Who did that for you?' he asked.

'I did it myself,' replied the girl. 'I found an old comb and...'

At a loss for words, Jürka merely stroked the child's head with his huge hand.

'You'll make a good mistress for the Pit,' he said.

One fine day he noticed that Riia was wearing a clean blouse. He stared in disbelief, too stunned to speak.

'Who washed your blouse for you?' he asked at last.

'I did myself,' came the usual answer. 'First I soaped it and beat it with the roller, then I dried it in the sun and put it on.'

A few days later, Jürka discovered that someone had washed his shirt. This time, he sat thinking for quite a while and did not speak.

'You've learnt to tell lies, silly child, haven't you?' he asked when Riia came and stood beside him.

'Yes, Father.'

'Who taught you?'

'The auntie next door.'

'Which auntie?'

'The one who has the baby.'

Clearly enough she meant the neighbour woman who had been going to embroider a blouse for Mall for a chunk of bacon fat and a ball of red thread.

'What did the busybody want here?' Jürka asked.

'Nothing. She came to see if I had anything to eat.'

'Hm.'

'I had a piece of bread in my pocket, and I took it out and showed her. She asked me if I had any milk to drink with it.'

'Hm.'

'I showed her the tub in the cellar.'

'Why did you tell me lies at first?'

'The auntie next door told me to.'

'What for?'

'Maybe you'd be angry at her for coming here and watching me play the mistress. She left her house on the quiet, and she came here on the quiet, and you weren't to know.'

As Jürka said nothing, Riia continued: 'Auntie left her baby

in the yard, and I played with it while she did things in the
house. And d'you know what she said to me? Little mistress,
she said, you live in a pigsty. And after that...'

She taught Riia how to dress, comb her hair, wash her hands
and face, weed the cabbage rows and give the grass to the pigs,
weed the potatoes and gather the grass for the cows, sweep the
house and the yard, and do other useful things.

Jürka listened but did not seem to take in what his daughter
was saying, and was busy collecting his thoughts. He had the
look of a hungry dog who had been given a piece of bread and
then patted on the head.

When Riia asked him if, now that he knew everything, he'd
let the auntie next door come over with the baby again, Jürka
replied:

'You've learnt to tell lies, haven't you?'

'Yes, Father. Auntie taught me well.'

'Well then, tell Auntie that I don't know anything, that you
didn't tell me a thing.'

'And if Auntie doesn't believe me?'

'It'll mean that you're not a very good liar yet.'

'Must I learn?'

'Yes, and how!'

Before Riia could learn how to be a really good liar,
something of far greater significance took place at the Pit. Jürka
was summoned to court with a subpoena. To be quite correct
there were two writs – he was sued for wages by Mall, and for
back rent by Ants. It was exactly as Ants said it was going to be.
He had a truly amazing knowledge of the ways of the world,
and was as good a prophet as any in the Bible. The only thing
that Jürka was seriously interested in was the day on which he
had to appear in court, and he made the messenger read it out
to him over and over again. Quite needlessly as it happened,
because Ants came to see him the next morning and he might
have asked him.

'I've received a court summons,' Ants told him with a
worried look.

'So have I,' Jürka replied.

'What do you think about it?'

'What's there to think?'

'Supposing you lose the case? Your livestock will be sold then.'

'I don't see why.'

'Mall, I hear, is claiming a year's wages. And I've already told you that if she sued you I'd sue you too. Where's our friendship if Mall receives her wages and I don't receive my rent? That's why I've put in my claim, you see. I've come to appeal to your conscience once more: please make it up with Mall before the trial, or else...'

'I'll never make it up with a thief,' Jürka replied.

Ants talked at great length about the forthcoming trial and the consequences, but Jürka remained adamant. As a matter of fact he was also trying to work things out in his own mind, but his reasoning stopped short at an obstacle he had not the wit to surmount: everything Ants said proved that he had better give up the Pit and move to Ants's place. Jürka wouldn't think twice about making it up with Mall if it meant keeping the Pit, but there was no sense in it now, and so he was utterly indifferent to Ants's further arguments.

Everything went the way it had to go: Mall and Ants confirmed their claims in court, and there was nothing Jürka could say in self-defence. Mall told the court that even if she had wanted to steal anything at the Pit she'd find nothing worth stealing, for even the mice and rats had all starved to death there. Jürka's poor, famished child would have been eaten alive by the bedbugs and the fleas if she, Mall, hadn't kept what scraps of food there were for the little girl, doing it in secret from the master. She had intended making him a present of her wages at first, but now that he had branded her a thief she demanded payment in full, a year in advance as agreed. Jürka's attempt to stain her good name had made Mall speak very angrily indeed.

When Jürka was called, he told the court that he couldn't understand why Mall was so angry. All he said to her at the time was that there could be no talk of wages as she'd probably stolen more than she was due. To be sure, stealing was considered not a bad thing if done in right measure and properly handled. His friend Ants would confirm this. Even robbery was all right if, for instance, one robbed the forest of mushrooms and berries, and a cow of her milk or her hide.

The wisdom of Jürka's speech was so profound, that all the judges could do was shake their heads and say:

'Old Nick will always be Old Nick.'

Mall won her case, of course, and so did Ants, and a deadline was set for payment of the former's wages and the latter's rent. The hearing went very smoothly and quickly because Jürka did not refute their claims, and when asked anything said: 'Oh well, if the court thinks so,' or his usual: 'I guess so.' He took the decision quite calmly, either agreeing with it or missing the meaning entirely.

When it was all over, Ants came to him and said:

'Mall is willing to settle for just the wages due her for the time she worked at the Pit, if you pay her the money right now.'

'I have no money,' Jürka replied.

'I'll lend it to you.'

'You are a wonderful friend to have, Ants!'

'I'll lend it to you on one condition.'

'What condition?'

'That you leave the Pit so I can let someone else have it for double the rent, and move over to my place.'

'No, Ants, I'm not moving out of the Pit.'

'There's no more to be said then.'

'I guess not.'

Jürka went home and calmly resumed his everyday work as if nothing had happened. And then, one fine day, a law enforcement officer came to the Pit to see what there was to distrain. He found no movables worth itemising in the house or the barn, and proceeded to list the livestock. There was one horse, two cows, and three sheep. He was going to put down the rooster and the two hens as well, but then decided not to, because they might take some catching when the time came.

'Aren't you coming to put down me, my child and the cat?'

Jürka asked.

The officer glared at him over the top of his glasses for a moment, and said:

'I have no time for jokes. The horse, the two cows and the three sheep must not be sold, slaughtered or mortgaged, bear that in mind.'

'But supposing the cow drowns?'

'Where and how?' asked the officer.

'How should I know? Cows do get drowned sometimes, or they get impaled on something.'

'You'll be answerable for that.'

'Not me. I never answer for my animals.'

'I'm warning you once more that the animals on the list are not to be sold or slaughtered.'

'Not to be sold or slaughtered,' repeated Jürka.

So the officer left, having tacked the notice about the forthcoming auction on a gatepost, and Jürka, watching him, asked:

'What's that?'

'A notice about the sale.'

'You can take it down, people hereabouts can't read.'

'Others will read it,' the officer said.

'What others?'

'That, I don't know.'

The officer left, and life at the Pit continued as before. Secure in his ignorance of the true state of affairs, Jürka cleared another piece of forest as he had been in the practice of doing for years. But this peaceful life soon came to and end. The officer came back, this time with Ants, the neighbour, and several total strangers. What could they want at the Pit? And then Jürka remembered the trial, the listing of his animals, the scrap of paper tacked on to the gatepost, and guessed that there was some sort of connection. And he was quite right. The auction began right there and then, and as the buyers were so few the animals were sold for next to nothing. Ants got the horse and one cow in payment of the back rent, and the neighbour bought the other cow for a price which just covered

Mall's back wages. The officer claimed that the costs could be covered only by selling the largest of the sheep. A little of what it fetched was given to Jürka, so that he, too, profited by the auction. As for the two remaining sheep, Jürka was again free to sell, slaughter or mortgage them.

'I guess so,' said Jürka, confirming the officer's words.

When the buyers began to leave with their animals, Riia ran weeping to Jürka and asked:

'Why are they taking away our animals?'

But the child waited in vain for an answer, as her father did not even hear her question. And then Riia clutched him by the sleeve, and, tugging at it with all her might, repeated her question.

'Because Mall held her hands under her apron when she went to see the neighbours,' Jürka replied at long last.

Riia gave him a wide-eyed look, and again asked:

'But where are they taking our animals?'

'How should I know.'

'When will they bring them back?'

'When we go to fetch them ourselves.'

'Will we go soon?'

'There's no hurry.'

Jürka would much rather not say anything, but the child kept asking him questions and he had to answer something. When he was silent, a mixture of thought and remembrance arose in his mind. And in this mixture he groped for an explanation of what had happened, or at least solace. But actually, matters weren't as hopeless as they looked. When he first came to the Pit he had nothing, only his old woman. He did have his old woman, however, and that was something. And the very day they arrived they got their first animal – a kitten, and it did not cost them any money, nothing but conniving at a bit of cheating. And how did they get their other animals? With Ants's help. Well, Ants was still very much alive, so there was nothing to worry about. Besides, Jürka was better off now than when he first came: he had a young pig, two sheep, two hens, a rooster, a cat, Riia, and a lot of household junk that had collected over the years. He had more hay than two sheep could eat in one winter, and so a horse and a heifer should be procured at once. If it couldn't be done, he could sell the excess of the hay, and live out the winter quite happily – the potatoes and flour he had would last him and Riia. He needed a horse, of course, to cart this and that. But he could do without, as he had done in the beginning, and fetch what firewood they needed for the house and hay for the sheep in bundles on his back.

All these rosy plans were upset by Ants, Jürka's best friend, whose good advice and aid were to help him start all over again. He brought two witnesses along the next time he came to the Pit and told Jürka in their presence that as he had no intention of renewing the yearly lease, Jürka would have to clear out come spring.

'And where will I go?' Jürka asked.

'You ought to know that,' Ants replied.

'I'm staying on at the Pit.'

'If you don't go nicely, I'll have the police evict you.'

'But you're my friend, aren't you?'

'Of course I am, but if you won't take a friend's advice...'

'What are you advising me to do?'

'To move into the cottage I told you about.'

'That's not a friend's advice.'

'It is, because only a friend...'

'I want to stay on here.'

'It won't work because you can't pay the rent.'

'I will if you help me as you did at first.'

'You were younger then, and...'

'Young or old, doesn't count.'

'What does then?'

'I'm Satan, that's what.'

'Here on earth you're a human being, that is if you want to earn salvation.'

'How can I earn it if you're going to evict me?'

'You can earn it elsewhere.'

'No, it's only here at the Pit for me. It's here I tilled the land.'

'My land.'

223

'The forest and the scrub are yours, but the fields are mine,
I tilled them with my own hands.'

'Listen, Jürka, my good old friend, I have a new tenant in my
sights who's willing to pay me double the rent I charge you. If
I let you stay on here, I'll lose money, see?'

'Will the new tenant clear more forest?'

'There's no need to clear more. The forest will stay as it is.'

'You mean someone else will be living on land tilled by me?'

'That's right.'

'Listen, Ants, you are my enemy.'

'Friend or enemy – what's the difference, the main thing is
to do a profitable deal.'

'People like you should be killed.'

'It wouldn't do you any good, my dear Old Nick,' Ants said
with a chuckle. 'There'll be others left, and you won't find them
any better, they also...'

'...bleed those who do the work,' Jürka finished for him.

'And eat the better food,' Ants said. 'Look here, Jürka, you
did the work of ten men all these years, and now that I'm
offering you a softer life...'

'I don't believe you, Ants.'

'Why should I lie to you.'

'You're after the land which I cleared and tilled with my own
hands.'

'I'll disposses you of it whatever you do, and lease it to
another tenant.'

'Who is this other tenant?' Jürka wanted to know.

'This man here,' Ants replied, indicating the neighbour who
had come as one of his witnesses. 'He'll pay me double the
rent. Is that right, Peeter?'

'Yes, I'll pay double.'

'And that other fellow, what is he after?' Jürka asked.

'He is a witness, he'll confirm what was said here.'

'You're wanting to evict me too?' Jürka asked.

'You'll have to move out, whether you like it or not,' Ants
said.'I've had enough of Satan, I want to have a man who'll go
to heaven with me when the time comes.'

'Hell is where all of you will be going,' Jürka said with complete confidence.

'Once we get rid of Old Nick here we'll be sure of going to heaven,' Ants said.

'And you, Peeter, do you think that you'll go to heaven too? Even though you're robbing me of the land I'd watered with my own sweat?'

'If I don't, someone else will. It's good deal,' Peeter replied.

'And many would gladly make that deal,' Ants said.

'Don't you want to be friends with me any more?' Jürka asked.

'It doesn't pay any more,' Ants said chuckling, and the two men with him roared with laughter.

'Very well,' Jürka said, and rose to his feet. He did not look in the least put out, and continued in the same calm tone: 'I know where we stand now: I am Satan, and you are humans. I want to save my soul, and you want to go to hell. That's why you rob me. Ants talks about friendship, but he is an enemy.'

CHAPTER TWENTY-ONE

With big strides Jürka walked back to house. The three men watched him, wondering what he was about. Jürka tore a handful of dry straw from the eaves of the roof and bent it in two. Now he was groping in his pockets for something.

'He wants to set fire to the house,' the two witnesses whispered to Ants.

'He won't do it,' Ants said through his teeth in which he clenched his pipe, thrusting his chin out.

Jürka found his tinder, steel and flint, and calmly proceeded to strike fire from it.

'I swear he's going to set fire to the roof,' Peeter said.

'He won't,' Ants said, his chin still stubbornly thrust out.

In the meantime Jürka had lit his tinder and thrust it into the bunch of straw he was holding, waving it to fan the spark into flame. Smoke trailed from it. All at once the whole bunch caught on fire and in the same moment Jürka thrust it under the eaves. The two witnesses rushed at him to stop him, but it was too late.

Ants, of course, had immediately guessed what Jürka meant to do and his confidence that he wouldn't go through with it was merely put on for the benefit of the witnesses. It suited him to have these buildings perish in a fire. They were insured for a good sum, and Ants would be spared any haggling with Peeter when sealing the deal. The impulse to stop Jürka at the last moment which both witnesses obeyed was born partly of man's instinctive fear of fire and partly of a desire, intuitive but very sound, to have something heroic to brag about afterwards. And Ants was mentally patting himself on the back: he had acted his part so well, that the Lord God Himself could find no fault with him on the Day of Judgment.

Could the men have averted disaster had they been quicker? That was another matter again. Could the buildings have been saved? The men's delayed intervention whetted rather than subdued Jürka's madness. He grabbed Ants by the scruff of his neck and would have finished him off there and then if the two witnesses had not come running to the rescue. Thereupon, Jürka picked him up as easily as if he were a length of oakum, and threw him over the fence on to a heap of stones that just happened to be there. Flying head first, Ants cracked his skull and passed out. Peeter – the braver of the two witnesses – took one punch from Jürka, and came to in the nettles growing along the fence. The other witness came nowhere near Jürka, leaving him free to set fire to the barn and the cow-shed. This done, Jürka strode off towards his neighbour's place. Peeter sprang to life and scuttled across the field to reach home first in case Jürka tried to set fire to it as well. Once there, Peeter armed himself with an axe for self-defence, and lay in wait for him behind the corner of the house. And what he feared did happen, for there was Jürka coming in through the gate. Peeter jumped out of hiding and raised his axe.

'I'll kill you if you come any nearer!' he yelled in a terrible rage.

But before Peeter could swing his axe, Jürka tore a hefty pole out of the fence and held it at the ready, forcing Peeter to retreat, and escape into the house.

'Damn me for not having a gun,' he cursed. 'He'll destroy everything there is!'

'Who will?' asked Peeter's wife, who sat serenely nursing her baby. She didn't see Peeter pick up the axe, as this happened outside in the yard where the firewood was stacked, and so had no idea that something was afoot.

'Old Nick. Who else?'

'What's he going to destroy?' his wife asked, still completely at sea.

'His home and ours.'

'Rubbish!' his wife said, and went out into the yard carrying

227

the now sleeping baby. She let out a scream when she saw the fire raging over the Pit. And Jürka himself stood in the middle of their yard holding a bunch of straw under his arm and striking fire from a piece of flint. She went to him with the sleeping baby, and said:

'Good heavens above, Jürka, your farm's on fire, and where's the child?'

'What child?' Jürka asked, and looked at the woman, her uncovered breast, and the sleeping baby nestling against it.

'*Your* child. Riia!'

'Huh?'

'Oh Lord, Jürka, where is she?' she asked, fearfully.

'With the sheep.'

'And where are the sheep?'

'In the field.'

'Thank God!'

In the meantime, the tinder in Jürka's hands had begun to burn. Seemingly lost in thought, he glanced at it, then looked at the woman and her baby, gave the tinder another look, dropped it on the ground and stamped out the fire. He swung round and quickly walked away, with the bunch of straw still under his arm. The woman watched him go, thinking he'd turn homewards, but instead he went hurriedly down the road in the direction of the village.

'He's gone mad,' Peeter said, running to his wife.

'What did you do to him?'

'Nothing much: Ants refused to renew his lease and told him to clear out of the Pit.'

'No wonder he went off his head.'

'What kind of tenant can he make? He'll never pay the rent.'

'And you can pay it, I suppose?'

'It wasn't my idea, it was Ants who asked me to come with him...'

'And where is Ants now?'

'He's lying on a pile of stones with a smashed head.'

'I see. His skull had to split in two to make him listen to reason, and I'm sure surprised that yours is all in one piece.'

'I am, too,' Peeter agreed. 'He's as strong as the Devil himself!'

'That's the whole trouble. He has the strength of a bear, and the mind of a child.'

'You think so?'

'Why is he so keen on salvation then? He does want it, terribly.'

Peeter would have gladly stayed chatting with his wife about Jürka, but cries for help were coming from the Pit and he ran there at once. Viiu went indoors to put the sleeping baby in its cradle.

The fire was out of control now, and was avidly devouring everything within reach. Even the barn Jürka had built in place of the one he had burnt down, had caught fire, for all that it stood at a good distance from the house, and, the wind was blowing away from it. The other witness had not deserted Ants and had heroically carried him to a safer spot. If he hadn't, Ants's goose would have been cooked. What were they to do with him now, that was the question? Peeter wanted to go home and harness his horse into the cart, but the other chap was afraid that the jolting would mean certain death to the wounded man. And so, the two of them carried Ants to Peeter's house. Viiu helped them to fix a stretcher of sorts out of her striped blanket and two poles on which the men laid Ants, putting a pillow under his head, and carried him to his own house to have his head attended to as quickly as possible.

All this took no little time, and meanwhile the buildings, fences and gates at the Pit burnt on, undisturbed. Viiu meant to go and look while the baby slept, but by now it was awake and crying. Changing and bundling it up took more time, and when at last she started on her way, carrying the bundle, she saw the fire subside, the roof fall in and the walls collapse.

She did not go straight across to the fire, but turned down the edge of the field to where Riia had to be tending the sheep. Viiu wanted to find her and take her home, because there was no knowing when Jürka would return. The sheep were there, but the girl was not, and she did not respond to the woman's hallooing.

Viiu's heart sank with a premonition of disaster. Was Jürka lying when he told her that Riia had gone with the sheep? Losing all hope, the woman returned to the fire with a heavy heart. She stood there for a while, and then sat down on a stone that lay clear of the fire, to suckle the baby. And suddenly Riia with the cat in her arms was there before her! She had come from the windward side where the smoke hung in a dense cloud, and where sparks were flying.

'Bless me, if it isn't Riia!' the woman cried as though she were seeing a ghost. 'Where did you come from? Straight from the fire? You might have burnt to death!'

'There's no fire there, only thick smoke high overhead,' Riia told her.

'And what about the sparks?'

'They flew together with the smoke, like the stars in the sky when it's dark, only the sparks did fly, and stars can't. The sun was so very yellow, as if it were setting in the middle of the sky.'

'How did you get into the smoke?'

'Oh, I stayed there for a long time. Once I thought I heard someone calling me, but the fire cracked so noisily that I couldn't make out the words. And when the smoke began to thin out it grew too hot, and so I came out because the cat got jittery.'

'Seems the cat's got more sense than you.'

'I wanted to have a look at the smoke, that's why I went there, I've never seen so much smoke and fire. The moment I saw it from the field, I ran here, but there was no one about, and so I walked right into the smoke – it was like a black roof over my head.'

While Peeter's wife sat chatting with Riia and nursing her baby, Peeter and the second witness hurried to the village with Ants lying unconscious on the stretcher. They had still quite a way to go to Ants's house when they saw black smoke pouring from it.

'Jürka's doing, d'you think?' Peeter asked.

'I wouldn't put it past him,' the other witness replied, and quickened his step.

By the time they reached Ants's residence it was engulfed in roaring flames. They looked about them forlornly, not knowing where to lay down their burden, and found no better place for the wounded master than the small house on the edge of the field where Ants wanted to resettle Jürka if he moved out of the Pit of his own free will. And that's where they carried Ants, seeing that the wind blew the other way and so the house was safe.

All hell had broken loose on Ants's estate. Jürka had acted as he had done at home: striking fire from the flint, he lit the tinder, then the bunch of straw he brought from his neighbour's yard, and thrust it into the first straw roof he came to, before people could collect their wits and stop him. Perhaps if Ants were watching he'd again say, 'Let him,' as in the case of the Pit, because his property was insured against fire and he had long felt the need for more comfortable and modern buildings. As fire insurance was a social business and Ants was a social creature to the core, he'd naturally build new premises for himself with the insurance money. A madman had started the fire, which was as much as to say that it was the Almighty Himself starting it with his lightning. Madman or lightning – both were the servants of God. And society had no nobler task than contending with these acts of God, even in those cases where these same acts of God promised good fortune for some.

With Ants lying unconscious in the little house, there was no one to ponder deeply on these social questions, and after Jürka set fire to the first house Ants's people attacked him en masse. But it was a losing battle, for even the strongest of them could not stand up to the hammer-blows of Jürka's fists, and collapsed on the ground. Two huge watchdogs were then set on Jürka, but one of them he killed right away with a stake, and the other barely escaped on the three legs it had left. Meanwhile, the fire had crept up to the cow shed, and the ferocious pedigree bull kept there had to be led out. Instead of driving the animal out into the field, and the farther the better, it was let loose on Jürka, in the hope that the roaring bull would make short work of this fiend whom neither men nor dogs could overpower. Alas, the bull was no match for Jürka, who found him an even simpler and easier job than the men and the dogs. No sooner did the bull go into attack with his

231

horns, than Jürka grabbed hold of them and the next moment the enormous bull was lying helpless on his back. That put the lid on any further effort to control Jürka's madness. Among the crowd collected by the fire there were people who sympathised with Jürka in their heart of hearts. Ants's watchdogs had bitten quite a few of them with impunity, and now, thank God, the curs got what was coming to them. People had gone in fear of the ferocious bull as, roaring and snorting, he pawed the ground, and here in the sight of women and children he had been thrown on his back, and lay like a lamb taken to slaughter or to be sheared. And so while some people yelled: 'Fetch your guns, shoot Jürka!' others shouted back: 'Why kill him when everything's burning anyway?'

It was, indeed. The fire had started on the windward side, and soon all the buildings were aflame. The onlookers, however, seemed not to notice it at first, fascinated as they were by the more exciting spectacle of Jürka scattering his assailants, killing one watchdog and crippling another, and throwing the pedigree bull which now lay at his feet, helplessly kicking his legs in the air, as if he were Jürka's horse whom he'd allowed to roll itself about after a hard ride. The women found the spectacle especially thrilling. Oh, how some of them longed to clutch Jürka with their arms – sunburnt or milky-white as the case may be – to see if he would get the better of them as easily as he had overcome the big strong men, the savage dogs and the ferocious bull. If none of the women assaulted Jürka it was certainly not because their willing flesh was weak, but simply because they had neither the time nor the opportunity. Having defeated all his opponents, Jürka cleaved through the crowd as though there was nobody there, and made for Ants's residence with the intention of setting fire to it as well. When he saw that it was already aflame and that people were trying to rescue their belongings, he instantly scattered the crowd and started tearing, breaking, shattering and smashing everything before him, as though he did not trust the fire to manage the destruction of Ants's property without his help.

The fire raged and roared. And in this fiery whirl Jürka went more and more berserk, and more and more people came running to the fire. The fire-brigade and the police arrived. A moment earlier someone had the bright idea of fetching Jürka's son Kusta, who might curb his father's fury, and so Kusta and the firemen dashed into the house together. Jürka threw out the firemen bodily and would have done the same with his son, had Kusta not screamed in desperation:

'Father, Father! Stop it, they've had enough. Father, it's I who drowned young Ants!'

'Huh,' Jürka growled.

'Please believe me, Father. I drowned him with my own hands, we're quits now. I told Mother, too, just before she died, so she'd tell this to God and to Maia up in heaven!'

Standing in a ring of fire, father and son took no notice of what was going on around them. Several firemen and policemen stole up closer and, on hearing Kusta's confession, pounced on the two of them. They seized hold of Kusta and dragged him out of the burning house, but their strength was no match for Jürka's. He hurled one of his attackers into the window, and the man flew out into the yard together with the window-frame and the smashed panes. When his second assailant drew a gun from his pocket, Jürka knocked him out with a stunning blow. The third fired several shots at Jürka and jumped out into the yard. Two more men – a policemen and civilian, gripped by the frenzy of battle – opened fire on Jürka through the window from the path.

God alone knows how this would have ended had not the fire spread over the entire building. By then many had procured guns, black and glistening, to shoot down Jürka, who could not be subdued by physical strength. There were not a few people there who were sorry the police had not arrived earlier, because then they would have seen for themselves if Jürka was really Satan or just an ordinary mortal who fancied himself a messenger from Hades. If he were Satan, he could only be killed with a silver bullet, and one that had a cross carved on the tip.

There were others who believed that a nickel bullet would do just as well as a silver one, and so a great argument ensued, which threatened to develop into a free-for-all or a skirmish, but in the nick of time somebody noticed that one of the policemen was missing. No one knew what had happened to him, and it was not until all the witnesses had been questioned at great length that it was ascertained that he had dashed into the house with the others to seize Jürka and Kusta. Orders were given to break into the house once more at all costs, as the policeman must be still there. And it was at that very moment that the missing policeman came flying through the smashed window.

'He's still alive!' one of the onlookers shouted, meaning Jürka.

'He lives in the fire!' screamed a second onlooker.

'He's really Satan!' shrieked a third one.

This shriek struck fear in the onlookers' hearts. 'Good Lord, he's really Satan!' And their souls quaked. Panic first gripped the middle-aged childless women, and then those who had nursed their babies at their breast; from the old women the fear spread to the old men, from them to the young women and young men, and finally to the children, whose hearts trembled with fear because they saw the trepidation of the grown-ups. For a moment everyone was petrified, and then an order was given and sprays of water were sent into the broken window through which the stunned policeman had come flying. Besides the fire-hoses, water was dashed at the window from bathtubs, pails, pitchers, beer mugs, soup bowls and tea-cups. Everyone did his bit so that the Lord might see from His heavenly kingdom how well men loved their neighbour, how charitable they were – old and young, men and women alike, and how earnestly they tried to rescue someone from the flames, even if it was Satan himself.

Alas, they did not succeed. The fire proved more powerful than the water dashed on it by people. Rafters and walls were collapsing, and the burning wreckage piled into precarious heaps. Still, people went on throwing water on these heaps as though their perseverance were a guarantee of salvation. Children who either helped to put out the fire or simply watched it, could not understand why the water failed to quench it and, if anything, seemed to add fuel to the flames.

'Could God put out a fire like this?' a little girl asked her mother.

'Keep quiet,' the mother hissed at her. 'Someone might hear

you, you little fool...'

'Why d'you call me a fool, I only asked if...'

'One fool can ask so many questions that nine sages will be stumped for answers, that's why!'

An older boy took the little girl aside and told her:

'Don't ask your mother things like that, it's silly.'

'But why?'

'Because your mother is afraid of God.'

'Why be afraid of God? It's not God who started this fire.'

'Who did?'

'Jürka did. Jürka from the Pit.'

'And who sent Jürka here?'

'He came himself, he's Satan.'

'Do you believe that Satan could come down to earth if God didn't let him?'

'Why not?'

'Look, this fire wouldn't have started without God's permission either.'

'But why did He permit it?'

'Because... Because He permits everything.'

'What everything?'

'Well, He permitted Jürka to kill that savage dog and throw the pedigree bull on its back...'

'Is it true about the bull?'

'And how! I saw it myself. That bull could have easily gored Jürka like he did that shepherd, but he didn't because Jürka grabbed him by the horns and threw him.'

Thus the question was solved as to whether the Lord could have put out the fire or not. Now, we can proceed to the next point, and see how people put out the fire that the Lord Himself was powerless to extinguish.

CHAPTER TWENTY-TWO

When at long last the fire was put out, Jürka's dead body was found under the wreckage and debris. The body was not charred at all and only slightly scorched and so wet that he may have died from choking on the water the place was flooded with. As Jürka himself believed he was Satan, and this belief was shared by many, the question now arose: what had killed him – fire, water, or bullets? The first cause seemed the least plausible, for what harm could fire do to Satan? Wasn't the fire of hell as hot as the fire that had devoured the house of a man as righteous as Ants? As no one had yet returned to earth after going to hell, the question remained unanswered. For the same reason no one knew if there was any water in hell and if Satan was drownable or not.

To ascertain the cause of death, an autopsy was made on Jürka's scorched body, and the results came as a most disappointing anticlimax. The doctor who did the post-mortem stated that the cause of death was a blow on the head! There were several bullet wounds on the body, but none of them were lethal. The obvious conclusion was that only a silver bullet could have killed Jürka, but no one had any to fire at him. The blow on the head was so strong that Jürka lost consciousness and was smothered by the smoke.

The question arose: how was this blow dealt, and by whom? Was it by the policeman whom Jürka hurled through the window of the burning house? And, in point of fact, was it Jürka who threw him out? Why would Satan want to save the life of a Christian, and a policeman to boot, by throwing him out of a burning house?

There were people who believed in speaking only well of their countrymen, and tended to hero-worship anyone who represented the authorities. They claimed that what had happened to the policeman was not chance but a consequence of his decisive actions. As to how Jürka was dealt that stunning blow, they saw only one possible explanation, which was quite natural and likely: it was dealt by the policeman. Recovering from the knockout, the policeman sprang to his feet. When Jürka attacked him again, he caught hold of the chandelier hanging from the ceiling, took a swing on it with his legs drawn up, and then, gathering momentum, went straight for Jürka, making him stagger back and hit his head on some hard object. On the return swing, the policeman let go of the chandelier and shot through the window. This proved that the policeman's flight through the window and his survival were his own doing, and not Jürka's, as some presumed.

However, other, equally acceptable explanations were offered. What if Jürka had been stunned by something crashing down on his head and not by a blow dealt by another person? Very well, but what could that something be? Say the chandelier that the policeman was clutching. Perhaps, but the order in which things happened was too difficult to establish. If Jürka was already down, the falling chandelier could not have knocked him off his feet. But if he wasn't, he might have well fallen down from the blow and lost consciousness. The condition that naturally suggested itself was that the fire engulfed him after he had lost consciousness, which circumstance allowed it to be assumed that Jürka was really Satan.

The condition of the policeman, who had been thrown or had come flying out of the window, was also most suggestive. When first aid had been administered and he opened his eyes, everyone naturally expected him to describe what really happened. But it turned out that the man had lost the power of speech. He was given a pencil and a piece of paper, but all he could produce was an illegible scrawl. One thing was obvious: the experience he'd had in the burning house was so fantastical that it could only be connected with Jürka. Everything about him was not ordinary, as

237

though he wasn't a mortal like everyone else. This was, in fact, confirmed by the doctor who did the autopsy on him, declaring afterwards that he never cut up anything like that before. Everyone guessed that there was something behind these unusual words. He didn't say 'such a body', 'such a man', what he said was 'anything like that', which, coupled with such an unmedical expression as 'cut up', froze the blood of those who knew how to read mysterious meaning into words. The implication was more than clear to them: human beings did not have such bodies.

The singularity of the case was confirmed by yet another circumstance. When the doctor was examining the wound on Jürka's head he discovered two little knobs like twin horns in his thick hair. This discovery aroused fresh interest in the research made into these same knobs some years ago, which had proved that they were of a traumatic origin. However, no one was impressed by that old diagnosis now. People were convinced that Jürka was Satan. And this was explanation enough for his physical strength and bulk. Since the beginning of time God had set down the measurements for Satan sent down to earth in the shape of man: he had to be not taller than a stack of five cartloads of hay and not smaller than an ordinary bedbug. As far as people could remember, Jürka had kept true to the prescribed pattern. However, they refused to believe that when he lived among them he was as huge as the scorched bulk now resting upon the ground. The question that remained unanswerable was: could he make himself small? And if so, to what extent? One thing was certain: the night he died many saw a strange, tiny animal, a black thing with a long tail. And none of them doubted for a moment that this was the dead Jürka and not an animal at all.

When the time came to bury him it was discovered that there was nothing to dress the body in. The rags he had been worn had been destroyed in the fire And nothing at all was found at the Pit, save a small pile of cinders.

'A real man can't be that destitute!' the community gasped in a body. 'A real man would steal a pair of pants, if he was too lazy to earn the price!'

In the end two young sheep, a young hog, two hens, a rooster, a cat and a child were what remained from Jürka. The sheep, hog, hens and rooster had to be sold to cover the funeral expenses. The child and the cat would have been sold as well, but there were no buyers: the cat was filthy, and the child turned out to be a girl, so what use was she? No one wanted them even for free, and so they remained where they were, in the home of Peeter and his wife, Jürka's neighbours.

A box, knocked together from unplaned boards, served Jürka for a coffin. He was placed in this coffin in the tatters he had on. Peeter's wife brought a length of unbleached linen for a shroud, but people thought linen was too good for Satan and replaced the new cloth with his rags. And so it was in rags that Jürka was to be buried.

And now there remained two essential problems to solve: where should Jürka be buried, and who would undertake the funeral arrangements?

At first, the overriding opinion was that he must on no account be buried in consecrated ground, that is, in the graveyard, but on the other side of the wall. There were also some who argued: why bother to take the body to the graveyard at all? A simpler and surer way was to dig a hole right here on Ants's land, and dump Jürka into it.

But here the womenfolk stood up for Jürka. There was no reason to treat him like an animal, they said, only because he was stronger than the men who were denying him a proper burial. And even if Jürka were Satan, he came down to earth on God's orders, and his going to church like everybody else proved it. He lived like a Christian, and so he should be buried in the graveyard and not on the other side of the wall. If the pastor was going to make difficulties...

But the pastor was not going to make difficulties, for Jürka was not a suicide, he was a victim of the fire.

'Does not the Reverend remember how strongly Jürka was against going to heaven?' asked the church warden. 'Surely he can't be buried in consecrated ground?'

'Jürka always said he wanted to earn salvation, and that's good enough,' replied the pastor.

239

'Yes, but he strove for salvation so as to be able to keep hell going!' protested the church warden.

'Ah, beloved soul, it was God's will to create hell, wasn't it?'

'Still, supposing Jürka was really Satan as he himself believed, and as many indications suggest? What then?'

'All I can say to this, beloved soul, is do not oppose Providence. If the Lord thought it necessary to send the devil down to earth in the shape of man, as once he sent His son, it is not for us, mortals, to judge His action. What we must do is examine ourselves to the innermost depths of our souls to make certain that we did not treat the devil in the flesh as unwisely as people once treated the Son of God. I had better put it like this: Jürka believed that he was Satan, and his faith was so strong that neither I nor anyone else could shake it. Do we not discern in this an inscrutable act of Providence? God willed superstition to prove stronger than true faith. We would move mountains if our faith were as unshakable as Jürka's superstition. And therefore, beloved soul, it is from Jürka, from this new Satan, that all of us should learn how to believe blindly, without questioning or doubting, like children. Although Jürka was possessed by superstitions, he was indeed a child professing our faith.'

The pastor wiped his eyes, for he was moved to tears by his own eloquence. As a matter of fact, he very often was. The churchwarden pulled a big, red handkerchief from his pocket and also mopped at his eyes, though actually he was completely dry-eyed, having understood little of what the old pastor said and even less of the emotion behind his tears. One thing was clear to him: Jürka would have to be buried in consecrated ground, against his better judgment. The churchwarden knew that the decision would be lauded mainly by the womenfolk who had seen Jürka overpowering that ferocious bull, and in his attitude to women this pious man was of a like mind with the Saviour who once said: 'Woman, what have I to do with Thee?' And, likewise, the churchwarden did not want to have anything to do with women in questions of religion. The pastor, unfortunately, did not see eye to eye with him.

And so the question of where to bury Jürka was settled. It was much harder to find someone who'd take the funeral arrangements upon himself, for there was no one capable of acting firmly and resolutely enough. Ants himself would have been the obvious choice, but his mind still hovered midway between heaven and earth. He did have his lucid moments, it is true, but even then he would not answer questions and merely kept muttering: 'Let it burn, let it burn, the money's rolling in!' What some people read into this muttering was this: Jürka had set fire to Ants's buildings not in a fit of raving madness, but by pre-arrangement, and none could know just what Ants had promised to pay Jürka for the arson. The more sensible said that Ants would not have stuck to his part of the bargain anyway, seeing how he had cheated Jürka all these years. If it was arson, then Ants alone knew it, and Jürka was simply his blind tool. Fate, however, decided the issue in its unpredictable way: the aim was achieved, but the man who achieved it perished, because no one had any hope left that Ants would pull through.

Were Kusta, Jürka's son, free, there'd be no problem about the funeral arrangements. But Kusta was under arrest, because the firemen and policemen heard him telling his raving father that it was he who had drowned young Ants. When Kusta was confronted with this statement, he said that it was a white lie, made up on the spur of the moment, to calm down his father. Kusta had heard from his mother that his father held young Ants responsible for the death of his daughter Maia, and threatened to break the necks of young Ants and old Ants if his suspicions were confirmed. It was Maia's death, Kusta thought, that was at the bottom of his father's fit of blind fury. That's why, when physical strength failed to subdue his father, he resorted to this ruse and told him that it was he who had drowned young Ants. These words had such a soothing effect on Jürka, that Kusta might have easily led him out of the burning house if the policemen and firemen had not meddled. Their interference ruined everything, otherwise they'd be hearing the whole story from Jürka himself now.

Although Kusta's explanation sounded plausible enough, he was not released, and Jürka had to be laid to rest by strangers.

241

None of the people who thought themselves better than others wanted to become involved, and finally a mason, a navvy, a peat worker, and a sewage swabber agreed to bury Jürka, and only then on condition that each would be given a bottle of homebrew before the funeral. No less than four men were needed, because Jürka was to be buried in the graveyard and the coffin had to be smoothly lowered on ropes into the grave and set down properly, not lying on its side, making it difficult for him to rise on the Day of Judgment. Now, if Jürka were to be buried beyond the graveyard wall there'd be no problem because resurrection was out of the question for anyone there, and just two men could have managed well enough.

As a one-horse cart wasn't roomy enough for the coffin and the four men, which meant that they'd have to set off in turns and walk, a two-horse cart was provided and thickly bedded with straw to make it easier on both the living and the dead. For safety's sake, the horses chosen for the occasion were two old, emaciated jades, lop-eared and downcast. Their backs under the saddle-cloth were covered with a scab; their necks were raw and bleeding under the collars; and their legs were crooked and swollen.

Everything was now ready for the journey. The coffin was hoisted on to the cart, two men sat on the lid, one squatted in the straw in front, and the fourth one picked up the reins. At that moment Viiu, Peeter's wife, came running with Riia, whom she had wrapped up in her old shawl lest she should catch a chill.

'Won't you please take this little ragamuffin along?' Viiu addressed all four of them at once. 'At least one of the family should attend the funeral.'

'You can't tell if it's a boy or a girl,' said the peat-cutter, who sat on the coffin lid with the navvy.

'Who'd ever wrap a boy in a shawl?' said the navvy, and spat with feeling on the ground.

'It it were a boy, then never mind, but seeing it's a girl...' argued the mason who held the reins.

'What's wrong with her being a girl? Can't a girl go to her father's funeral?' Viiu protested.

'If you come too, it'll be another matter,' said the peat-cutter.
'I can't, the baby will cry for me at home,' Viiu said.

The men couldn't decide what to do. At last the sewage swabber who sat in front on the straw turned round to see who was being foisted on them, and after a long look at Riia asked:

'What's that you got under the shawl?'

'Look,' Riia cried, letting the black cat with the yellow eyes poke out its head.

The cat decided the issue. The sewage swabber was fond of animals, and this was probably his only real love.

'Come here and sit at my feet in the straw, it's softer here,' he told Riia, and Viiu quickly helped her up.

And now they could start on their journey. The mason tugged at the reins and swung a stick at the horses, who seemed to fear threats more than actual beatings, remembering very, very dimly that years ago people beat them and it hurt. The cart rocked, and here the sewage swabber suddenly shouted:

'Stop, dammit! Stop your pedigree stallions!'

He pulled out the bottle of homebrew from his pocket and holding it out to Viiu, said:

'Take a drink to his soul.'

'I don't drink, you see, now my old man...' Viiu demurred.

'Then you should have sent your old man here with the kid! What kind of funeral is this if we don't even drink to his soul?'

Viiu took the bottle and drank a tiny sip from it, fearing that if she didn't the men would refuse to take Riia and the cat along. Next, the man offered the bottle to Riia.

'Not to the child, you oaf!' Viiu cried indignantly.

'I won't give her much, just a gulp,' the man insisted. 'She's burying her father, after all.'

There was nothing for it, and Riia had to take a drink from the bottle. To be sure, Viiu didn't let her take more than a sip.

'Don't give the child any more on the journey, for mercy's sake,' Viiu invoked, as the cart rolled off.

'Not on your life, we'll need it ourselves,' all the four men shouted together, and as if in confirmation of their words tipped their bottles and drank with a loud gurgle. The cart clattered

243

down the road.

'What a shameful way to bury a man!' sighed a woman who happened along.

'How d'you know he was human?' a man asked her.

'Human, human,' another passer-by mimicked them. 'What things a human being can be!'

The men in the cart did not hear this senseless bickering. They were heading for the church. Once they were out on the smooth road, they took a drink now and then, each from his own bottle, and long before they reached the church they were hollering songs. Not psalms, naturally. The sewage swabber tried to quieten the men at first, because the child and the cat had fallen asleep at his feet. But, as if to spite him, the men hollered louder and louder, until at last he also started yelling with them. People hearing their bawling came out to see who the merrymakers were and what they were celebrating. The four drunks waved their arms and hats at everyone they saw and shouted in hoarse voices:

'We're on our way to bury Old Nick! We're on our way to bury Old Nick!'

The church service went off almost without a hitch, except that when the chorister began his chant, the drunks joined in so boisterously that the poor chap had quite a job hushing them. Still, the limits of the permissible were not overstepped, and the drunks were, in fact, above reproach. The sewage swabber was so moved that he picked up Riia and the cat and held them in his arms until the end of the service. True, he swayed a little and stank of homebrew, but Riia felt safe in his strong arms and enjoyed listening to what was being said and watching what was being done, holding her cat close under her shawl.

The pastor spoke in simple words, but they came from his heart.

'You were the poorest and lowest among your own kind, and yet you felt rich and great because you had firm faith. You left us as simply as you have lived, but all the brighter you will shine where you will dwell.'

These last words impressed the sewage swabber, and he said to his friends:

244

'Hear what the pastor said? He's not letting him go to heaven.'
'I guess not, all he said was 'where you will dwell'. And
where's that? As if we don't know!' said the mason.

They pulled out their bottles and in full view of the
congregation took several gulps of the homebrew for courage.
This done, the mason and the navvy sat down on the lid of the
coffin, while the peat worker and the sewage swabber decided to
walk the half-kilometre or so to the graveyard to stretch their legs
a bit. They forgot all about the girl and the cat. Riia was used to
being left behind with her cat, so she was not upset by the men's
neglect. And so they were off again, the horses pulling the cart
with the coffin and two men on it, the peat worker and the sewage
swabber walking behind it with their arms about each other –
bosom pals thanks to the funeral and the homebrew, and Riia
with the cat in her arms, bringing up the rear. She also walked in
the middle of the road, dragging her feet to raise clouds of dust
and make the trudge more fun. At first, the two bosom pals talked
about something in loud voices, but when the two sitting on the
coffin lid started a song, they couldn't help joining in, and never
mind if it wasn't the same song, not even the same song for each
pair of them. Each of the four men found the lyrics and the
melody after his own heart.

This singing, in which only Riia and the cat took no part, had
its fatal consequences. Had the drunks kept quiet or just talked,
the dogs from the roadside yards would have allowed them past
without a sound, because so many different carts clattered down
the road here all day that no self-respecting dog would bother to
bark every time or run out to see who was coming and what he
was carrying. But the moment they heard singing, all the dogs
down the street jumped out to see what was going on. Among the
curious there was one old lapdog who knew less than nothing
about the customs of the watchdogs. Through ignorance and
stupidity, she tilted her head and gave a tentative yelp, and as her
voice was too husky for a proper bark, she began to howl at the
top of her voice, as though she were stirred to her depths by the
drunken singing. The other dogs could not keep quiet either, for
such is the canine custom: if one of them starts to do something,

the rest must follow suit, no matter if the one they are copying is a downright fool. The origin of this custom still puzzles scholars, but some of them are of the opinion that dogs must have adopted it from people, their masters. It has been observed that no madman, however erratic or unbalanced, could invent an absurdity so gross that it would not be immediately picked up by people who are reputed to be intelligent and have no doubt that they really are.

But never mind the origin of the tradition for the moment. The canine chorus swelled to such a volume of sound that it drowned out the bawling of the drunks. The terrible howling both frightened and intrigued Riia's cat, and slipping out from under the shawl, it flew past the singers and the horses, and made for the nearest tree. Riia stopped kicking up the dust and, screaming, ran after the cat. As she came level with the cart, the sewage swabber grabbed her and asked what the matter was. Words stuck in her throat, and all she could utter was: 'My cat, my cat!' pointing helplessly with both arms.

'What happened?' the man asked.

'It ran away, up there!'

'Up where?'

'Up that tree.'

'Which tree?'

'That one there!'

Now that he understood what was up, he turned to the men sitting on the coffin lid and shouted:

'Hey you, drivers! Stop yelling, and hold your horses for a minute!'

He told them about the disaster that had befallen the little girl, and clambered on to the cart together with the peat worker. The sewage swabber thought that if he stood on the coffin lid he would be able to take the cat down from the tree where it had fled from the dogs. However, a drink was obviously indicated before tackling a job as novel and unexpected. This done, the men stood up, ready to step on to the coffin lid together the moment the cart came abreast of the tree under which the dogs were barking in a frenzy of excitement.

246

'Hold on to one another now, I'm going to make it hot for these nags,' the mason shouted.

'Whip them on, we can take it!' the men yelled back.

The horses started off, and the cart rolled towards the tree. Everyone was curious to see how high the cat had climbed and how it could be retrieved. They were so preoccupied that they did not notice one wheel crashing into a stone, and another one slipping into a rut. The cart lurched, and the jolt sent the men tumbling on to the road. Luckily, the Lord had endowed both horses with a quickness of wit and a mild temper, and so they came to a halt the moment they sensed disaster. Thanks to the horses the men were not too badly thrown. The first man got up with a chuckle, the second one with curses, and the third with exclamations of astonishment, wondering how this could have happened to such fine fellows who had carted more manure than they could remember in their lifetime, standing in the cart too, and never a tumble yet among them!

The fourth fine fellow – the sewage swabbler – made no attempt to get up. He remained lying in the ditch where he fell, hitting his head against a stone. The other three heaved him on to the cart, discovering in the process that the man was unconscious and there was blood on his head. Small matter, they decided. First, they'd find the cat, for no one wanted to listen to that kid crying her heart out. The cat, however, didn't seem to be in the tree. To let Riia take a good look, the men stood on the coffin lid, lifted up the girl and showed her, at close range to the branches, that the cat was really not there. The yelping dogs had also vanished without a trace. The whole thing was like a bad dream and as there was nothing more they could do about the cat, they began to bring the sewage swabber round. There was no better medicine than homebrew, of course. They pulled the man's bottle out of his pocket and poured the few drops left in it down his throat. When this didn't do the trick, they added a little from their own bottles, and at last he opened his eyes.

'Listen to this. The cat isn't in the tree, how d'you like that?' all three said together as soon as he opened his eyes.

'I know,' the man replied, as though suddenly sobering.

247

'How can you know when you were asleep, you dirty liar?'

'I saw it.'

'Saw what?'

'Didn't you see it?'

'What?'

'He raised the lid, stood up, and took the cat down from the tree.'

'Who raised the lid?'

'Old Nick, who else,' the sewage swabber replied as calm as you please to his horrified friends.

'Who're you fooling?' all three yelled, more to reassure themselves than anything else.

For answer, the sewage swabber climbed on to the coffin, put his left eye to the chink between two unplaned boards, and peered for a long time into the coffin. Lifting his head at last, he said with dignity:

'Look yourselves. There it is. Only its yellow eyes look blue in the darkness.'

Shaking in their boots, the three men leaned over the chink in the lid. The mason was the first to peer inside.

'Like sparks from flint,' he pronounced.

'Like flax in flower on black bog,' stated the peat-cutter in turn.

'Like little blue stars in a dark sky,' said the navvy.

What the sewage swabber said was true. And terror struck at the hearts of the men.

Suddenly Riia's ringing voice shattered the stunned silence. Standing on the ground and watching the grown-ups, she craned her neck to see over the side of the cart.

'I want to look too!'

The men jumped, because in the bustle they had forgotten all about the girl, and couldn't understand where the voice came from. The mason was the first to recover from the shock as he had noticed a child's head showing over the side of the cart.

'Look at the young devil!' he shouted for courage. 'Why, it's that kid, the little girl!'

'Show it to me too,' Riia responded to his shout.

248

She was lifted up, shown the chink, and told how to peep inside. Riia tried it, but did not see a thing.

'A child's eye can't make it out,' said the mason.

'She just doesn't know how to look, the silly kid,' said the navvy.

'Here, take a good, long look,' the sewage swabber instructed Riia.

She did as she was told, and then said:

'It was dark at first, then it turned blue, and sort of shone.'

'She got it,' the navvy said enigmatically to his friends, and added: 'Come on, all of you, sit down on the lid.'

They sat down on the coffin lid, and all four took their bottles out, draining the homebrew to the last drop. The sewage swabber's bottle had been emptied earlier, but still he tipped it and drew something from it, quite as though he were having that last drink together with the others. This done, they drove the horses as fast as they could go, and flew into the graveyard gates at such break-neck speed that Riia screamed with laughter, forgetting all about her cat for the moment.

'Keep sitting,' the mason said when the cart came to a stop. With the rope they had taken along to lower the coffin into the grave, he first tied up one end of the coffin and then, chasing off the men one after other, wound the rope all down its length.

'There we are! The devil himself can't do a thing to us now,' he said. His friends, grasping at last why the coffin had to be tied in such a strange fashion, unanimously applauded his cleverness.

Hoisting the bound coffin on their shoulders, they carried it to the grave. The only mourner was young Riia who started weeping again over the loss of her cat. The gatekeeper's wife thinking that the child was weeping for her father, borne to his grave by drunks, walked behind the weeping girl for a long time, herself moved to tears and crooning piteously: 'Oh, my poor little mite! Oh, my poor little chick!'

The thought uppermost in the minds of the four men as they stood before the gaping grave was how to retrieve the rope after lowering the coffin on it. But the mason found the right solution, and said:

'To hell with it. Let it perish together with Old Nick and the cat.'

'Let it,' said the navvy and the peat-cutter.

'It wouldn't be fit for good Christians to use anyway,' said the sewage swabber.

Without further ado, they lowered the coffin into the grave, and picked up the shovels to fill it in, when suddenly something struck the sewage swabber again. 'Hold it,' he said, stuck his shovel into the pile of earth, took Riia by the hand, stood her on the edge of the grave, and showed her how to take a handful of earth and throw it into the grave, repeating it three times, and saying: 'With this handful of earth I cover thee forever.' In a sing-song voice he chanted the words together with the girl.

The mason pulled off his cap.

'What're you doffing your cap for?' the peat-cutter snapped at him. 'This is no prayer.'

The mason put his cap on again, noting that the sewage swabber had kept his on while performing the rite with the child. For a while the men stood with lowered heads, as though reading 'Our Father' under their breath. Riia threw three handfuls of earth upon the coffin, chanting the prayer-like words, and then took a last look into the open grave. With a scream, she freed her arms from the shawl and stretched them out towards the gaping hole where she must have seen something out of the ordinary. The men flinched from the child's scream. The sewage swabber, standing on the edge of the grave with Riia, couldn't help looking down at the coffin. He sprang back, as though stung by a viper: on the coffin lid sat a small black animal with a long tail. A pair of sky-blue eyes glittered in the animal's small, round head, and they stared up unblinkingly at the sewage swabber. Speechless from fright, he pulled away the screaming child, grabbed a shovel and started filling in the hole. The other three followed suit. But as the first clods of earth hit the coffin lid, the black animal with the sky-blue eyes and the long upraised tail, jumped out, scurried for a moment between the graves, and vanished like a ghost, leaving but a faint trail of blue smoke which disappeared as quickly as it arose.

Riia was still screaming in a shrill voice, now stretching her arms out to the grave, now after the little beast with the sky-blue eyes who had vanished into thin air. The sewage swabber, who had got his tongue back, thought that Riia was crying for that little beast, and said: 'Did you see that?'

The others did not hear him, or else they had been struck dumb, and none of them uttered a word in response. They shovelled the earth furiously, never pausing until they had the grave filled in and a small mound built over it. When they were ready to go, they couldn't find Riia, there was no sound or sight of the child. They went to the cart, thinking that she had run there ahead of them, but she wasn't there either. The men stared in dismay at one another, and a terrible fear gripped their hearts. They were all gripped by a single wish: to get out as fast as possible. Getting in each other's way in their haste, they untethered the horses and clambered on to the cart. And at that precise moment the gatekeeper's wife came up to them and asked:

'Where's the little girl?'

All four pretended not to hear, and the woman asked again:

'You had a little girl with you, where is she?'

'She went after the little animal,' replied the sewage swabber, whose head was bound up.

'What little animal?' asked the puzzled woman.

'The one with the blue eyes,' the sewage swabber clarified.

'Listen, you, something's not quite right here. What have you done with the girl?' the woman persisted, feeling her blood run cold.

'I told you, she went after that animal,' the sewage swabber repeated.

'That's right, that's all we know,' the mason supported him.

'Have you all gone out of your minds?' the woman shouted. 'If you don't tell me this minute what you've done with the child I'll notify the police!'

But the men had already started off, whipping the horses for all they were worth. The clattering cart cleared the gates, and went jolting away down the road. The woman watched it out of sight with wide open eyes, and then made her timorous way to the fresh grave. She was afraid that if she saw something horrible she'd get a boil from fright, or some kind of inflammation. She'd been warned against this by the Gipsy who read her hand, and also by her second cousin who was good at fortune-telling from cards.

But she found nothing frightening beside the fresh grave. Taking the short cut back, she walked between the graves, trying to puzzle out the disappearance of the girl. And suddenly she stopped short and whispered in amazement: 'Why, there she is!'

Riia was sleeping sweetly under a lilac bush, with her head pillowed on a grassy grave mound. For a minute, the woman gazed upon her with a smile. She remembered how piteously the child had wept as she followed the coffin, and how she herself had been moved to tears, and she repeated the words she had said then, only more tenderly still, more lovingly:

'Oh, my poor little mite! Oh, my poor little chick!'

And, carefully picking up the sleeping girl in her arms, she carried her home.

This was not the first time that he came knocking on the gates of heaven to find out whether he had earned salvation while living on earth in the shape of a man or not. He knocked for a long time, and at last the Apostle Peter opened the gate.

'A hundred years have passed, and here I am back again,' Satan told Peter.

'So soon?' he exclaimed.

'Time drags terribly when you're waiting.'

'The Lord's long-sufferance is great indeed.'

'You mean, nothing has been decided yet?'

'Not yet.'

'Couldn't you sort of get a move on?'

'Alas, that is possible only on earth where relationships and connections are taken into consideration.'

'But this might drag on till doomsday, you know,' Satan said hopelessly.

'It can't be helped. At the moment, additional data are being collected on your earthly life.'

'And in the meantime, what's going to happen to hell?'

'That's your headache, you know. Couldn't you think of something new?'

'My boys are so bored that they've taken to experimenting. The latest hellish punishment they've devised is to make fine ladies launder their children's clothes with their own hands. For another thing, they have the paint peeled off their faces and all their wrinkles stand out for all to see. My old woman says that after this their soul looks like the milt of a sprat, and their flesh like shrivelled beet greens. We have mirrors all over the place, they can look at themselves all they want for free.'

'And what do they do to the men?'

'The way we treat them is like this: if they're going some place for pleasure they must foot it, if it's on business – they may ride. As a result, the cost of paving the roads in hell has been reduced by seventy-five per cent. We also test the effects of a certain procedure on boxers, weight-lifters and suchlike: they sit and learn to pick up the runs on women's stockings. We haven't found out yet which factories put out the rottenest stockings so we could use them in our experiments, but in any case we're making headway. One of the targets in our plan is to make it so that motors would operate men, and not the other way about. In this way we hope to relieve the crematoria of their overload, and reduce the price of burial plots, because the way things are now we've nowhere to put the poor. We're also thinking of...'

'Well, you see, my dear Satan, something new can be created from old junk too, if it's properly handled,' Peter interrupted.

'But without an inflow of new souls, my boys will soon rebel. I'm warning you once again: if hell falls apart, paradise will soon be finished too, because fear has a stronger hold on man than promise of bliss.'

'Such is also my opinion and, therefore, I think we should stick together and continue hand in glove.'

'The heavenly policy will have to be reconsidered then. Actually, it won't be difficult to do. You can see what's going on down on earth, can't you? Faith, which is supposed to lead people to salvation, wears out the poor and the weak, while the rich and the strong prosper with its help.'

'My dear Satan, it may be that God has willed it so in His wisdom. And surely we must not condemn anyone for living as God willed him to live? You must also remember this: Judge not, that you be not judged!'

'But you're judging me all right, and it's been going on for hundreds of years!'

'You're Satan, that's why.'

'On earth, I was a human being.'

'That is precisely why it's so difficult to decide one way or another about the salvation of your soul.'

Satan turned to go, but before he left he took another look at his old friend Peter and said in a sad, sad voice:

'My life on earth got me nowhere, I guess.'

'You still have hope left.'

'What hope?'

'That you'll eventually earn salvation and thus be able to keep hell going.'

* * *

VIIVI LUIK

The Beauty of History

(translated by Hildi Hawkins)

1968. Riga. News of the Prague Spring washes across Europe, causing ripples on either side of the Iron Curtain. A young Estonian woman has agreed to pose as a model for a famous sculptor, who is trying to evade military service and escape to the West. Although she has only a vague awareness of politics – her interest in life is primarily poetic – the consequences of the politics of both past and present repeatedly make themselves felt. Chance remarks overheard prompt memories of other people and places, language itself becomes fluid, by turns deceptive and reassuring.

The Beauty of History is a novel of poetic intensity, of fleeting moods and captured moments. It is powerfully evocative of life within the Baltic States during the Soviet occupation, and of the challenge to artists to express their individuality whilst maintaining at least an outward show of loyalty to the dominant ideology.Written on the cusp of independence, as Estonia and Latvia sought to regain their sovereignty in 1991, this is a novel that can be seen as an historic document – wistful, unsettling, and beautiful...

Viivi Luik is one of the most highly-acclaimed and well-known writers in Estonia today. She has published eleven collections of poetry, as well as three novels.

ISBN 978 1 870041 73 7
UK £9.95
(paperback, 152 pages)

For further information, please contact:
Norvik Press, Department of Scandinavian Studies, University College London, Gower Street, London WC1E 6BT, England
e-mail: norvik.press@ucl.ac.uk
or visit our website at www.norvikpress.com

Lightning Source UK Ltd.
Milton Keynes UK
UKHW020158010619
343685UK00006B/377/P